SUNDAYS

James McLaren

For Dad.

ONE

Now. Today. Sunday. Morning time.

Silhouettes of the last autumn leaves dapple upon the window as they glide across its surface. Pinpricks of bright light pierce through the shadows, momentarily blinding me as I lookout. I can see the arching branches reach above us and join hands with the trees on the other side of the road. Their gnarled fingers interlock, and their dead leaf skin blend together, creating a continuous tunnel.

We sail through the arteries of the county side. Shadows sweep across the car like a multitude of small hands that cannot quite grip us as we pass. They won't catch us. Nothing will catch us. Everything is ahead of us. This day could hold anything.

There is no better time than this, waiting to get there. Wherever we are going today.

We have a number of regular places we go to, but we all have the same favourite. We usually discuss where to go and what to do. But today, we did not. We had our breakfast and left. I think I know where we are going.

I *hope* I know where we are going.

I turn from the window. The flickering light has started to make me feel queasy despite the pink travel sickness pill I crunched down before we left. The fragments of the pill must be trapped in my teeth, and the taste is enough to bring on the nausea.

The brown covered seat spills out from beneath me, and my short legs jut out. I consider the distance between my boots and the driver's seat. I've been told countless times not to press my feet against the driver's seat, but what if I've shrunk?

I push my legs out, but I stop when a movement draws my eyes to the front of the car. The head in front of me has made the familiar jerk upwards and now looks off centre. His eyes catch mine briefly in the rear-view mirror. They are knowing but smiling. The eyebrows raise expectantly and are enough for me to resist the urge to test the boundaries of my legs. The back of the driver's seat remains unpressed, this time.

From where I'm sat, my view of the dashboard is limited. I can see the left side of the radio. It is turned off at the moment. We will listen to it on the way home. If the aerial can pick up a strong signal. There will be a constant backtrack of crackles as we listen to the time tunnel countdown. The crackle will fade in and out as we roll up and down hills. I am an expert in the signal coverage for our routes home. I know the exact points where we will lose the station entirely. I hope that it won't be during a song I like.

I don't know why we never listen to the radio on our way out. I start to hum a tune in my head instead. An adventure tune. Something to fit the soundtrack of our day, of the adventure to come. Something like Indiana Jones but not exactly the same. I refrain from humming out loud. My legs start to jiggle as a tune runs around my mind.

The part of the radio I can see looks back at me. I see the tuning knob, black and round with an inner trim of blue that is chipped and faded. The pre-tune buttons, big and clunky, line out below it like a row of straight, black teeth. I wonder what song would be playing if we turned it on now?

I look down at the handbrake sat atop its orange carpeted hump. It lies there like a disused black knobbly bone. The carpet slopes away to the passenger side footwell, and I catch sight of Tessa's red wellies. Her bobbed hair turns to the right. Not to look back at me but to look up at Dad. He is quiet. We don't usually sit in silence like this. Something is wrong. He seems preoccupied.

We usually chat. I love it when Dad tells us about a film he stayed up late to watch the night before, after Mum goes to bed. If he can stay awake. These are the type of films Tessa and I are not allowed to watch. They are grown-up films. Not the grown-up films with rude, fast forward bits, but grown-up adventure stories or scary stuff. I like to hear about those films.

As our self-proclaimed entertainments manager, Dad has to vet everything we watch. His catalogue of films recorded from the tele is vast. He can get at *least* three films on a video if he uses the long play function. There is a whole shelf in the fireplace of videos. Every one of them has a card slipped in its sleeve where Dad has written the names of the films he has recorded in his pencilled scratch.

Westerns and war films are saved for whenever Dad and I are on our own when Tessa's doing homework and Mum has gone to her diet clubs.

Our weekends run like this. On Friday we watch 'Cheers' first and then 'Roseanne'. We get to stay up late for that. Saturdays are film nights. I know some people rent expensive videos from the corner shop, but we don't need to thanks to our entertainment's manager. We have *loads* of films on tape.

Dad knows what he has recorded, and when it comes to dinner time, he tells us the outline of a few of them so we can decide which one to watch. Mum *always* gets the deciding vote. Then, she gets cross with Dad as he rummages on all fours to find our choice amongst the anonymous videos. His tea has often gone cold, and mine is all gone by the time we start the film.

In amongst this selection are a few videos at the back. Those are for the grown-up films. I have learnt the hard way not to watch them when no one is around. I did that once and had nightmares. It was *really* embarrassing. I woke up crying my eyes out. I had dreamt about the little aliens from the film. They were trying to take over the world. The film was so scary I had to stop watching. I knew that was a mistake. If I had kept watching, maybe I would have been reassured by the end of the film when the aliens *must* have been defeated. At least then, I would have known that the world was safe again. But as it was, I stopped it before the end, which meant they could still be out there! So that night, I woke up and cried my eyes out all because of those stupid, little aliens.

When Mum and Dad came into my room at the sound of me blubbing, I had to confess. I had to tell them I snuck in a grown-up film after school. I should have just told them it was a bad dream and I didn't know why I was scared, but when Mum asked me what was wrong, I *had* to tell her the truth because that makes a bad dream go away. I think I got Dad in trouble for having the film on tape in the first place, but he never said.

Since then, I've known not to even look at the cards in those videotapes. The titles alone might spark something in my imagination, which I have been told is overactive. I might have a nightmare inspired by just the name of the film.

However, I still like to hear about those films. Usually, Dad will tell us the story on the trip out. We've listened to loads of different stories. Hearing them from him seems to stop the nightmares from getting through. He's a good filter.

We heard about a man that travelled the world in the future when the whole population is dead. His only companion was a panther that was forever by his side. The only other living things were witches and warlocks and nasty mythical creatures.

Together they walked the earth, going into battle with every strange creature they met. Deserted supermarkets were home to hidden trolls, but the hero had to go into them to get canned food. Rooftops were full of gremlins, and witches lived in the forests and tried to seduce him and *even* kiss him! I enjoyed that story, and I didn't have any nightmares about the trolls or the gremlins.

We heard about a young girl who could move things with her mind and threw knives without touching them. In another, we heard about a man trapped in a haunted house, and his pet dog got so scared it killed itself by pushing its head into the wall to get away from all the ghosts.

I wonder if Dad has any more of these stories to tell us today, but he keeps quiet. Tessa is obviously wondering the same thing because I keep seeing the flick of her hair as she looks at him, waiting and hoping for him to say something.

I feel the car slow as we approached a turning. I see Dad's hand grip the rounded top of the gear stick and move from fourth to second, then into first and then we slow to a stop.

Sometimes, only sometimes, Tessa gets to change gears for him on the way home. On those occasions, she leans forward tentatively, her hand on the gearstick and waits for instruction. She's usually pretty good at it. Finding second gear is the hardest, and we've only stalled once.

When it's just Dad and me in the car, I get to sit in the front seat. I'm the third reserve. When Mum is with us, she's in the front seat, and Tessa is relegated to the back seat next to me. When it is just the three of us, Tessa is promoted to co-pilot. I am only the co-pilot when there is no one else around. The selection is based on our age. The curse of being the youngest is you have to watch everyone else do thing's first before you get to have a go.

When I do get to be in the front seat, I rack my brain to remember all the things Tessa got to do when she was co-pilot. I am usually desperate to do everything she has done, so I'm overeager, which can be annoying, I know. I have to wait to be asked, but sometimes I can't wait. Sometimes I just lean forward and go for it. I grab the gear stick and wait. Sometimes I'm allowed to do it, and sometimes my hand is slapped away.

The funniest thing is when Dad hasn't noticed my hand is on the gear stick, and he just changes gears over me. I get wrenched back and forth with the shifts up and down the gears until I laugh so much I have to sit back in my seat. This is always followed by a glance from Dad, and then he says, "What are you laughing at?" which makes me laugh even harder.

He must know that my hand is there, it must feel different, but he never seems to notice or notice me flying back and forth in my seat as he changes gear.

My favourite feeling when changing gear is when we are waiting to turn or at a traffic light, and the gear stick is in neutral. I love the soft shake of the rounded grip beneath my hand as the engine idles. In those moments, I feel like I'm the one who is driving. I feel in tune with the car as it softly communicates its gently throb up through my hand, along my arm and into my chest. It's even better when Dad closes his hand over mine to shift the car into first. His hand, which is always rough to the touch, focuses the vibration from the gear stick. It tightens the rattle to an almost imperceptible movement. Then we are into first gear and off again.

I love being in the front seat, but I don't get to do it much. The third reserve co-pilot is rarely deployed.

We are waiting to turn, and I watch the gear stick vibrate as it sits in neutral. Dad's hand moves down and grips the gear stick, and I hear the rattle of his ring finger against the plastic top of the gears knob. I hear the whoosh of the passing car, and the gear stick is clunked into first, and we turn. We move on to a road cast deeper into shadow by the trees that seem to huddle closer together, trying to block out every last ray of sunlight.

The road is narrow and bordered with high grey old, crumbling walls. Behind them are the enormous trunks of the towering trees. The road winds downwards, snaking left to right like a labyrinth.

I know where we are. If we stop just before the humpback bridge at the bottom of the hill, then we are going on the riverside walk, and we will probably play on the stone turret that juts out from the riverbank. If the tide is out, maybe we can see how far we can walk out into the mudflats, hearing the suck and slap of the mud as it tries to take our wellies away from us forever. No doubt I'll fall, I usually do, and I'll get covered in mud and told off by Mum when we get home. We'll have to throw our hats into the house first by way of an advanced apology. That's the tradition.

The car nears a blind bend, and as we slow down, the three of us make the same noise.

"Fffmeep, fffmeep!"

This is promptly followed by Dad pressing the car's horn to warn anyone coming around the blind bend that we are there. The car's horn lets out a feeble ffmeep ffmeep sound. It sounds like the crack in a prepubescent boy's voice. The car wants to sound like a grown-up, but it's not quite there yet.

Once Dad has pressed the horn, we laugh at the pathetic sound and at our united prediction that it was coming, and then we edge slowly round the bend.

Our car is not the biggest, it's not the newest, and it's not the fastest or even the most reliable, but it's *our* car. It's been ours for as long as I can remember, and I know every inch of it. But it does have the weakest sounding horn I've ever heard. I'm not embarrassed by our car, not like Tessa is, but I am embarrassed by the car's horn. Now it's just funny, but if it were to sound when I have my mate in the car, or near school, I would *die* of embarrassment.

Whenever we drive down this narrow road and approach the blind bend, we always make the 'Ffmeep, ffmeep' noise. It's another Sunday tradition. These traditions come from years of our Sunday outings. Sundays, for us, are steeped in our Sunday adventure history. 'Ffmeep, ffmeep' is part of this.

Loads of Sundays ago, we were driving down this stretch of road. Despite being a two-way road, it's so narrow that only one car can fit down it, and the crumbling stone walls get even closer as it bends. If you take the bend wrong, you have to wind down the window and pull in the wing mirror just to be sure they don't break off as you slide through. That is why we honk the horn before we go through. Actually, the word *honk* sounds too loud and impressive... that is why we *ffmeep* the horn before going through.

Anyway, ages ago, we were driving down this road. Back then, Dad didn't ffmeep the horn before we went round the bend. He just placed his hand on the vibrating gear stick, the car would go quiet, and he would edge slowly round the bend. It was like looking around the corner in a scary film, the type that would give me nightmares. Everything would be still and quiet as you hoped nothing would be on the other side and would leap out at you.

On this occasion, something did leap out at us. As we neared the bend, a huge, silver, metal beast roared around the corner. Dad had to jerk the car to the left to get out of its way, narrowly missing the brick wall but getting close enough for the bramble vines to scratch their clawed barbs against the windows. The sound was like someone scratching nails down the chalkboard at school.

This hulk of a car tore past us. It just missed taking our wing mirror with it, and as it went, it let out a tremendous blast, like a giant bellowing at us to get off his road. Its car horn was *so* loud it sounded like an American car from the movies. It must have had the type of horn in the centre of the wheel, in a prime place for the driver to blast whenever they get annoyed. The car was so high up that all I could see from my window was the silver glint of its metal armour as it flashed by. I couldn't *even* see their windows, but I bet they were tinted black like some kind of steely street tank.

Our poor cars front was angled in towards the wall. It must have looked like the dog from that ghost story Dad had told us about, boring its head into the wall with fear. Dad fumbled to return the horn blast, but, unlike the road monster that had just bullied its way past us, our car's horn is not in the centre of the steering wheel for easy and angry access. It is on one of the function sticks angled out from the steering wheel column. It is the one on the left. You push it up and down for the windscreen wipers, pull it towards you for the screenwash, and you have to push the whole stick in towards the steering column to make the horn sound.

In his fumbling to return the cars war cry, Dad managed to activate all the other functions. He set off the wipers and then splashed the windscreen with washer spray, and then finally managed to unleash our cars retort. What came out was the feeble cry of a boy nearing puberty. In response to the street tank's awesome blast, which still echoed down the brick-lined road, came our cars mouse-like *fffffmeep, ffmeep*. By the time our car had managed to deliver this squeak, the monster of the road must have been halfway to Exeter.

We sat in the car facing the brick wall, stunned into silence. After a glance at each other, Dad raised his hand to the stick horn and gave two more *ffmeeps*. "Take that, you big bully!" he said and raised his fist in mock threat at the rear window. Tessa and I laughed, and then Tessa did an impression of the cars exchange.

"HHHHHOOOOOOONNNNNNKKKKKKKKK!!!" She said, followed by a *"ffmeep, ffmeep..."*

I laughed from the back seat again, but stopped short, recognising the link between my laughter and my suddenly full bladder, and Dad gave her a wry smile. He patted the dashboard.

"That's okay, my friend," he said.

He set the wipers off, on purpose this time, to clear the washer liquid from the windscreen and inched the car back to manoeuvre us away from the wall. As we re-approached the bend, Dad let out two *ffmeeps* before we cautiously edged around the bend. "Is there anybody there?" he said in his best Herman Munster voice. I laughed again, but I quickly shut up, feeling the wee come too close to the surface.

That is the reason why we all make that sound as we approach this particular bend in the road.

The car weaves its way down the hill, and we pause at the bottom, just before the humpback bridge. I start to think this is it, this must be our destination, and Dad will swing the car left and in through an open gate. The tyres will crunch over the dusty and uneven car park, and we will slow to stop. That won't be so bad, I think. We have fun wherever we go. We always have some kind of adventure or funny moment to share with Mum when we get home. I enjoy the riverside. Its surrounded by thick, lush woods where we can trek through and find a good tree to climb. We've been here so many times, but there is still a lot of unexplored territory. There is a lake somewhere in the woods, and we could build a raft and paddle out to the middle. No doubt I'll fall in... I normally do.

I've settled my mind on the river walk. This will be another good Sunday. I'd be happy with that, but... but... I can't shake the hope that we will drive on over the humpback bridge, and then we will be a little bit closer to where I *really* want to go. Where I am sure we *all* really want to go. We've not been allowed to go there for weeks.

I sit in my seat, idly tugging in my seat belt, feeling it lock tight when I yank it too hard. The chunk, chunk, chunk sound of the safety mechanism draws Dad's eyes to the rear-view mirror. His head moves almost imperceptibly, and his hazel eyes beneath the full eyebrows ask me to stop. I stop instantly, the seat belt snapping back into place against my chest, its edge digging into my neck. I finger the edge of the belt away from my skin and keep my hand there to stop it from pressing against me. The eyes in the rear-view mirror nod their acceptance of this and then return forward.

The car idles where it is a moment longer. I feel the swish of a car drive past us, and I catch a flash of colour. Dad had been waiting for another to car drive over the humpback bridge. I see the shunt of the gear stick into first, and we drive forward, over the bridge.

We are not going to spend this morning by the tidal river. Hope springs back up inside of me, and Tessa turns in her seat to look at me. She bites her lip and raises her eyebrows. She's hoping the same as me, and she too thinks we are a step closer to getting there.

I start to pick at the white stitching in the red plastic of the door interior and then stop, knowing this will only get me in trouble. If I carried on, the stitching would hang down in a loop, and the next time Dad opens that door, I will get *that* look. The one that asks the question I never have an answer for, the question that would draw an irritation inducing silent shrug from me. The question that asks in an exasperated tone, "Why do you do these things?" And the answer is always honestly... *I don't know.*

I don't want to spoil anything today, so I stop and do my best to look out the front window. Tessa glances back at me again as we near a T-junction. We both know that if we go right, then we are on the right track. She looks back at the road, and I keep my stare locked on the back of her head, where her eyes just were, as a thought dawns on me. For once, I might know more than Tessa. This morning was one of the few times Dad asked me to do something for him instead of going straight to my big sister.

I turn to look at my satchel beside me. I always carry this with me on Sundays. It is a green satchel with a brown leather strap. I always wear it across my body so that it hangs down to one side of me, just like Indiana Jones. Dad got it for me from the army surplus store, and it has been my Sunday bag ever since.

I don't get to carry much exciting stuff, not usually anyway. I'm not entrusted with our picnic or anything like that. But today, I have two things of importance in my satchel. I have Dad's slim grey walkie-talkies. These are proper real walkie-talkies that you can use over a decent distance. Not like the ones I play with where you have to be in the same room to talk over them, or at best stand on the other side of the bedroom door. These are the ones I am not normally allowed to play with, but I have them right here in my satchel.

The second thing I have in that satchel is what gives me the edge over Tessa, and it was Dad who told me to get it before we left. I lift the flap of my satchel and peer inside. There are the walkie-talkies and next to them is the pocket tide timetable.

It was up on the pinboard along with the old ones. I don't know why Dad keeps the old ones. It gets to the point when one pin cannot hold them all, and if Mum or Dad walks past it too quickly, they all fall down. That's when Dad has to get rid of the old ones. Mum gets sick of them falling, so she tells him to throw them out. I had to get on a chair from the dining room to reach the pin to release the latest timetable. Even then, they all fell on the floor. I hurriedly picked them all up and stuck the pin through the old ones as I didn't want Dad to have to lose his latest collection.

Now, there it is, sat in my bag. I swell with pride thinking back over how I was asked to get it and didn't sacrifice the others in my haste. Dad won't ever know that I saved his collection, just like he frequently saves me. There is a part of me that wants to tell him right now, but I refrain. If I tell him, I would reveal to Tessa that I have the timetable, and that will give away my advantage. I now know for sure... well, pretty much for sure that we are going where we both want Dad to take us. There is no other reason for us to have the timetable. We *must* be going to our coastline

Tessa will know soon anyway. Once we wind our way down the next hill and do the U bend that is yuppievile, or as others may know it, Noss Mayo, there will only be one place we could be heading towards. We are going back to our coast and we are going to have the best adventure ever. We are going to race against time and tide.

TWO

Before – Six Sundays ago. Evening. Past bedtime.

"You can't go back there again. I don't want you taking them back there again. I mean it!" says Mum.

I hear the quiet thrum of Dad's voice rumbling his response. I strain to hear what he says, but he must be in the dining area bit of the kitchen. That part of the downstairs is furthest away from the stairs and the hardest place to hear what someone is saying if you are eavesdropping from the top of the stairs, the way Tessa and I are.

If I were my parents, I would have figured this out as a matter of priority when I moved in. Grown-ups seem to forget about the important things, and there is nothing more important when choosing a house than finding the best spot to talk in where *no one* can hear you from the top of the stairs. We all know that the top of the stairs is the most likely place for someone to eavesdrop. When I get a house, I am going to find that spot first. I am also going to have a cellar and a huge loft. The cellar is going to have a secret entrance you access from the bookshelf.

Tessa jolts me back to what is happening downstairs by grabbing my arm. Mum has opened the kitchen door. She must be checking to see if we are where she thinks we might be. I hold my breath. Any movement now will make the stairs creak, and she will know we are here. I don't move an inch. I focus on Mum's shadow, which is cast into the hallway by the kitchen light. From her silhouette, I can see that she is holding on to the door handle and leaning partway out into the hall, her head cocked. She must not want to break her conversation for long because she doesn't come out all the way to do a proper check and turns back to Dad. In her haste, she forgets to close the kitchen door, which is a blessing for us as we will be able to hear more now.

Mum was *really* annoyed. She has been grumpy with all of us since we got home. I thought Dad's idea of not actually walking back into the house but just opening the front door and throwing our hats onto the doormat would have won her over. It did not. When she saw the state I was in, I could see the vein pulsing in the cleft of her neck. This was not going to end well.

"I mean it, Ray," Mum says, resuming her irritated tone. "You take too many chances."

Dad must have come back into the kitchen part because now his low voice has words and not just sounds.

"They were safe. I always make sure I'm careful."

"Really? Well, what happened today?" Mum's voice has an edge that I've not heard before, "Billy could have been swept out to sea!"

I can see in my mind Dad's hands rise in a placating gesture.

"And don't start telling me I worry too much! I'm not overreacting!"

"She is," I whisper to Tessa, who looks at me but doesn't say anything. "I was *fine!* I *would* have been fine. I was just caught off balance."

Tessa nods and smiles. "I know," she says. "But you know what Mum is like. She worries about everything." She looks back down the stairs to the conversation.

I follow her gaze and start to tug at the threads of the carpet on the top step. Our carpet is swirls of browns and creams. It is made up of lots of tiny different colour threads that build up to make the pattern you see when you are standing up. There are partings in the pattern. They snake around and help make the swirling effect and are shorter threads of carpet weaved back into themselves. The carpet looks like it has tiny lanes or roadways curling through its surface. Sometimes, I like to imagine that I've been shrunk to miniature size. If that happened, the only way you could get anywhere would be to follow the weaved partings, like a trail through a gigantic carpet jungle. You would have to be careful because not all the miniature paths take you somewhere. Some circled back on themselves in an ever-decreasing spiral. If I were shrunk and ended up on the carpet, I would be okay because I have already traced the route across the majority of the house *and* committed it to memory... Just in case.

I pull at the longer threads of carpet. I don't know what they are made of, but some of them have developed and a hard, coarse end. Maybe it's after they are stepped on or scuffed several times that the end goes like that. If you find one of these and pull on it hard enough, it unravels, and you end up with a really long thread. It's like three times the length! I feel a rush of satisfaction each time I pull one of these out. I tend to do this if I'm bored or worried. I can't do it too many times in one place because if I do, I reckon Mum and Dad will be on to me. Dad especially. He would guess it was me rather than general wear and tear. Maybe he does it too sometimes? Maybe after Mum has gone to bed tonight, he might sit downstairs and pull at the threads.

My fingers weave across the carpets, and a rough end brushes against my fingertips. I pinch it between my thumb and forefinger and start to pull, gently at first.

"I'm not saying you are overreacting. All I'm saying is that you weren't there. It sounds a lot worse than it was." Dad says.

"A lot worse?" Mum shoots back. "It sounds dangerous because it WAS dangerous!"

I pull at the strand a bit harder. This one is going to be tough to unravel.

"He was fine," Dad says.

"Falling from a cliff face into the sea is not fine, Ray! What if there was a rock under the surface? He could have cracked his skull open!"

"It wasn't quite like that, Jan. He slipped, but he didn't fall far. The kids are always falling over or slipping off things. Especially Billy, you know how clumsy he is." Dad says.

I frown. I'm not sure if I'm frowning at what Dad said about me being clumsy or with concentration at trying to pull this thread clear. I can feel the carpet lifting off the floorboards. The part of the carpet my bottom is on strains as it lifts with my pull. I shift my grip so that I now have the thread edge between the nails of my thumb and forefinger.

"Besides," Dad continues. "He didn't fall from a cliff face, we weren't scaling some sheer cliff, and he didn't fall that far."

I can visualise Mums stance. She's stood leaning against the sideboard facing Dad, her arms folded, her lips pressed thin with pressure. Either that or her hands are on her hips.

Dad's voice dips lower, trying to get beneath Mum's frown and crossed arms. "We were going around the coves. You know, the way we usually do. The tide was going out. It was higher than I thought it would be, granted, but it was *going* out."

"So, what was he doing on top of one of those rocks?" Mum's voice has eased slightly, trying to get the facts by sideling her annoyance.

"We got around the first few coves. The kids were great. They counted the waves, just like I've taught them. They waited for the lull, and then we all ran out and around the rocky headland and back into the next cove."

"So...?" Mum asks, prompting Dad to get to the bit where I fell.

"So, we got to a cove where the headland goes out a bit further than the rest. You know the one, you've seen it."

Silence from Mum.

My nails click against each other as I lose grip of the carpet thread. Without looking down, I fumble to grip it again. I don't want to lose this one. It's proving to be my trickiest one yet.

"The tide hadn't gone out far enough on that one yet. It was still half filling the cove. So, we decided to climb over the rock to get to the next cove."

"*We* decided? Come on, Ray, the kids will do whatever you tell them to." Mum says.

"Okay, Okay. I decided to take them over the rock. The tide was going out. The kids love that stretch of coast. It's a real adventure for them."

"You and your *bloody* adventures." Mum's words jab at him.

"We've climbed so many rocks, run that stretch of headland against the tide so many times, they love it, and it *is* safe, I promise," Dad says.

"You should have turned back."

Tessa leans around and sees my plight to pull the thread clear.

"Stop it!" she whisper-shouts as loud as she dares. She tries to slap my hand away, but I nudge her off. We suddenly become aware of the pause in the conversation downstairs, and we freeze. We look at each other. Have they heard us?

We stare down at the corridor. There is a thin line of light cast by the crack in the kitchen door. If Mum had heard, she would have been straight out of that door and halfway up the stairs before we could even scrabble to our feet.

"Maybe," Dad says, the conversation resuming and with it, our fear of getting caught ebbs away. "I just didn't want to disappoint them. You know how much they love running against the tide. They're free down there. There are no problems or stresses down there. They leave all that behind. You should see their faces. They are bright and filled with excitement. They get to escape. It's important to them, especially with all the trouble Billy is having at school."

I start to feel hot, my face flushes with embarrassment. I know Tessa knows I hate school, but I don't like to talk about it at home or hear anyone else talk about it. If it's not talked about at home, then home remains safe and mine. I don't want school to get into my home.

My frown deepens. I adjust my grip on the carpet thread. I can feel my fingernails turning white with the pressure. I don't want to talk about it. *I don't want to talk about it!*

I can see my eyebrows as my face almost falls in upon itself. I can feel Tessa looking at me, and *I don't like it*. I don't look at her. I just sit and frown and pull at the carpet. I want Mum and Dad's conversation to move on.

I feel Tessa's arms curl around me, and she leans towards me. I let her hug me even though I stay ridged. I bury the urge to shrug her away, and I feel my face slowly start to relax.

The dark shadow at the top of my vision lifts as my frown eases. I feel hot tears burn at my eyes, and they start to blur my vision. I hope and hope *and hope* they don't spill down my cheek. I don't want Tessa to see them. I try my best not to blink. If I do blink, then the tears *will* start to roll.

I breathe deeply. I try to fill my lungs slowly with a nice, even, comforting rhythm. My body starts to relax a bit, and I let Tessa pull me near.

"It's okay, Billy boy," she whispers, "It's okay."

With my head resting against her, she cannot see my face anymore, so I let myself blink. The tears roll down my cheeks. I don't rub them away because that would let on I am crying.

"Jan," Dad says, his voice soft. "The tide was going out, we climbed over the rocks, and we were almost down the other side. There is a ridge on that rock. It was above water level. We were going to sidle along until we got to the sand. From there, we were just going to jump down and run across the cove to the next rock. It was an accident. Billy just slipped. I had hold of him the whole time. He could have probably touched the ground, but the water was so frothy you couldn't see."

"You had hold of him?" Mum asks.

"Yes," Dad says and there is a slight laugh in his voice. It catches in Mums voice too.

"What do you mean?" She says, and I can hear the smile in her expression.

"Well, I know what he's like," Dad says. The humour has increased. I smile, even though he is telling this story at my expense. I like that the argument they were having has passed.

"I went down to the ridge first, and the kids came down on either side of me. Tessa was first, and when Billy boy came down, I saw him start to slip. It gave me a shock at the time but..." he lets out a short bark of a laugh. "...but thinking back," his grin is wide now. I can tell by the stretch in his words. I realise that I'm grinning too. I can feel Tessa's body shake as she holds in her laughter.

"He just about gets to the ridge, and I see his footstep onto a wet bit of moss. Before he knows it, he has slipped backwards... I grabbed him by the scruff of the neck. I've got his collar in one hand and the rock face in the other." He pauses while he catches his laughter. "He swings out beneath me, and he's just dangling there like a worm on a hook!"

Mum's voice is trying not to laugh. "Don't, Ray. It's not funny."

"You're right. It's only funny now because he's okay... But thinking of him just hanging there. His poor little face, trying to be brave. You know the froth that builds up on the top of the tide?" he pauses while Mum must give him a nod. "Well, we call that stuff 'spew'. It builds up when the tide thrashes around in those coves. Anyway, I've got him hanging there, and all he's saying is, "The spew! The spew! Dad, the spew's going in my mouth!" He lets out another laugh, and Mum joins in, letting out a stifled snigger.

“Stop Ray, it’s not funny,” she says, trying to gather herself.

I have tears of laughter rolling down my cheeks now, and Tessa is almost convulsing as she tries to keep her giggles suppressed. She whispers, “The spew, the spew!” to me, which makes the back of my neck ache with the laugh I must not let out.

We try to get ourselves under control as it has gone quiet downstairs. I sit up straight and resume my pull of the impossibly tricky carpet thread. The air seems to have gone serious again after that brief relief.

I think Mum must have gone to stand next to Dad because her voice sounds as far away as his now. "Look, Ray, I know you won't let anything happen to them, but I worry. Accidents can happen, and I think that stretch of coast is taking a risk."

I start to feel the end of the thread give. I grip it harder between my nails and double my efforts.

“They’re okay with me. I promise. Even puddin' head.” Dad says, and with that, the end of the thread gives way, and it unravels. As it does so, I hear the throb of the movement reverberate through the carpet and the floor. I stun myself into silence. It’s never been that noisy before. Tessa turns to me and cuffs me on the back of the head. The noise of my head against her hand is too loud. We look at each other like condemned prisoners who find their sentence hilarious.

“What was that?” Mum says, her voice punching through the partly closed kitchen door.

Tessa and I simultaneously look down the stairs and then back at each other. We hear the slap of Mum’s Scholl slippers against the kitchen linoleum floor, and we scramble to our feet. I know the sound of her walking will mask the sound of us standing up. We pause on the top stair holding hands. We have to run back to our beds, but we need another sound to cover the noise we’ll make in our retreat.

Like a gift granted by the patron saint of eavesdroppers, we hear

Mum's voice. She must be talking more to herself than to Dad.

“They better not bloody well on the top of those stairs again!” she says.

Her voice provides us with the best cover we could have hoped for. Her words cover us as we dart for our rooms, parting at our doorways and slipping as silently as we can into the bedroom’s darkness and the beds themselves.

I just slide under the covers in time, but I haven't had a chance to make myself comfortable when Mum stops mid-way up the stairs. She's listening for any giveaway signs. Giggles or the sound of beds creaking in response to us just jumping into them or, as my body aches to do, sounds of us readjusting ourselves into a more comfortable position. The silence seems endless. Eventually, I hear her turn. The bannister creaks as she turns around, and the familiar slip slop of her slippers sounds out as she goes back downstairs.

In a rare moment of defiance, I use the sound of her on the stairs to cover getting out of bed and creeping down the hallway. I want to pause by Tessa’s door and whisper for her to join me, but if I do that, I will miss out on the camouflage Mum’s shuffle offers me.

I make it to the top of the stairs just as Mum gets to the kitchen. This time she hasn’t bothered to close the door at all. I can hear how close she is standing to Dad.

“Anything?” he asks her.

"No, I think they're both asleep," she says.

"Look, I know you worry," Dad says. "I understand, but the kids are safe. I would never put them in harm's way."

“I know, but....” Mum says, trying to interrupt, but she must be silenced by Dad’s look. “What?” she asks him. “What is it? What’s wrong?”

“Nothing. It’s just... Jan, no matter what happens, I promise you,

I will always get them home safe. I'll always get them home to you."

Mum is silent. I guess she's hugging him. I feel a warm smile flood my face as I lean against the wall of the corridor. I feel a happiness that cannot be dulled by the impending Monday. Dad will always be there. He'll always get us home.

THREE

Before. "Think of it as an adventure."

All good heroes have a catchphrase. John *'Hannibal'* Smith from The A-Team has *I love it when a plan comes together*, Sledgehammer has *Trust me, I know what I'm doing.* My Dad's catchphrase is, *Think of it as an adventure*. He uses it on the most appropriate of occasions, usually when you are facing a problem. Recently I have been facing quite a few.

I used to think he just meant it for Sundays. Sundays are our adventure day, and whenever something seems like a challenge or a bit scary, Dad tells you his catchphrase. He means that if you think of what's in front of you as an adventure, it won't seem so daunting. I'm sure the A-Team get scared sometimes. Even Indiana Jones must get worried about trying to get the Ark before the Nazi's. They all have adventures, so why can't we? And all adventures *must* be scary at some point, just like real life.

At the end of Empire Strikes Back, Han Solo is frozen in carbonite and taken by the bounty hunter. That *had* to be scary, but they got through it, and they really were in an adventure. Our Sundays are just the same because we have faced some pretty scary things too.

There was the time when we had to go past the wolf's cave in the noisy woods, and I got really scared. We were playing hide and seek. I had found Dad, but I was still looking for Tessa. Dad was sure she was on the other side of the cave near the loud river (that's why it's called the noisy woods), but that meant walking right past the mouth of the wolf's cave. This cave is just like the type you hear about in fairy tales. Its mouth yawns open as though it is a rock mouth that was frozen when it first woke up. Inside there are long and pointy cave spikes, and it goes back really, really far.

When Dad first told us about the wolf that lived in there, the three of us were having our picnic sat on the rock right outside of it. He said it was fine because he could tell the wolf had left for the day from the tracks. He pointed out a few markings in the soft wet grass, and I nodded as if I agreed with his deduction, but I couldn't pick out any definitive markings. I took his word for it, but I was sure that the more I heard about this wolf, and the longer I looked into that impenetrable darkness, the more I could see two red eyes looking back at me.

At first, they were just pinpoints of red, but as Dad's story went on, they seemed to get bigger. In my mind, I could see the hulking, shaggy shape of the wolf-beast padding slowly towards the cave mouth but staying back just out of sight. Dad and Tessa didn't seem to notice that it was there. I was the only one who could see the red eyes that had gotten bigger the closer it got, drawn by the sound of Dad's voice telling us about the wolf within.

When we were playing hide and seek, I stood on the rise to the south of the cave. Dad, who I had found in the waist-high ferns near the crowman's tree, had already walked past the cave. He stopped when he realised I was no longer next to him. He turned to see me frozen to the spot, biting my nails and not wanting to move. He waved me towards him (he couldn't shout because that would have let Tessa know that we were on our way), but I just shook my head and tried to force my tears back down again.

Tears are so annoying. They come out so easy, and when they do, they don't stop, and you can't hide them because they get everything wet. And half the time, they bring out all the snot from your nose to join in. I have no control over my tears.

I know that if Tessa were there, she would have laughed at me, but Dad did not. He seemed to know what was wrong and didn't make me say it out loud. He walked slowly back up to me as my eyes scoured the ground outside the cave. I was frantically trying to make sense of any tracks so I could figure out if the wolf had left or not. If I knew the wolf had gone, maybe I could push the tears away. I would need to ask Dad to teach me how to read tracks.

Dad crouched down beside me and looked down at the cave. “It’s okay, we can go.”

"No," I said. If I had to tell him why I knew I would cry.

He nodded and rubbed his thumb across his chin. On the weekend, he doesn’t shave, and so by the time we get to Sunday, there is some grey stubble on his face. When he rubs his chin like this, there is a very distinctive scratching sound. It’s not like anything else. I reckon if I were blindfolded, I would know that sound anywhere.

“You know, lots of people get a bit frightened. Even grown-ups.”

I looked at him. Grown-ups didn’t get scared, did they? They never looked scared.

Dad nodded. “It’s true. They just don’t show it as much.”

I looked at the ground. It was strange. Even though what Dad was saying made me feel better, it made me want to cry even more.

“I get scared,” he said.

I looked at him dumbfounded. He never looked scared or looked like I felt on the inside.

“But do you know what I do?” he continued.

I shook my head.

“I think of it as an adventure.”

“Like Indiana Jones?” I asked cautiously, not wanting to get it wrong.

He nodded. “Just like that. Being scared is another word for being excited. Anything scary is an adventure. Think of it that way, and you'll be fine."

It must have worked because I was able to walk past the wolf cave, even though once we had gotten past it, I still felt the need to run.

I thought that thinking of things as adventures was just for Sundays, but Dad told me to take the same approach with problems outside of Sundays as well. It's not easy or straightforward, and I have tried, but, you see... Sundays are my safe place, even though Mum seems to think we are in constant danger when we go out.

One Sunday, we went for a hike along the cliffs. It was a bright sunny day, but there was no one around because it was so windy. That was when we learnt to judge if the wind was strong enough to lean on. We spent a lot of time on the top of the rise, leaning against the wind. It is quite a skill because the wind isn't constant. It can be strong one minute and weak the next, which means if you are leaning on it and it drops away, you fall on your bum. I had ended up on my bum quite a few times, as you would expect, but even Tessa and Dad fell once or twice.

When we walked down the other side of the rise, the wind fell away completely. That was where we had our picnic. We looked out across the sea. The sunlight caught the tide as it moved, and the light twinkled and danced on the crests of the waves. It looked like a glinting ocean of diamonds.

I had already started to hate school by that point. We sat quietly eating our ham sandwiches and adding crisps to them when Dad said to us both, "Peaceful, isn't it?" We nodded. I was eyeing Dads bag, wondering if he had brought KitKats or Penguins for pudding.

"You know, whenever you feel a bit upset or worried, you should think of this," he said and pointed the crust of his sandwich out towards the sea. I felt that he was talking to me more than Tessa. I looked at him, and he gave me his reaffirming nod. "Whenever you are somewhere you don't want to be or doing something you don't want to do, but you can't leave, take a moment and think of this place. Whatever it is won't last, and you can come back here again."

I nodded at him, caring a bit less about the chocolate biscuits in his bag.

"If you have a problem," he said, turning to us both, "Remember, think of it as an adventure."

It's not as easy as that in real life. Sundays are not *real life*. Real life is when Mum wakes me up on Monday morning. One of the most annoying things about the week is that my favourite day and my worst day are right next to each other. It's not fair that I spend all week wishing that Sunday will come only for Monday to be hiding to pounce on me right behind it.

I've tried to think of the bay of diamonds when I'm sitting at my desk in school, but it only seems to make me feel sadder. I try to think of the problems I have at school as an adventure, but there is no happy ending that I can see. The problem with problems is that you don't know where their story is going. In adventure films, you know that there will be an exciting bit, then a bit when it looks like the goodies will lose, then there will be an even more exciting bit before the goodies win and everyone is happy. Then the credits roll. Everyone in the adventure is lucky because after the credits have rolled, they all must have a rest from their adventure. If my problems at school really are an adventure, like in the movies, I wish the credits would hurry up and roll so I can have a rest.

I often wonder if Dad thinks of his own life as an adventure. Sundays are adventures for him, so are Saturdays because we fix things around the house or on the car. But I wonder if he sees work as an adventure. I don't think you get the same worries at work as you do in school.

I wish I could leave school and go straight to work. I'm sure Dad doesn't have to deal with big grown-ups who aren't very nice at work. I reckon no one bothers him because he is tall. Not like me.

I'm short. It's the thing that no one talks about. As if I am, or my height is an embarrassment. It's not fair because the rest of my family are tall.

Our cousins are tall as well, and they always get told how tall they are. Aunties and Uncles *always* bring it up when they see them. They talk about it as if they've passed a very difficult test at school. It's so stupid. You can't revise to be tall. If you could, I would have stayed up all night to revise. But no one mentions how *short* you are in the same congratulating way. You can be in the same room as everyone else, and they all say how lovely and tall the cousins are, and then the best I get is my hair ruffled or a patronising pat on the shoulder.

Mum thinks that's why I don't make friends very easily, even though she never says it. My best friend is average height, but he still makes me look small. Mum thinks no one apart from Steve likes me because I'm little. I'm not sure which word is worse, little or short.

I don't think other kids don't like me because I am short. I think they just don't notice me. The first thing they think if they *do* notice me is that I must be younger than them. Then, if they pay enough attention to see that I am their age or a bit older, that's when the teasing starts.

It's not just my height. I don't really know how to make friends. I've been friends with Steve for as long as I can remember, so I can't think back about how we became friends and then do the same thing with other kids. It's hard to make friends. It takes a lot of thought. You have to say the right thing at the right time, otherwise, you look stupid.

I've tried to say something cool or funny before to impress other kids, but I always seem to get it wrong. Then the other kids either just look at me, or they laugh. Not the kind of laugh that includes me but the kind of laugh that makes me feel very hot under my skin. I feel my neck starting to burn, and my cheeks go red. I hate the feeling because I can't make it stop once it starts. I can't control the heat and switch it off like the radiators at home. I wish I had an internal thermostat I could switch to 'cool'.

I get the same feeling when they just look at me. Sometimes that feels worse than when they laugh at me. If they laugh at me, then that's as bad as it's going to get. They may laugh for a long time and even give me a shove, but they usually walk away soon after. Then they go on my list. The list is quite long these days. If they are on the list, it means I have to try and avoid them.

It gets very difficult to navigate my way around the school with a list as long as mine. I have to take the long way round as the shortcuts are normally where the kids on my list are walking or hanging out. I've been told off for going out in the rain and running the length of the main building to avoid walking down the dry corridor because that was where the 'List kids' were. I turned up late in my classroom, the windows were all smudged with steam, and I got told off for being soaking wet and tracking water all over the floor. When I didn't answer my teacher when she asked why I chose to go outside and get wet, she whispered under her breath that I was "bloody-minded." I had to ask Tessa what that meant when I got home.

When kids just *look* at me, it feels worse than when they laugh. A *look* is the start of something, a *laugh*, while humiliating, is usually the end. The *look* means they are thinking more about me and will come back later to do something worse. The ones who say nothing are the ones that are the most dangerous. They become curious, and they go to the top of my list. I can't avoid everyone on my list, but if it has to come to a decision between running into a *laugher* or a *looker,* I would rather run into a *laugher*.

I don't think the teachers like me very much either. They are always telling me off for staring out of the window when they are talking to the class. After a parents evening, I heard Mum telling Dad that the teacher worries that I'm not paying enough attention.

I sat on the top of the stairs on my own that time. The teacher said she thought I'd rather watch what was going on somewhere else than be involved in something right in front of me. The problem is that being involved is not my choice. I can't make myself be involved or get invited to be involved. I'm either ignored or picked on. If those are my choices, I'd rather look out the window and pretend I am somewhere else. Or even better, someone else.

That's why home is the best thing ever, and Sundays are brilliant. On Sundays, I can be the adventurer who is six feet tall, the person my weekday problems won't let me be. Sundays are when I can be the hero and not the strange quiet one you either don't know or want to pick on to make yourself feel good.

FOUR

Before. Five Sundays ago. Early.

There is a crunch from the crispy bread as Dad's knife cuts deep into the stack. The tower of lightly fried sandwiches lifts on one side like an accordion threatening to spill out the bacon within, but Dad is a practised hand at this. Before there is any spillage, the crusts are neatly separated from the fried bread. He shifts the discarded crust along the wooden chopping board and onto his own plate with the knife edge. He rotates the block of sandwiches and repeats the action three more times, and then finishes his dissection by cutting the sandwich tower into four squares. He divides the squares up onto our plates and hands them to us.

I look at the fluffed-up topside of my sandwiches. This is another Sunday tradition, fried bread. Dad used to make these for himself when he lived on his own in his bedsit before he met Mum. Dad knows a lot of one-pan recipes. His descriptions of his old bedsit in town make me think of the bedsit John lives in, in *Dear John.* Dad only fries one side of the bread; he uses the dripping from the green casserole pot that sits on one of the rear hobs of the stove. I've never seen that pot anywhere else. I think it must be glued to the stove's surface. Frying just one side means the other side of the bread looks puffer than it really is. Inside the sandwich is a mix of red and brown sauce and a strip of bacon.

Before I graduated to the *closed Sunday breakfast sandwich,* I used to have the open kind. The principle was the same, but I didn't have bacon because that used to make me gag, but I had the red and brown sauce. On my plate would be a collection of lightly fried squares with swirls of brown and red. I liked looking at the pattern on them before I ate each one. Although I much prefer that I now eat the same style of breakfast as Dad and Tessa, I miss looking at the swirling pattern. Sometimes I peel the bread back from each sandwich to check the pattern before I eat it. This is one of the oddities I'm sure Dad would question if he saw me doing it.

"Why can't we go to our coast today?" Tessa asks.

This is a redundant question. I know she knows why. We both know why. We both heard how worried Mum was after last week's incident. If Dad knew she knew, he'd say Tessa is *chancing her arm.*

We take our plates over to the dining room table. I shuffle into the L-shaped bench, and Dad moves in next to me. As he sits down, he looks briefly at the cushioning of the bench. I know immediately what he is thinking. Dad made this bench to fit our dining room. The seats lift up to reveal hidden compartments. The only problem is that sometimes the foam Dad used to upholster the bench goes a bit flat and needs replacing. The look he just gave means he has clocked this, and it has been logged in his brain as a job for next weekend. I realise that I must not be the only one who keeps mental lists, although I'd rather be making one like Dad's than my list of bullies.

Tessa is sitting in the chair opposite me, and the ordinance survey map is sprawled out on the table between us.

"We'll go again, but not for a bit," Dad says. Tessa's question hung just a bit too long between us.

"Why? I want to go there. We both do, don't we, Billy Boy?" Tessa says.

I find it hard to swallow my mouthful of sandwich. I was not expecting to be pulled into the conversation so early. I rarely am involved until the end, and I hardly ever start a conversation. I look blankly at Tessa, who gives me a hard stare. I turn to Dad, who is considering the map as he chews his food.

"Can we go?" I ask tentatively, not wanting to let Tessa down.

Without looking up, he says, "Not this week."

"But *why* Dad? We had so much fun last week! It was such an adventure!" Tessa says, her hands raised for dramatic effect.

I frown. I don't want to be reminded of my fall, which is clearly the reason why we can't go back to our coast. I feel that Tessa is *chancing her arm* way too much.

Dad is just about to take another bite of his sandwich when he pauses and says, "That's exactly *why* we can't go back yet. It was *too* much of an adventure."

"But *Daaad...*"

Dad holds up his hand to silence Tessa while he finishes what is in his mouth and then says, "We'll go back there again, but in a while, once things have calmed down."

I look at Tessa, hoping she won't push it any further. We all know what is going on, so why is she asking?

"You mean once Mum has calmed down," she says, almost to herself.

Dad stops and regards her. I feel myself sink into the now hard seat of the bench, wishing it had more give. Dad's look doesn't wavier, and I can see Tessa wants to squirm on the inside. His look isn't cross or cruel. He just has the look that says *you've pushed it too far.* It's the look I get when I get too excited playing, and I'm acting up a bit. It's a *Dad* look. Not as strong as Paddington's *hard stare,* but a look that either makes you straighten up or want to shrink into the background. From the look of Tessa, she wishes she could shrink rather than straighten.

In a very even voice, Dad says, "She got a scare. We all did."

Dad glances at me, and I realise that I can still be seen. The bench didn't swallow me whole as I had hoped.

"The sea can be rough." he continues, "There are many accidents that happen if you don't respect it. We made a mistake, and your Mum is more comfortable if we give the coast a rest for a bit. I'm more comfortable with that too." Dad lets out a small sigh and pushes his plate away so that it just catches and lifts up the edge of the map dividing us.

"She does worry, but with good reason. The sea can be dangerous, you both know that. Besides, there are plenty of places for us to go."

Tessa nods and shoots him a dipped smile. Dad pulls his plate towards him again, and I resurface to table level, like a submarine coming up for air. Dad gives her a smile from his eyes. I'm not sure I would have got away with *chancing my arm* so easily. Dad points at the map with one of the fried crusts he removed from our breakfasts.

"What about the noisy woods?" he says.

Tessa, her confidence returning, tilts her head to look at the map from Dad's angle. "Dartmoor?" she offers.

Dad scans the map looking at the Dartmoor bit.

With Tessa now back on an even keel, I feel more confident again too. I shuffle up so I can see the map from above like them. In order to do this, I need to put my knees on the hard bench. This means my feet press against the backrest, and I know if Dad sees me, he'll tell me to put my feet down, but I want to be involved in this with them. Without putting down my sandwich, I adjust myself and tilt my head in a mirror image to Tessa. I look at the map, doing my best to imitate Dads understanding of it.

"How about we do something new?" he asks and then slaps a finger down on a wooded section of the map. "There!" he says with mild triumph, "Let's explore there!"

"Yes!" I say excitedly, and in my enthusiasm, I squeeze my sandwich too hard. The result is a brown and red sauce covered slice of bacon spurts out of my sandwich and slops onto the ordnance survey map, not far from where Dad's finger lies. Dad and Tessa both look at the ear-shaped piece of bacon, and then they look at me. Dad's eyes are smiling until he sees my feet on the bench, then I get the *why do you do these things* look from him, and a bowed head shake from Tessa.

FIVE

Before. Five Sundays ago. Late morning.

"Are there any snakes around here?" I ask Dad and Tessa's retreating backs.

I know that Tessa is probably rolling her eyes at my question. She still thinks I'm only scared of snakes because I'm trying to be like Indiana Jones, but I'm not. I genuinely am afraid of snakes. I can't even watch the whole *Well of Souls* bit in Raiders of the Lost Ark without using a cushion, and yet she still thinks I'm making it up.

I must admit, I have a strange fascination with snakes, even if they terrify me. The last time I had a nightmare that was not inspired by watching a grown-up film was when I woke up terrified because of a snake dream. I had been flicking through the television channels because there was nothing good to watch. It was early evening, and Tessa was doing homework. Mum and Dad were looking at bills. I was entertaining myself by flicking up the channels and back down again, hoping that something of interest would start soon. I went all the way up to channel four and then back down again to BBC1.

The rotating golden globe had appeared on BBC1, which meant the man in the tele was about to introduce the next programme. Probably *Open All Hours* or something like that. Not holding out much hope, I carried on my channel flicking. I thought my best bet was on Channel Four. As I got to BBC2, a nature programme had started. Not wanting to break my rhythm, I carried on up the channels. By the time I got back down to BBC2, I found myself transfixed to the screen.

What I saw was horrific! I don't even know how they could show it before the watershed. I was so close to the screen that what I saw was huge. I took my hand off the channel dial and shuffled back on the carpet, away from the screen.

That was a mistake because then I was too far away to turn the channel over or switch the tele off. I didn't dare go closer to the screen because that meant I would have to go closer to the *thing*, and what if it could reach through the glass and bite me? I was gripped with horror. Mum and Dad were just in the next room. I could see them in my periphery through the open door, but I still felt scared. How could something so terrifying be so close to such a feeling of safety?

On the screen in front of me was the close up of a snake's head. I think it was a cobra. Its jaw was distended as it took into its mouth the impossible size of an egg. It looked like some horrific, laughing comic book villain. There was no way that that should have been possible! The egg was *twice* the size of the snake's head, and yet there it was, its mouth wrapped around the egg, slowly sucking it into its body. Even the soothing tones of David Attenborough could not make this freak show feel safe.

What was worse was how its mouth hung, misshaped by what it had just absorbed as the bulge of the egg travelled down its throat. These creatures are not normal. They have to be some kind of demon. I turned to look out at Mum and Dad, but they were absorbed in bills and receipts. I could have just left the living room, but then I would have been called back to turn the tele off and told that we aren't made of money, and I should turn things off when I've finished with them. I couldn't close my eyes and reach for the off button because what if I missed and my hand touched that despicable *thing* on the screen?

In the end, I did the next best thing. I squinted my eyes shut so that the lashes joined, but I could still see through them, like when you want to pretend you are asleep but still see what is going on. With my vision slightly hooded, I reached out my hand, bracing myself for the snake to burst through the screen and sink its fangs into me. I paused just before the screen and then summoned my last piece of *'think of it as an adventure'* courage and hit the off button. The button made a loud snapping sound as the screen went dark. I felt relief wash over me, and then I heard Dad's voice.

"Oi! Gentle with the tele, we're not made of money!"

"Sorry... I Just..." I had no good excuse in my catalogue of reasons to suit the situation. "I just... I... I... dunno," I cringed.

Without looking, I knew Dad was shaking his head in disbelief. This was confirmed when he said to himself, but loud enough for me to hear.

"Puddin' head."

This was his affectionate name for me when I did something silly. Puddin' head.

"Are there any snakes around here?" I shout again, pulling my arm free from the thorned blackberry barb that had snagged me. I had dropped behind and was starting to feel a little bit scared...

"Maybe," Tessa throws the comment back at me.

"Come on," Dad says, "There's a clearing just up ahead."

I trot to shorten the distance between Tessa and me, and as I do, I scan the ground for any slithering movements. The image of the snake eating the egg comes back to me, and then in my mind, the egg changes into *my head*! I try to shake this thought out. Why does my brain do this? Why does it take a situation and then make up an even scarier alternative?

We are walking through a pathless patch of wood. I slow to a walking pace behind Tessa, still scanning the ground and doing my best to dodge the occasional tree branch she holds back for a second too long, only to release it as I approach to try and whipped in the face.

"*Pack it in*, Tessa!" I say.

"*What?*" She says back over her shoulder with mock innocence.

"Dad?" She calls forward, "How fast do snakes strike?"

"*Shut up, Tessa!*" I whisper at her.

"Oh, I dunno," Dad says, as though he's not aware Tessa is trying to wind me up. "Pretty fast, I reckon."

"How fast?" Tessa continues.

"*Stop it!*" I plead, hating how weak I sound.

"Well..." Dad calls back, "It depends. If there were some people walking in the woods and a snake was asleep, I reckon the first person would wake it up, the second one might stun it and then it would strike the third person."

I am about to repeat my *shut up!* at Tessa before she has a chance to respond, when I realise what Dad has said. I quickly scan the areas to either side of us, and then it dawns on me... I *am* the third person!

Not wanting to fall behind, I keep up my pace. I catch sight of a slight clearing to the left that is coming up next to Tessa. I don't hesitate. I bolt into the clearing and run clear past Tessa to fall into position behind Dad, leaving Tessa bringing up the rear. Now *she* is the third person, and *she* will be the one to get bitten. I stomp my boots extra loudly to make sure any snake Dad wakes is stunned enough to let me pass before attacking my sister.

"You sure about that, Dad?" Tessa calls over me.

Dad pauses for a moment and looks through the trees at the clearing up ahead. His hand rests on a branch while he makes the scritch-scratch sound along his stubbled jaw with his other thumb. He starts walking again, and I follow, making sure to keep my position in second place.

"Come to think of it," he says, "Snakes *are* pretty hard to stun. I reckon the first one wakes it up, and the second one gets it."

I stop for a moment. If that is true, then I am in a prime position to be bitten. Tessa pushes into the back of me and shunts me forward.

“Come on, snake bait,” she whispers.

I use the momentum from her shove to bolt forward again and slip in front of Dad, who almost trips on my heels as I resume a walking pace. I really want Tessa to get bitten. If Dad’s smart, he’ll drop back a place now he is in second. I hear him recover from his stumble. I stride out, flaunting my position of safety for Tessa to see. The clearing is near, just a few paces away, and then I will be free from the *wood of snakes.*

“Come to think of it,” I hear Dad say, “Snakes are deadly fast... I reckon they would wake up and strike in one go. Yes... I think the first one would definitely get it.”

I stop dead. *What?*

Dad walks past me into the clearing and shoots me a smile. “C’mon puddin’ head.”

I stay where I am, not wanting to be second place either anymore. Tessa shoves past me and gives me a smug grin.

"Dweeb,” she hisses goes to stand next to Dad in the clearing.

I am the last one in the wood. Dad and Tessa are standing in the sunlight, the grass shining with bright dew. I give the wood of snakes one last look. One thing I am sure of is that in those scary grown-up films, the person at the back always gets snatched first so as not to immediately alert the rest of the group to the fact they are under attack. I feel the fear on the back of my neck, and I sprint forward to join them. As I stop, the dew grass makes me skid, and I slip. Dad's arm shoots out, and I catch it. He steadies me back to a standing position, smiles at me, and then looks around the damp green field. The woods restart across the other side of the field, behind a waist-high wire fence. I can't see a gate or a sty to climb over.

Dad is looking around, taking in the early autumn view. He grew up around the bombed-out docks in Liverpool, and he never fails to appreciate the countryside or a coastal view. He takes in a few deep breaths.

“Ahhh! Just breathe in that country air!" he says, continuing his surveillance of the field. He catches sight of a steeple to the left of us. He rummages in his bag and pulls out the ordnance survey map, and unfolds it.

“Okay!” he says with authority. “Bilbo! If you would be so kind,” he says to me and gestures to the area in front of him and Tessa.

I know what this means, so I stand near them, facing the fields incline and bend over so my back can be used as a table for the map. Dad spreads it out and I can feel them both peer over it and prod at landmarks to decipher our exact location.

“Right then,” Dad says to Tessa, “Where are we?”

Tessa makes an *ummmm* sound as she pours over the map glancing up now and again to look for landmarks.

“So, there is an incline there,” she says and points in the direction I’m facing, “And… A church back there.” She points in the direction my bum is facing, “and so that puts us about… Oh… what’s *that?”* she says, and I feel her lift up the edge of the map.

"Where?" asks Dad.

“That, there,” she says, disgust in her voice.

“Umm… That is ketchup… or bacon grease.”

Tessa laughs, and I join her. Dad gives me a nudge. “You’ll never get in the A-Team Billy-Boy, leaving grease everywhere, yuck!”

You’ll never get in the A-Team. This is another of Dad’s catchphrases, reserved for when I have done something particularly stupid.

As Dad looks back over Tessa’s navigation, I look up from the dewy grass beneath me to the top of the field. Just beyond it, practically out of view, I see a series of shapes appear in silhouette. They look like small black triangles in a row. Occasionally one of them flutters.

"Dad?" I say, but he's still talking with Tessa as they pinpoint our exact location. He has his compass out now resting on the map.

"Okay," he says to Tessa, "Turn the dial, so the lines match up...."

"Dad?" I say again.

"Hmmm?" he says distractedly.

"Dad, what lives in here?"

Tessa's voice chimes in, "So that puts us here, just outside of that wooded area." she jabs her finger roughly into my back, and I flinch.

"Whoa, boy!" Dad says to my reaction, and he pats me like I'm a horse. Then to Tessa, he says, "That's right! Well done. Now, see if you can fold this thing up the right way?"

I stand, relieved of my table duties and rub the sore point on my back made by Tessa's finger. I take a step further up the rise and shield my eyes to try and make the odd shapes against the sun. More have appeared.

"Dad, what lives in this field?"

"Eh?" he says, turning his attention from Tessa, who is wrestling with the map. He stands next to me.

"What are those triangles up there?" I ask.

Dad shields his eyes from the sun. "Triangles? What Triangles?"

"Up there, just over the hill. They move every once and a while."

"Dad!" Tessa calls out, "This thing is impossible, and it stinks of bacon!"

The silhouettes grow in size until there are multiple round bodies lined up on the horizon, like woolly Indians ready to ambush in a cowboy film.

"They're sheep," Dad says, his voice flat. "Lots..." he pauses as he takes in the increasing mass of bodies, "... and lots... and lots of sheep..."

"Dad," Tessa says as she stands next to us, handing an enlarged folded map to him, "I can't do it, and it's full of grease." She wipes her hands on *my* jacket and then looks up the hill. "Wow," she says, "that's a lot of sheep. What are they looking at?"

The hill is now full of sheep. Their shadows span out in front of them. One of the sheep steps forward, like a native chief offering to barter or trade, or to threaten an attack. This really does feel like a cowboy film.

"What are they doing?" asks Tessa.

"Is that one the leader?" I ask Dad.

Some of the sheep at the back are jostling forward as if trying to get a better look at the trespassers. The one at the front, the chief sheep, bends its head down and sniffs the grass.

"Are we *allowed* to be in this field?" Tessa says.

Dad looks to our left at the fence and the woodland on the other side of the field. "I think we better head for the woods," he says. "DON'T RUN," he barks to my initial instinct to bolt.

I halt my brief sprint and draw alongside Dad, on the side furthest from the army of wool. Their heads follow our progress, slowly turning as we make our way across the width of the field. I look at the wood up ahead. It still looks far away.

Tessa hangs back, covering her eyes from the sun and looking up at the pack watching us.

"What do sheep eat?" she calls out.

Dad turns to her and gestures her to follow us, "Come on, Tess, let's go."

I stop and look back. She points up and the chief sheep. "That one is stamping its foot like a bull."

Dad and I take this in. She's right. The leader is digging at the soft wet ground with its hoof. It lifts its head and calls back a bleat to its army as if calling them to arms.

Suddenly the whole tribe of sheep burst into a charge. They veer to our right as if trying to block off the route we came by. The three of us watch with dumb fascination as they cut us off. Tessa leans closer and squints. “Dad, do sheep have horns?”

"Don't worry," he says, "They're not running at us. They must be heading back to the farm. Maybe it's feeding time."

At the phrase *feeding time,* Tessa and I exchange a look. What if there is no farm? What if they *ate* the farmer and his family, and now they only like the taste of *human flesh?* Damn my imagination! Why do I do this to myself?

I can feel the thunder of their hooves as they stampede in perfect formation. As they reach the bottom of the hill, they change direction and veer directly towards us like a flock of birds.

“Um... Dad... I don’t think they’re running back to the farm... I think they are running at uh-”

Dad sprints forward and snatches Tessa's hand. He yanks her around and runs with her back towards me, grabbing my hand as he passes, and we all start running, hand in hand, for the wood on the other side of the field.

“DAD?” Tessa calls out in a breathless gasp.

“Just run, Tess!”

In my awkward sprint, I chance a glance behind me. The sheep pack have gained on us. They are holding a perfect inverted V formation with the Chief Sheep dead centre, his head down and his eyes fixed on us from beneath its curled horns. He seems to notice me looking back and doubles his effort, and the whole pack lurches forward, closing the gap between us.

“DAD!” I shout out, *“They’re going to eat us!”*

We are now at full pelt; my heart is pounding in my chest, and my vision is blurred by our jolting run.

“Get ready!” Dad calls.

As we near the fence, I try to slow down, but the wet grass makes me slip, and I land on my bum and skid the rest of the way to the fence. A tree root slices underneath me and right up the crack of my bum. I howl in pain as I hit the fence.

Dad and Tessa reach the fence. He grabs her under the arms and launches her over and into the wood. From my lying position, I look back at the demon sheep. They are on us. The first sheep in the V formation hit the fence on either side of us. In the centre, the evil leader, the Ram, lowers his head. He is on a course to hit us dead on. Bodies of sheep blast the fence on either side of us. The space between us and the chief ram closes as the woolly V collapses upon us.

The next thing I know, Dad has me by the belt of my jeans and the scruff of my neck, and he throws me over the fence. He grips the fence post with one hand and leaps over the top wire just as the Rams head collides with the base of the wooden post.

I lie, crumpled on the other side of the fence and look directly into the eyes of the Ram. At first, it looks like his eyes are doing circles in their sockets. I half expect to see a loop of birds flying around the top of his head. He staggers for a moment and then gains his balance against one of the sheep next to him. Then his eyes lock on mine, he dips his head, and if he could talk, I'm sure he would say, "*Next time, Billy Boy, next time....*"

SIX

Before. Five Sundays ago. Picnic Time.

We were trapped. After we had caught our breath and laughed at what a sight we must have seemed, running from a pack of sheep, we tried to continue with our walk. But we soon discovered that what we thought was a continuation of the woods was actually a small cluster of trees in the centre of the field. We were in a fenced-off wooded island. What made matters worse was that as we walked around the perimeter of the fence, the pack of sheep, led by their leader, Butt-Head I had called him, followed us wherever we went. As soon as we stood before a clear patch of the field, it would suddenly be swarmed by the woolly mass.So, without anything else to do, Dad looked at his watch and deemed it picnic time.

*

I try to avoid looking at the woolly gang as I eat my sandwich. That brief moment of laughter we had when we first made it over the fence seems a long time ago now. The sheep feel ever-present, glaring at us as we eat. I'm standing because my bum is too sore to sit on. Dad and Tessa are sat opposite each other on logs.

"What do you think they want?" Tessa asks Dad.

"Our *flesh?*" I offer.

"Don't be stupid. Sheep don't eat people," Tessa says.

"No, they don't," Dad says. "And don't call your brother stupid." He surveys the pack of sheep. Some of them are now nibbling at the crisscross wires of the fence. There is a flicker of concern on his face. Can they eat through wire? He turns and puts on his Herman Munster voice, "Unless they are *mutant sheep*!"

"Really?" I say, but Dad gives me a glint of a smile.

My bum is sore to sit on my discomfort makes me jitter, hopping from one foot to the other.

"You okay?" Dad asks, indicating towards my fidgeting.

I look at the ground, ashamed. "I hurt my bum," I say.

Up to this point, I had been able to hide my rear end from both Tessa and Dad as we had all been so intent on the sheep. "I caught it on a root when I skidded." I point vaguely out at the offending root.

He finishes his sandwich and, with a sigh, dusts his hands free of crumbs. "Show me," he says.

Reluctantly I turn around, displaying my rear end to both Tessa and Dad. Tessa bursts out laughing, and I hear an exasperated *"Blimey..."* from Dad.

When I turn back, he is shaking his head and looking off beyond the sheep who are still tugging at the fence with their thick yellow teeth.

"This was supposed to be a *safe* Sunday," he says and then looks at the floor. "Your Mum's gonna kill us."

"Is it bad?" I say.

"Can't you tell?" Tessa says, panting from her hysterics. "Your bum is completely out!"

"What?" I say, trying to look at my own backside, pulling at my jeans to see if I can get a better view. What I can see is a tear up the middle of my jeans. I gingerly touch the skin I can feel through the hole. I realise my underpants are torn through as well.

"How did you do that?" Dad asks.

I look at the ground, "When I skidded, I went straight over that root," I point out at the root and this time, I notice it still holds a strip of fabric from both my jeans and my underpants. It seems to wave the tufts in the wind in celebration.

"You look like a baboon!" Tessa says and lets out another burst of laughter.

Dad smirks to himself and tries to look away. Then, refocussed, he waves me towards him. I stand in front of him. Tessa is on her back, still gasping for air.

"Turn around, let's see the damage," he says, and I silently obey.

His hands pull at the tatters of my jeans. "*Strewth* Billy-Boy... You don't do things by half, do you? Hold still. This will feel cold." I feel water pour over my exposed rump, and Dad's rough hand rubs at my bum, cleaning away the congealed mud. I wince at the cold, and my body jerks back and forth with rubbing motion.

Tessa gathers herself enough to look at me, only to fall back down again at the sight of me spasming as Dad works on me.

"You look like you're hula-hooping!" she yells and roars into new guffaws of laughter.

When Dad has finished, I have been cleaned, disinfected, and the cut up the back of my bum bone is plastered with several small plasters. These are the only type Dad carries in his first aid kit. He looks me over and then pulls a jumper from his bag.

"Here, tie this around your waste. Save you getting a frostbitten bum," he says. "We can't have a full moon in broad daylight."

With my pale and bandaged bottom covered, Tessa manages to pull herself together. "How we gonna get out of here?" she says.

I look at the pack of sheep, who are tugging at the fence in a frenzy. Have they eaten through one of those wires? I'm not sure, but I don't think that strand was broken before.

"Don't worry," Dad says, "What we need is a sheep charmer."

"A what?" I ask, looking back at him.

"A sheep charmer, like a snake charmer but for sheep. I reckon I can summon one up, hang on," he says, and he roots around the dirt in front of him. He rubs leaves and twigs between his hands and looks up at the trees. "Please, sheep lord, send us a sheep charmer in our time of need." He scatters earth and debris over the ground and looks at us.

"Did it work?" I say, gripped and trying not to itch my bum beneath the scratchy woollen jumper.

"*AFTERNOON!*"

The voice comes from behind Tessa and me. Dad meets the thick Devon brogue with a broad smile. We turn and see a lean man with a lopsided toothy grin beneath a flat cap. His clothes are as mud-splattered as his wellies, and he carries a black bucket containing something I can't see. Dad *must* have seen him coming.

"Got you cornered, have they?" he says. "Little beggars."

"Is he a sheep charmer?" I whisper to Tessa.

Dad stands, "They gave us quite a chase too."

Tessa crosses her eyes at me and sticks her tongue out one side of her mouth as if I am some kind of idiot.

"You ain't from around here, I take it? Accent gives you away," he says and offers a hand over the wire fence.

The man has waded through the mass of sheep bodies and seems utterly unperturbed by them. The sheep are still focussed upon us. The odd one absently nibbles at the farmer's jacket edges, and he good-naturedly swats them away with a granite slab of a hand.

"Not originally, no," Dad says, shaking the enormous, outstretched paw.

"Northerner, are you?"

"Liverpool settled down here sixteen years ago."

"Accent ain't left you."

Dad nods. One of the sheep must have nibbled at the farmer a bit too hard because he gives it a good wallop this time.

"Pack it in, you!" he says and then looks back at us. "They are a playful bunch, this lot. They were probably just funnin' you by giving you a chase."

Tessa and I exchange a disbelieving look.

"That one is the friskiest," he says and points at the Ram, who eyes me with what I think is irritation. "He'd do no harm." He says the word *harm* as *AAARRRRMMM*, "But he's playful, to say the least."

With that, the Chief Ram takes a mini-run and butts the fence post again, making the whole fence wobble, and making the three of us jump.

"Hmmm, I call him Rammers. You can tell why."

"You think you can help us out?" Dad says.

The Farmer gives an embarrassed look as if he had forgotten to offer us a cup of tea.

"Course, sorry. Don't you worry. They'll follow me now." He gives the black bucket a shake, and the loose rattle it makes causes the entire flock to twitch in his direction. "They're hungry is all, probably thought you were gonna feed them."

Or they thought we were food, I think.

"C'mon, you bastards!" he says, shaking the bucket and turning up towards the rise.

The flock turn and follow him as he goes. He lifts a hand in good-bye, and Dad waves his thanks back. As the bodies thin out, the Ram remains. It stares at me. Soon it is the last one, just standing there, glaring at me.

Tessa leans into me, and I hear her voice close to my ear. "I think he fancies you."

I say nothing, scared to break eye contact with the beast. I've heard that indicates you are weak. There is the distant rattle of the bucket again and the far off voice of the farmer. "C'mon Rammers, heal buoy." He says it as *buoy,* not *boy.*

With that, Rammers bolts away and joins the pack.

"C'mon," Dad says, "Let's get outta here before they finish their lunch and want dessert."

He hoists us over the fence, and we walk cautiously back the way we came. I hang back slightly, keeping my eyes fixed on the retreating flock. I want to make sure they don't change their minds and rush us again. The dark figure of the farmer dips out of sight behind the rise. His flat cap is the last of him that bobs out of view. The shadows of fluffy bodies follow him like a river flowing upstream. I watch as the last of the sheep disappear.

I pause, looking at the now empty hill, just to be sure they've gone for good. I'm about to run after Dad and Tessa when a solitary figure trots back into view. Its woolly bulk is silhouetted against the high sun, and I realise it is the Chief... the Ram, Head Butt or Rammers as the farmer called him. While the figure is far from me and the sun is behind it, I'm certain he is looking at me. He lifts his head and lets out a final bleat which, if I understood sheep talk, would say, "*This ain't over Billy-Boy!*" He then turns and slowly walks over the hill and out of view.

SEVEN

Before. Four Sundays ago. Morning.

The blue weaved rope sails over the branch and falls back down, splashing into the water. The river pulls at it, but Dad snags it with a long stick, pulling it back to him and snatching it up. He holds both bits of rope together and looks at them.

"Will it hold?" Tessa asks.

"It will," Dad says.

"Why can't we go back to our coast yet?" Tessa asks, out of the blue.

I look at Tessa in disbelief. She knows why. We all know why. I don't understand why she keeps asking. I decide to stay quiet. As with most conversations, there is little value I can add. Dad tugs at the rope to test the strength of the branch. As he does so, he says, "You know why, Tess."

"But last week, Billy got into a right mess, and we weren't even at our coast," she says.

Dad, satisfied by the integrity of the branch, tucks both bits of the rope behind the twig of a nearby tree. He seems to ignore her question. Tessa looks at me for backup. I look off to the tree branch that Dad has looped with his rope which will soon be our rope swing. I do not want to be pulled into her challenge.

She was right if you thought about it. I had been more injured by our escape from the sheep than I have ever been at our coast. That night we had both sat at the top of the stairs again, listening to Mum and Dad talk. Mum wasn't as annoyed as she was the week before. Her voice had more of a sparkle to it.

“So, the sheep really *did* chase you?” Mum asked.

The silence between them must have been a Dad trademark nod.

“Why?” Mum said.

"The farmer reckoned it's because they thought we would feed them," Dad said.

"And why were Billy's trousers ripped to shreds?"

“Exactly as he told you, at the last minute, he slipped and went scooting on his bum over a root. The damn thing still had hold of some of his pants when we looked back,” Dad said and let out a small laugh that distorted his last few words.

“Stop it, Ray,” Mum said, but I could tell she didn’t mean it. “The poor thing, he couldn’t sit down all afternoon!”

Dad laughed again and then got himself under control. “I know, it’s not funny. But... But he had to hold himself off the car seat all the way home. His arms were killing him by the time we got back!”

Now Mum laughed, but she tried to snort it back into herself, as though that erased her humour at my pain, “Poor thing.”

I didn't mind them laughing like this. It feels different from when I'm teased at school. This kind of teasing at home makes me feel a part of something, not outside of it.

“I had to throw his jeans away. They were beyond an iron patch. Maybe we can go Trago next Saturday and pick up some new ones.” Mum said.

Dad let out a groan, “They got a great deal happening,” he said, in the same jingle style as the Trago Mills radio advert.

Mum didn’t seem to hear him and mused to herself, “Unless Tessa has any she’s grown out of.” Then something dawned on her, “Ray, what about school? He won’t be able to sit down all week!”

Hope fluttered up inside of me. Maybe I could stay home from school!

She went quiet and then said, “Unless I send him with a cushion....”

“Christ, no!” Dad said. “Poor devil. He won’t live it down at school.”

On the stairs, relief rose inside of me. At least Dad understood what school was like. I was on my knees on the top stair. I had to keep moving up and down to relieve the discomfort the position had on my bum.

“Keep still!” Tessa hissed as the stair creaked beneath me.

“I can’t help it,” I loud whispered, “It really hurts!”

"Maybe I should start coming out with you on Sunday's," Mum said from below.

Tessa and I held our breath. We love Mum, but she *could not* come out on Sundays. They were our adventure days! If Mum came along, she would stop us from doing all the exciting stuff. She would worry us all into boredom.

Dad gave her his quiet voice. “The kids love our Sundays. Of course, you can come if you want to, but I enjoy the time with them alone. Remember, we did this, so you had a bit of time to yourself, and I get one morning just me and them.”

“I know. And I *do* like my Sunday mornings,” she said with a smile in her voice.

I am never a hundred per cent sure what Mum does when we are out. I think she watches shows that Dad won't watch with her. Stuff like *The Waltons* or *Little House on the Prairie.* Stuff that has no chases or punch-ups.

“And your right, it is your time with them. I just worry,” Mum said, and I heard her kiss Dad, and I pulled a *yuck* face, but then smiled because Dad had managed to keep Sundays as they were without upsetting Mum.

“I just worry about you all, especially Billy. And especially after he ripped up his arse!"

At that, Tessa and I snorted with laughter and then slapped our hands over each other's mouths.

"They're bloody well up there again!" Mum said, and we heard her hard-soled slippers squeak on the linoleum as she turned for the stairs.

"Can we go back next Sunday?" Tessa asks Dad.

Dad seems purposefully distracted, looking out over the river. "So… Who wants to go first?"

He looks at Tessa, who looks back at him. Then they both look down at me. Their faces share the same expression. They don't trust me to use the swing first. They look back at each other and, as if some silent agreement has been exchanged, Dad rubs his hands together. "Right then! I'll show you how it's done."

The morning is crisp with hints of early autumn. The trees running along the side of the uneven riverbank are turning shades of brown and deep crimson. The river is fast and deep in patches. Mossy rocks jut up at intervals. I look across the river, trying to pick out a route I can take if I need to cross it, jumping from rock to rock. I reckon I could get halfway, but then the rocks are too far apart. This river is wide, and when we swing out across it, we will only be able to swing out over the deepest part of the river. We won't get anywhere near the other side. We will be like Indy swinging out over the river in Raiders of the Lost Ark when he has to get to the plane-boat.

As Dad takes the rope from the tree, I stand on the bank and look down. It's a short drop. If I jumped for the first rock and missed, I'd fall into at least a foot of water. I start to thrust my arms back and forth to see if my body can build enough momentum to carry me to the first rock *if* I try to jump. I sense Dad standing behind me.

"*Don't* even think about it," he says in a low voice.

I play innocent. "I wasn't..." my voice trailing off. But I *know* he knows what I was thinking.

In a louder voice to include Tessa, he says, "Right! There are two sides to this rope. Make sure you hold on to both. One side has a loop at the bottom, put your foot in there," as he says this, he does it for real. "Make sure you hold *both* pieces of rope and hold them tight to you. And then, just swing."

With that, he launches himself from the riverbank and swings out over the river. As he gets to the furthest part of his arc, he twists himself around and faces us as he swings back to us. He sails back to the riverbank and lets the foot that is not in the rope's loop drop down to the ground. He lands next to me. My mouth drops open in amazement.

"That was just like Indian Jones!" I say. "Can I go next? Dad! Dad! Dad! Can I go next?"

I can see the reservation in his creased brow. "Let Tessa go first," he says.

I kick at the muddy earth with my welly boot and slump down hard on a rock. I instantly regret my protest when my bum reminds me of the root scraping skid I took last Sunday. I quickly stand again, hoping Dad and Tessa didn't see me wince. I stuff my hands in my pocket and watch as Tessa takes the ropes and holds them tight. She hooks her foot in the loop, and Dad catches her elbow to keep her balance.

"Ready?" he asks.

Tessa focuses on the fast-flowing river and nods.

"Don't worry, I'll catch you when you swing back," Dad says.

I watch her knowing that I will be *so* much better at this rope swing than she is. Dad steadies her shoulders, and then she's off. She's not as good as Dad at swinging out across the river. She spins around more than he did. As she starts to swing back towards us, she doesn't even let out a Tarzan cry or *anything*! What a waste! She just clings on with both hands. I decide that I am going to show them both what a great rope swinger I am. I am going to look *so* cool when I'm out there.

Dad catches her as she gets to the bank, and her face breaks from concentration into elation.

"That was amazing!" She says. "Can I go again?!"

I stand and run over to them, snatching the rope just beneath her hands. Dad looks at me, and I know he's worried I'll mess it up.

"Just give her another go, Billy-Boy," he says.

I step away and fold my arms in a huff. Tessa lifts her feet again, and she swings out. She's better at it this time. When she gets all the way out, she leans her head back and looks up at the branch that supports the rope. By leaning back as far as she does, she makes the rope swing in a wider arc. I have to jump out of the way to make sure she doesn't hit me when she swings back to us. I know she was just trying to show off in front of Dad and kick me.

I push past her before she even has time to unhook her boot from the rope's loop, "Can I go now, Dad? Can I? Can I? Pleeeeeeaaa-seeeee?"

Dad pulls an expression that is uniquely his. He frowns and smiles at the same time. It means you're never sure if he's happy, grumpy or yet to make up his mind. His face eases as he relents.

"Okay. But do it exactly as I showed you. Exactly the way Tessa did. Hold on to *both* ropes with *both* hands. Get it?" he says.

"Got it," I say.

"Good."

But I'm not really listening. I just want to be out there, swinging across the chasm. If only I had a fedora and a leather jacket. I look out across the roaring river and see a rock that is just beyond the reach of the rope. I start to envisage letting go mid-swing and landing on the rock in a crouch, just like Spider-Man.

"Okay... ready?" Dad asks.

I nod.

"Go!"

I lift my foot, and I sail out from the safety of the riverbank. Beneath me, the ground drops away to the coppery water that seems to rush over itself in a hurry to get to the sea. From up here, I notice how the water froths and bubbles around the rocks. As it's annoyed at them for being in its path. I look out to the rock I think I will land on, but I am much higher up than, and it looks further away than it did from the bank. Suddenly, I hear a crack in the branch above, and I look up and see the rope stretched taut over the bark, creaking as it holds my weight.

I'm at the highest and furthest point of the swing, and I start to head back to Dad and Tessa. The roar of the water is deafening. Their faces reflect a worry that has begun to fade into a pleasant surprise, as I might actually make it out of this adventure unscathed.

I can't believe it! I *really am* swinging across a river!

I remember thinking Tessa should have done something cool at this point, and so I let out a Tarzan cry and let go of one of the ropes with one hand to wave it above my head in triumph. As soon as I do, I see Dad's hand shoot out as if to catch me, even though he's too far away. Suddenly the support of the rope beneath my feet feels slack, and I grip one rope with both hands, yanking it hard, desperately trying to steady myself. Before I know what's happening, I feel the foot caught in the loop get hoisted over my head. I spin upside down, still clinging to one strand of the rope. My head is plunged into icy water that fills my mouth and my upside-down nostrils. I garble out a scream, but I'm met with more dark, gingery rushing water. I am hooked by the rope like a bandit in a snare trap, and I am mouth deep (upside down) in a river that is trying to whisk me away.

I hear splashes over the sound of the river, and fingers start prising at my hands, trying to release my grip on the rope. My head is hauled out of the water for a moment, and I hear Dad's voice calling, *"LET GO OF THE BLOODY ROPE!!!"*

Despite the instruction, I grip tighter, and Dad practically has to break my fingers to release me. I feel him tug at my boot that's caught in the loop of the rope and then my legs flop into the water. Then my head is up and out of the river and vomiting water over Dad's arm.

Dad shouts over my head to Tessa, *"GET HIS BOOT BEFORE IT ENDS UP IN WEMBURY!"*

Dad wades to the riverbank with me under his arm, pulling me against the rivers grip. The water is ice cold, and I'm dizzy. He slops me onto the mud slope and wades back out to grab Tessa, who is struggling to push her way back against the current. She is dutifully holding my lost boot above her head like a talisman that must remain dry, even though it is pouring water all over her. At the sight of my boot, I look down at where it should be. My sodden sock looks back at me.

Tessa and Dad clamber up onto the riverbank. The three of us lie on our backs, shivering and gasping for air.

"What did he do?" Tessa asks, exasperated.

"He..." Dad is panting. "He held on to one end of the rope, and bloody well pulled himself upside down." He says and looks at me. He wipes water from his face and looks down at his soaked and muddy body. He shakes his head, and over the roar of the river, I hear him say, "You Puddin' head!"

EIGHT

Before. Four Sundays ago. Picnic Time.

We are all wrapped in blankets from the car, huddling around Dad's portable gas burner next to a fallen tree trunk. We don't always bring the gas burner with us. Usually, our picnic is made of sandwiches and crisps. On occasions, Dad brings the burner so he can heat up some beans. I'm glad of the warmth today.

Our jeans are hanging from the branches that spike out from the trunk's thick dead body. Tessa is sitting in the middle, and I only catch sight of Dad when he leans forward to stir the beans. A tin mug is passed to me, and Dad leans around Tessa to pour me some tea.

"Drink up. Otherwise, you'll catch a cold," he says. I try to pick up on any irritation in his voice.

"Can you tell us a story, Dad?" Tessa asks. "One of the ones from when you were a kid, one of the ones with Uncle Bert?"

I'm relieved because this takes the silent focus away from me and my head dunking stunt.

"You don't want to hear those again," he says.

"We do, we do," Tessa says.

"You know them all off by heart by now."

"Please, Dad."

"P-P-P-P Please, Dad," I splutter out, the cold taking over my voice. I sound like the advert for the Penguin biscuits.

Tessa mimics me and laughs. Dad leans forward again to run the spoon around the inside of the saucepan, removing the congealed bean sauce and stirring it back in.

"I don't know why you kids like those stories so much....

NINE

Back when the world was black & white.

I was sneaking out to meet Eddie and Gobber when my Mam called after me.

“Don’t forget to take your Brother!” she said.

I rolled my eyes and tried to open the front door without making a sound. She must have had ears like a hawk because the latch barely made a sound when she shouted, "Don't you be pretending you can't hear me, Raymond!"

She used my full name, which meant if I carried on, I would be getting a clip round the ear when I eventually came home, and the belt from my Dad when he got back from work.

I sulked in the living room, where my Nan was poking at a pot of boiling water on the cast iron range. She looked at the bubbling contents, appraising its progress. Then, she tonged out her enormous white bloomers and inspected the gusset. As if still unsure, she gave the fabric a quick, efficient sniff. Dissatisfied, she dropped them back into the pot, a splash of hot water scolding her hand. I heard it sizzle on her flesh, but she paid it no mind, barely wiping it on her once white but now brown apron.

“Where is he?” I asked her.

Her voice was deep and gruff. She tugged at the spindly whiskers that jutted out from the mole on her chin. Without looking at me, she pointed her tongs towards the kitchen.

“Ask your Ma. I don’t know what you little scally’s get up to, and I don’t care.”

I trudged into the kitchen, the metal studs on the sole of my boots announcing my arrival. My Mam was hunched over the porcelain basin. In those days, the sinks were as big as small baths and just as deep. She was scrubbing at a frying pan.

Not turning, she pointed out to the backyard. "He's in the outhouse. He's trying for his morning movement... again."

I hooked my thumbs in the top of my shorts and pushed through the door to the yard. I clumped up the cobbled path to the back of the yard. My boots were too big. The newspaper stuffed at the end of my boots to make them fit dug into the webbing between my toes.

The concrete outhouse had a wooden door. The bottom of which was splintered and jagged, probably from the rats either trying to get in or get out if Nan was in there. Her movements were as stern as she was and twice as deadly.

I kicked the bottom of the door, and it rattled all the way to its hinges.

“Hey,” came Bert’s nasal voice.

"Come on, Mam says you got to come with me."

"I'm just trying to get this out," he said, his voice trailing off into a squeezed groan.

I never knew a kid as constipated as he was. I rubbed my neck and inspected a slight stain on my hand. I wasn’t sure if that was there before or after I rubbed my neck. I rubbed my hand on my shorts and kicked the door again.

“Stop it, Raaay!” Bert’s voice was always whiney, and he said my name in such a thin way it made me hate it.

I tried to figure out the time by looking at the sun, but there was only grey cloud. Everything in those days was grey. Grey from soot and grey from dirt and grime. If I didn’t leave soon, I’d miss Eddie and Gobber at the docks. We were supposed to be heading out to explore the quarry.

“Right, well, if you’re busy, I’ll see you later.” I spun on my heels, but Mam was looking at me from the kitchen door. With her arms were folded, she pointed at the outhouse with her chin.

“But Mam! He might be in there all day!”

It was true. Burt was almost as bad as Nan. He seemed to spend hours in there, although what he produced was not nearly as impressive as Nan or as satanic.

He must have gotten piles by now with his bum hanging over that drafty drop. I looked around to see if there were any rats I could coax into paying him a visit. I looked back at the kitchen door. Mam had gone back inside. I kicked through the wooden boxes and tins to see if a rat was hiding under any of them. Nothing. I went over to the washing line and pulled down my black woolly hat, and rolled it up as best as I could. I stood in front of the outhouse door and let out a dramatic gasp.

“*OH JESUS! OH JESUS MARY!*” I said.

“*Wha?! Wha* is it?!” Bertie shrieked.

“Bertie, don’t come out, whatever you do! And get your feet up against the wall!”

“What is it?” he yelled.

“BE QUIET. IT’LL HEAR YOU!” I said in a loud whisper. “Jesus, it’s the biggest one I’ve ever seen!” I said to myself but loud enough for Bert to hear. I heard his cobbled soled boots clack against the walls of the outhouse.

"Stop it, Ray, you're scaring me!"

“Scaring you? Think about me! You haven’t even seen it yet!”

His voice dropped to a conspiratorial whisper. "What is it, Ray?!"

I whispered back, “It looks like a rat, but it’s as big as a cat.”

“Is it a cat?”

“No way, it’s definitely a rat, but...*OH MY GOD!*”

“What? What!”

"I think it must have eaten a cat or something. It has flesh and fur in its teeth, and its eyes are...." I paused for effect, "... Its eyes are red!"

"*Where is it?*" Bertie whispered.

"*Shhhh! It's right by the door,*" I told him.

"Oh god, oh Jesus. Please don't let it come in here," Bertie started whispering to himself. "Ray! Help me!"

I stood close to the door and nudged it with my foot making it rattle again.

"*Raaayyy!*" Bert whispered. "*I can hear it! Ray... Are you there?*"

I nudged the door again, and I heard his bum rip out a squeak of fear which echoed around the porcelain bowl.

"*Oh no,*" he muttered to himself, "*Now you're coming?*" He was, and maybe still is, the only person I know who talks to what comes out of him as if it's a close friend.

I nudged the door and heard a plop from the other side followed by a short, high pitched "Oh!".

"*Ray, are you there?*" Bertie said.

"*Yes!*" I whispered back, "*But you got to get out of there....*"

"*I can't. My movement is coming!*"

I bit my lip, trying not to laugh. *Oh, Jesus, I didn't realise they could climb so good!*" I say.

"*Oh, oh, oh,...*" Bert whispered

"*It's climbing up the door!*" I said

At the top of the door, there was a gap for natural ventilation, and it was just big enough for a cat to climb through.

"*Bertie, I'm gonna get Mam!*"

"*No! Don't leave me! Ray... Ray... Ray...? RAY?*" Desperation sent his already high pitched and panicked voice up a few more octaves.

I snuck around the back of the outhouse and lifted a box crate, placing it as silently as I could next to the door. I reached around and gave the door a nudge mid-way up. Then another nudge at the top to give the impression something had climbed up the outside of the door. Each rattle was met with a higher pitched "Oh!" from Bertie. I stood on the box crate, which gave a small squeak. It sounded a bit rat-like which drew another, almost imperceptible squeal from inside the outhouse. From the box, I gave the top of the door a massive bang, and like a soldier throwing a grenade into an enemy bunker, I tossed my woolly hat in through the gap.

The noise from inside the outhouse was a mixture of screams, liquid squirts and a final yelp. The door banged open, and Bertie shot out of the outhouse. His shorts were still around his knees, his grey/white bum was out, and his arms were flailing in the air as he ran, panic-stricken, down the path. I fell back off the box crate and sat creased with laughter.

Bertie must have had his eyes closed because he ran straight into the firm and steadfast bosom of our Nan. Her arms were folded, and her face was so closed in upon itself with fury, I couldn't make out her eyes. My laughter choked off as soon as I saw her.

Bertie bounced off Nans unmoving mass and landed on the cobbles with a skin on brick sounding splat. He looked up at her, bemused, forgetting about the flesh-eating rat he had just evaded. She looked down at him over her own mass and let her eyes take him in, head to toe.

Her voice started low but grew louder. "Just what in the name of *feck..!* Are you doing running around with your Hoo-Haa out?"

Bertie looked between his legs and tried to cover what was there and stand at the same time. He turned to point back at the outhouse, its door still swinging to and fro. He was about to point towards the *rat* when he saw my woolly hat lying just inside the door, disappearing and reappearing from view with each slam of the door. They both looked at me as I peered above the box crate.

My throat closed, and my ear could already feel the wallop it was about to get.

*

I still couldn't hear through my ear as Bertie and I scuffed down the street, dodging the scraped stains of horse muck as we went. The street was lined on one side with tall narrow houses with steps leading up to front doors. On the steps were either gangs of yobbo kids who would eye you and rattle their railings if they didn't like the look of you, or neighbouring women who would stand in mirror image of each other, their hair up in handkerchiefs and arms firmly folded. They would occasionally stop gossiping to shout at the yobbos or join them in their disapproving glare at those who dared walk past.

A group of lads were stood by a gasp lamp. They were using it as their starting point to spit hockers as far as they could to see who had the greatest range. One boy was poking the remnants of horse muck with a stick to find a juicy part. When the stick was adequately covered, he chased the girls down the street, mucky end out, trying to catch their pinnies or their retreating hair as they ran.

On the other side of the street was the dock lined with boats, cranes and shouting men. Bertie watched them as they groaned and griped, clanked and chuntered through their daily grind. I finger my swollen ear, it felt hot to the touch and twice the size it should be. My Nan should have been a bare-knuckle boxer. She'd be a one-hit-wonder.

Bertie turned his attention back to me, and I dropped my hand, not wanting to show how much my ear hurt. He said something I couldn't hear over the swelling and then trotted round to my good side to say it again.

"Serves you right, you stinking bumhole," he said. He looked pleased with himself.

"Shut your trap, squirty-Bertie, at least I got your *movement* out of you. *If* it wasn't for me, you'd still be trying to squeeze one out till supper."

He fumed in his quiet way. "Where we going?" he huffed.

"*I*", emphasising the singular, "was going to see Eddie and Gobber,"

Bertie huffed, "I don't like Gobber."

"Well, he don't like you much either."

"He calls me Bert-Twerp to my face," he said.

"You should hear what he says behind yer back."

He shot me a look of indignation. "They're not nice boys. Why don't you hang out with nice boys?"

"You sound like Mam, you old biddy. Besides, don't worry, he won't call you Bert-Twerp anymore."

He looked at me with a mixture of surprise and admiration, "Why, you gonna tell him something? You gonna punch his lights out?"

"No, but when I tell him about this morning, he'll call you Squirty-Bertie until you're fifty!" I said and shot off, running down the street shouting "Squirty-Bertie! Squirty-Bertie! Squirty-Bertie!"

Bertie chased after me shouting, "Shut UP! SHUT UP, RAY! IT'S NOT FAIR!"

When we caught up with Eddie and Gobber, they were picking through an old bombed out house. Eddie was, as always, looking for some kind of impressive weapon to wield. One that would define him in the eyes of all kids and make the Proddy Dogs run for cover as soon as we walked around the corner. His list of weapons to date consisted of an iron fireplace poker, a pitchfork, both items his Dad had taken for the house and the yard. He once found a knife that Rozzer took away from him when we all caught scrapping with the Proddys. His most recent find was an iron which he fastened to his belt and leant on it whenever we stopped, as though he cowboy surveying the open range. He eventually discarded the iron, saying it was too heavy for a quick getaway, but Gobber reckoned it was because the girls kept asking him to get the creases out of their pinnies. But it was probably his mam that took it off him. Irons were expensive back then.

Gobber was sat against the wall, intently picking at a scab on his knee. He was going through his usual routine with scabs. He would pick at them until they started to peel away from his skin. Then he would do his best to examine the gap between the scab and his flesh to assess whether he could pick the whole scab off in one complete piece. If he lifted it too far and it started to bleed, he would frantically blow on the scab to try and stop it from bleeding. He seemed to think that the cooler the scab was, the less likely it would bleed and the easier it would come away in one piece. Either way, he always seemed to have bloody knees and pockets full of crusty scabs.

Occasionally he looked away from his task and threw some slate at Eddie, who would tell him sod off and get back to his scabbing.

“What you divey’s up to?" I said as I leant in the destroyed building's doorway. The doorway was to only thing standing on that side of the building. I was trying to look as cool as I could.

“Stop beating your gums,” Gobber said without looking up from his knee.

Since we saw the gumshoe movie at last Saturday’s matinée, he had been trying to drop in Yankee slang whenever he could.

Eddie looked down from the hill of slate he was stood on and currently rooting through, "Alright, our kid!" he said, as good-natured as always, and then he saw my ear. It must have been glowing for him to see it from all the way up there.

“Bloody Nora!” he said, “What happened to your ear? It’s the size of my bum and as red as me Grannies knuckles!”

He said the word *Bum* as *boom.* Up in Birkenhead, words sound thin and narrow, not fat and round like down here in Devon. Eddie half walked, and half slid down the slate pile to take a closer look. He stepped right up to me and peered at my ear. He leaned so close I could feel his breath on my hot ear, even if I couldn't hear him.

"By the cringe!" he said, impressed. "I think I can see it pulsing! Who did it to you? The Proddys?"

Gobber finally looked up and pulled an expression that meant he was mildly impressed, but only mildly.

"No, it was our Nan," Bertie said, stepping out from behind me.

"Y'alright, Bert-Twerp?" Gobber said, piping up at the site of Bertie. He enjoyed poking fun at my kid brother almost as much as I did.

"Yer wha?" said Eddie, getting even closer to me. "Yer Nan did dat?"

"Have ye seen 'is Nan?" Gobber said, getting to his feet and giving Bertie a shove. "She's the size of a brick shit 'Ouse."

"She clobbers like one as well," I said, pushing Eddie away, who was now on tiptoes trying to get an even closer look. "Get outta it. You wanna climb in or wha?" I said.

"What she cuff you like dat for?" Eddie asked, regaining his balance and then picking his nose. He let his finger do a full rotation in his nostril and seemed surprised and impressed by what came out of it. He looked at each of us and then held up the offending boggie for us to see.

I shoved him away before he had a chance to flick it at one of us, "Get away with you, yer animal." I turn to Bertie, "She cuffed me cos I gave Bert ere a scare in the outhouse. He squirted so hard he almost turned himself inside out."

"Bert did a squirt?" Eddie said, wiping his finger on the back of his shorts.

"Bert-Squirt!" Gobber shouted out with a laugh and then started singing the tune to *any old iron*, hooking his thumbs into the edges of his sleeveless pullover. "Oh! Bertie-squirt, Bertie-Squirt, little old, little old squirty. It's hard work, when he needs a squirt, gotta get his kecks off before he lets it squirt!"

Eddie and I fell over laughing while Bertie's face grew redder and hotter. Gobber was about to launch into another verse when Bertie stormed up to him and punched him right in the groin. Gobber let out a hefty wheeze of air and slowly doubled over, a high-pitched squeak straining out of him as he folded in on himself.

"Jeeze, Bertie! His nuts will be as big as Ray's ear!" Eddie said. He turned to me. "Wha's a matter wid 'im?"

"Don't pay 'im no mind. He's had a right cob on since I scared 'im. You alright, Gobber?"

Gobber rolled over onto his side. "sssssoooouuuunnnndddd," he said in a thin voice.

*

We weren't supposed to go into the quarry, as we called it. It was more like a dumping ground for old bits of furniture and bric-a-brac. We called it a quarry because all the junk was in the middle of what looked like a crater. The slopes that encircled the carter were the same sliding grey slate that seemed to carpet the whole of Birkenhead in those days. There were tufts of mud and thick, coarse weeds that erupted from the steep, sheer slopes. At the bottom, the junk lay in brown water, the depth of which was impossible to define. The quarry was unofficially owned by the rag & bone man. He collected all the junk from his weekly trips around the neighbourhood on his horse and cart. The rest of the time, he just seemed to sit around watching his collections pile up. I was never sure if he lived there or not. He was intent on protecting his junk from the local kids who were always trying to either steal anything they could carry or dare each other to get to the bottom crater and back without getting caught.

The four of us stood at the top of the crater, looking down into its belly. Gobber, who had limped all the way here, gave Bertie a shove. Bertie's arms wheeled out, trying to steady himself from falling in. His hand blindly reached out to grab my shirt, and I stood back, letting his fingers grab at the air before I caught hold of the back of his shorts and steadied him.

He gasped back his initial fear, and then in his whiney voice, said, "Don't Gobber! I almost fell!"

"Alright, alright," Gobber said, holding his hands up, "Keep your squirt on!"

Eddie and I let out a smirk, but all of us quieted down when we saw Bertie frown and clench his fists.

He turned to me and, in the same irritating whinge, said, "Ray, what are we doing here? The old Ragman will kill us if he catches us."

"*We* are going down der," I said pointing to the centre of the crater.

"What?" Bertie said, "Why?"

Eddie cut in, "Cos dat's where the old Ragman keeps his Nazi gold."

Bertie looked at each of us in turn and then settled on me, "What's he on about?"

"It's true-" Gobber said, but his voice cracked in a squeak. He cleared his throat and started again, making his voice as deep as he could. "It's true. They reckon he found it in when he cleared out old man Sterner's place after he died. They reckon Sterner was a Nazi spy who had a stashed as much gold as he could carry and hid right here in Birkenhead.

Bertie looked amazed for a moment, and then his frown returned. "Yer avin me on. Old man Sterner lived here for years. He was too old to be a spy."

"That was the perfect cover," Eddie said. "No one would suspect and 'auld codger like Sterner. They said he was a Gerry and that when the war broke out, he pledged his allegiance to Adolf and hid his gold. That's why his house never got bombed. They knew where he lived, and the bombers were under strict instructions not to bomb his house."

"Geeraway!" Bertie said. His accent got thicker when he was excited or scared. "That's a load of rubbish!"

"It's true. There is a safe down there that Ragman has been trying to crack ever since he got his grubby mitts on it."

Bertie looked down at the jumble of mess at the bottom of the slope, his eyes wide. All I could see was stagnant water and a load of old rubbish.

"It looks like a used bog down there," I said. It was true. The water was thick and brown with flies buzzing all over it. "I'm not going down there, Nazi gold or not."

"There could be a fortune down there," Gobber said.

"Even if there is, how you gonna crack a safe that Ragman has been trying crack all this time?"

"We'll figure something out. I reckon he hasn't hit it with a brick because he wants to sell the safe once he gets the gold out." Eddie said.

"Yer what?" I said, "You really believe you can smack a safe open wid a brick? Safes are safe because you can't break 'em," I said.

"S'Not true", Gobber said. "I saw dat film once where you just have to know the safes weak spots. It's the hinges, one or two good smacks on de hinge, and the door will pop right off."

I took a step back and folded my arms. "Alright... Go-ed den. Yous get down der and have a go."

Gobber looked down at the sheer slipping slate and licked his lips. I looked at Bertie, who seemed transfixed by the jumble of mess far below us. If his eyes could have rung with dollar signs, they would have. I nudged Eddie and quietly pointed to Bertie.

"How would I get back up again wid all dat gold?" Gobber said.

“I dunno,” Eddie said. “Maybe you could pull yerself up on dem der weeds un stuff.”

“*You* pull yerself up.” Gobber shot back.

“Why me, it's your idea.”

“One of us has to keep dixie in case Rag man shows up. We can lower one of us down on a rope, ders bound to be some round ere.”

“Come’ed den, let's find some rope," Eddie said.

“Hold on,” Gobber said, holding his hands up and adopting an American twang. “Who’s doing the lowering, and who’s getting lowered?”

“I’d better stay up here. I’m the strongest and can pull any o’ you lot up,” Eddie said.

“Yer Mam!” Gobber said, the scouse accent back in his voice. “You ain't bigger den one of dem dare weeds! I'll stay up here, and one of yous lot goes down dare.”

“The lightest one of us has to go down,” I interjected, my eyes fixed on Bertie, who was still looking at the jumble of metal, his face riddled with greed.

“Dat’s easy den. It’s auld Squirty- Bertie den.” Gobber said, lightly covering his groin with his hand and crossing one leg over the other.

“You up for it, Bertsquirt?” I said.

He nodded silently and then, without looking at me, said, “Don’t call me Squirty.”

“Alright, *Cuthbert*,” I said, dragging his full name out as long as I could. This broke his focus, and he turned to me.

“Don’t call me dat! I hate dat name!”

“Speak to Mam and Da, dey gave it to you. You up for it or what?” I said, nodding at the mess at the bottom of the crater.

Bertie took a step and leaned out to assess the drop and the distance to the bottom. “I could make it. I won’t need a rope.”

“Don’t be a div, course you’ll need a rope.” I turned to Eddie. “How long a rope d’you reckon Ed?”

We all edged closer to the lip of the crater. Our collective weight sent some slate slipping down from beneath us. Before we had the chance to step back, a voice boomed out at us.

“OI, YOU LITTLE SCALLYS!”

We all twisted around, and the slate under Bertie's feet gave way. He lurched forward to regain his balance and grabbed Eddie's shirttail that poked out from beneath his jumper. Eddies footing slipped, and he grabbed Gobber, who in turn grabbed me, and we all started to shoot down the slate slope on our bellies.

The noise we made skidding across the loose slate was deafening, and dust billowed up, marking our speedy descent. I flailed my arms back and forth, desperate to grab onto a mound of dirt, a weed or anything to stop me from slipping straight into the skanky water at the bottom. I felt something sting my hand, and I grabbed hold of it, and I jerked to a stop. It felt like my arm was almost ripped from its socket. We must have been falling fast.

As the dust settled, I tried to pick out if anyone had splashed into the stagnant brown water at the bottom. The sound of slipping slate dried up, and I caught the side of Gobber far over to my right and slightly below me. He was sat proudly astride a mound of earth with a branch erupting out of it.

“You alright, Gobber?!” I shouted.

“Me nuts!” he wailed back. “This branch caught me right in me nuts! I won’t have any left by the end of the day!”

Despite my precarious position, I smiled and looked below me to see what had happened to Eddie and Bert. The dust had almost cleared, and I saw Eddie to my left hoisting himself up onto a mud bank by a root. “Jeeze, Ray, that was crackers!" he said as good-naturedly as ever. No matter what predicament we found ourselves in, Eddie never seemed phased. He always just seemed happy to be along for the ride.

“Did Bert bite the swamp?” I shouted.

Eddie squinted into the dusty distance below. “Nah,” he said. “He’s just down dare, wriggling like a worm on a hook.”

He said *worm* as *weeerm.* You have big fat worms down here in Devon. Up there, our *werms* were small and wriggly.

Bertie was below me. He was clinging to a vine and writhing back and forth, trying to get and better grip.

“Y’Alright down dare, Bertie?” I called.

"No, I'm bloody not!" his whining voice called back. “You wait till Ma hear’s about dis. She’s gonna string you up by your hoo-ha!” he said.

“Only if you get back alive,” I said.

I started to look around. How the hell would we get back up to the top? I had lost interest in finding the Nazi gold now and hoped the others had too.

I heard the tinkle of fresh slipping slate come from above. I tried to look back up. I had completely forgotten what had caused us to fall. The Ragman. He had shouted out at us. I saw the tips of his feet. Above that his gaunt twisted face glared down at us.

“Little feckers..." he said and shot out a bullet of spit from between his crooked and yellow teeth. "In trouble now, ain’t ya? Little feckers.”

He crouched down and looked out across the mouth of his pit, scratching his chin with an audible rasp. He returned his gaze to me. Although I was a third of the way down the slope, I was the closest to him.

“Do I know you, boy?” he said quietly.

I shook my head.

“Do you know me?”

I nodded.

"You heard what I do to little feckers like you and your friends who come a trespassing?"

I didn't know for sure, but I didn't want him to tell me either, so I nodded again and felt the bramble vine I was clinging to start to give.

"Who's down there wit'cha?"

I stayed quiet. Did he want names?

"How many?"

"F-F-F-Four," I stammered, and then I quickly tried to explain ourselves. "It was me brudders idea, mister! He wanted to have a look at yer stuff down dare!"

He held up a hand to silence me. "Ain't nothing down there but dirt and horse shit," he said and stood.

He took a moment to look at the other three boys dangling at various points in the pit. Then looked back at me before he stepped back and disappeared from view.

I looked over at Eddie. "Bloody hell Eds! We gotta get outta here! He's gonna kill us!"

I tried to pull myself up, but I felt the vine give again. I froze. The last thing I wanted to do was slip down into that toilet water. I glanced down at Bertie, who was still wriggling.

"We still getting the gold?" he shouted.

Ignoring him, I tried to pull myself up, but the root broke. Suddenly I was sliding down again at a ridiculous speed.

"Oh! He's gonna get a dung dunk!" I heard Eddie shout to Gobber, who replied with a high-pitched squeak.

I tried to dig my feet into a slate as I plummeted, desperate to slow myself down. As I shot past Bertie, I grabbed hold of him, and the root he was clinging on to snapped with a loud whip crack. Then we were both clinging to each other as we hurtled towards the stagnant, festering brown filth.

"OHHHHHH EEEYYYYYYY!" Eddie narrated, "De brudders are in it together!"

In a flash, I saw a muddy brown mound coming up on my left side. I pushed Bertie away from me and caught the mud bank, jerking myself to a halt. I looked back and watched as Bertie's shot down the last stretch of slate. His eyes were fixed on mine, his face a mixture of shock and then confused disbelief at how quickly I abandoned him. I couldn't help but give him a little wave before he plopped into the water, disappearing completely. From the sound he made when he hit the water, I could tell it was more sludge than liquid, and the smell it released made me wretch.

"Oh, that's nasty," Eddie said

We all stared at the now smooth surface of the gunk lake.

"Oi Ray. Do you think he's dead?" Eddie shouted.

I surveyed the brown water. Where was the little squirt? A moment later, Bertie burst out from the gunk and stood waist deep in the filth. He was completely covered with brown dripping ooze. The flies that had been hovering just above the surface of the water now relocated to buzz around him. His two white eyes glared up at me.

"Oh, Ey! Dats Rank!" called Eddie.

Godder squeaked something I didn't hear, and I sniggered.

"Y'all right down dare Bertie?" I said.

"Squirty-Bertie!" Eddie added and chuckled.

"You found dat gold yet?" I said, as good-naturedly as possible.

Bertie just glared at me, his fist clenched before him. His head started to shake, and if he were the tin man, I'm sure he would have let out a *POOP POOP* sound from his tin hat.

The Ragman wasn't so bad after all. He sent down a rope with a hook on the end and tied the other end to his pony. We each took it in turns to wrap the rope around us, and then we heard the slap of his rough hand against the rickety old horses' rump, and we were each slowly dragged up across the shingle surface.

He was about to give us a gob full for trespassing when he clapped eyes on Bertie, who was the last of us to be pulled up. After that, he kept erupting into laughter and had to bend over to catch his breath, slapping his hand against his knee. In between this, he tried to tell us all off, but his sentences would get lost as his voice would get higher, and his whitter would turn into another attack of husky giggles.

In the end, he undid the chain from around the gate, wiping the tears from his eyes and let us out, settling to give the last of us a solid kick, right up the arse. His boots were something to be reckoned with, and I heard the crack against the bum bone. Fortunately for the rest of us, old Gobber caught it. He proceeded to waddle home, one hand clutching his wounded crotch, the other over his freshly booted bottom. He chuntered away to himself that he never should have come out today in the first place and that this type of thing never happened in America.

When Eddie and Gobber left us, I took a look at Bertie. He hadn't spoken since we left the 'quarry', and I wasn't sure if it was because he was still mad at me or because he was afraid he'd get some of... whatever it was on him.. in his mouth. The worse thing was that we were almost back to Price Street, and he was still soaking wet. Whatever he was covered in, it didn't want to dry. And he stank. Every once in a while, the wind blew past him, and I'd get an acid wrenching feeling of bile swell up in my throat.

"Jeeeezzzze Bertie, you don't half hum!" I said, looking at him from a safe distance.

Bertie just looked at me and fumed silently. Maybe the heat from his furry stopped the sludge from drying on him. I needed to at least get him dried out. I looked behind him and realised he had left a dark brown sloppy snail trail behind us. You could follow it all the way back to the Ragman's place.

"Jesus," I said to myself, "Dad could pick up your trail and follow it all the way home."

I delayed heading straight home because I knew what would be waiting for me. My good ear started to tingle at the very expectation of the wallop coming my way. I took Bertie down near the train tracks and got him to run around a bit to see if that would dry him out. All it did was make him sweat, and that just made him stink even more.

I was sitting on a pile of disused rail tracks, throwing stones, when I heard the *toot toot* of the 604. It would be chuffing its way right past us any minute. In a flash, I had a moment of inspiration.

"Come on, Bertie, there's hope for us yet." By us, I meant *me.*

I half shoved him up the grass bank and up onto the cobbled street, trying to wipe my hands clean of his smear on the grass as I went. He even felt smelly. On the street, we ran out onto the bridge that ran over the tracks.

"Ger yer head over dare Bertie!" I said.

He was too small to reach the top of the bridges brick wall. I heard the trains chunter and saw the thrusting plume of steam roaring towards us, chuff after chuff. With slight disgust, I grabbed Bertie by the bare legs and jerked him up so that his top half dangled over the top of the bridge. He let out a small shriek of fear. Maybe he thought I was trying to throw him off the bridge. I clung to him tightly and felt the thrum of the steam engine ploughed beneath the bridge. Then, like a whales spume, the steam erupted like a volcano on the other side of the bridge, breaking free of its stone captor and hitting Bertie directly in his face and upper body. I felt his upper body get blown back by the force of the steam, and I pulled his feet to the ground.

He looked back at me dazed as the sound of the train shunted off into the distance, the throng of the steel animal retreating as it went. What I had hoped for was an instantly dried little brother. I could not get rid of the smell, but if he were dry, he wouldn't seem such a mess and surely the smell would decrease slightly.

He was still wet, soaking in fact. But now, his top half was also caked in black soot. So far today, I had managed to soak him in sewage and roll him in soot. I pulled at my good ear, enjoying its normal feel for however long it lasted.

Bertie said nowt all the way home. He still stank, and he was still leaving some kind of wet smear behind him as he walked. We both stood in front of the steps to our house, not wanting to go in. I looked him in the eye and shrugged.

"Come 'ed," I said, "Let's be men about it."

I got my key out and opened the door, graciously allowing Bertie in first. He trudged in, and before he could call out from the matt, I whispered, "Tell Mam it wasn't me!" and I slammed the door and shot off down the street as fast as I could. Just as I turned off Price Street, I heard my Nan's booming voice calling for me to come back.

I scuffed around the street a bit longer. I knew I had only made it worse by running off and leaving Bertie to take the flack, but the longer I could hear from both ears, the better. Eddie and Gobber were nowhere to be seen, so I flicked stones into the dock for a bit and then went down to the train tracks and flatted a few pennies.

As it got dark, I knew the trouble I was in was getting worse as each minute passed. I stood on the street corner and watched the lights go out in a zig-zag across the front of the house. My Dad was methodically going to bed. Before I approached the front door, I gave it another ten minutes – he was the last to bed and fell asleep quickly. It was dark outside, and I was freezing. My hand shivered as I reached for the lock, and a pulse throbbed through my bad ear like the devil's steam engine. It was so loud I thought the sleeping house would hear it.

Once inside, I snuck through to the kitchen, rubbing my hands together to generate some warmth. On the hot plate was a covered dish. I was starving. I lifted the cooling plate covering the dish, my hands aching in its warming embrace. Underneath, I saw a pie of some sort. This was a good sign. Mam, at least, didn’t want me to go hungry.

I had just clawed in a mouthful of the pie when I heard a creak on the stairs. I knew which one it was. It was the one I avoided when sneaking out. It was four stairs from the bottom, my early warning step.

With my mouth fit to burst with pie, I quickly and silently replaced the cover on the dish. If I left it uncovered, whoever was coming would know I was home. I looked for somewhere to hide. Everywhere was too noisy to open or climb into... except under the sink. I swept back the curtain and slipped into the dark space pulling the curtain back just before I sensed someone enter the room. I held my breath which meant I couldn’t chew my food. My cheeks were bulging.

I heard the fat padding of bare feet and ill-tempered muttering. I thought I could make out curse words in this chuntering, but they were said so quietly and quickly I couldn't catch them. The flat-footed steps slapped up to the hot plate, and the muttering seemed to acknowledge the dish was still covered. The feet turned and smacked, heavy and irritated, over to the back door. The muttering and the hefty gait sounded like Nan. If she caught me, my good ear wouldn't stand a chance.

She opened the back door, and I felt the icy breeze blow in and whirl around the kitchen. Newspapers on the table fluttered, and a few daring leaves skidded like mice across the tiles that reflected the moonlight. She was going for the outhouse. Once the door closed, I would have my chance to shoot up the stairs and into my room.

I heard her curse the cold. I knew she wasn't looking forward to sitting on a freezing seat. The door slammed, but I paused before making my escape. I heard the slap of her feet again. She hadn't gone out! She padded to the sink. I could see her gnarled and fungus-infected toenails beneath the edge of the curtain. This was it! She must have heard me! I held my breath. I felt a cough rise in my throat, so I slapped a hand across my food filled mouth. I waited for the curtain to be yanked back and for the vice-like grip on my ear to jerk me out from my hiding space. But it never came.

Her feet turned so that her ankles faced me. I couldn't work out what she was doing. Maybe she was sleepwalking? And sleep swearing? She backed up to the sink. I heard her gather up her rustling nightie, and then she let out a groan as she squatted. The next thing I heard was an enormous and powerful jet of wee. I heard it swish around the basin and rattle down the plughole that was directly above my head. I wanted to laugh. I *needed* to laugh! I couldn't wait to tell Eddie and Gobber already.

I put both hands over my mouth, which was still bursting with pie, I had to spit it out, or I'd choke on my internal hysterics. Over the sound of her endless flow, I heard her even longer sigh of relief. I couldn't take much more. I started to convulse, my shoulders shaking, the back of my neck aching. This was worse than trying to stifle a laugh in Sunday Service.

As the flow slowed, so did her sigh. I was almost through it. I just had to last a few moments longer. I heard her start to groan as if in pain. Then she let rip with the loudest explosion of flatulence I had ever heard. The basin amplified the sound, and I swear I felt it rumble through my bones. At the release of her gas, her flow restarted and... and... well... that was it for me.

I spat my food out with a projectile laugh. I can still see the semi-dissolved slice of pie shoot out across the moonlit black and white tiles, making the short curtain I was hiding behind billow as it went. I lapsed into manic hoots of laughter, clutching at my belly and letting my legs kick out from under the sink.

From her squat position, I heard Nan exclaim, "*WHAT IN THE*

NAME OF FECK…?" And the next thing I knew, I was dragged out by my legs. My memory of this is that she held me upside down by my ankles. She drew my upside-down face to hers. She fumed like an enraged giant. Either way, I went to bed with two ears that couldn't hear and a bum that wouldn't let me sit down for a week.

TEN

Before. Four Sundays ago. The end of picnic time.

I love Dad's stories of when he was a lad. There are a few special ones we get him to tell us whenever we can. If we're lucky, we can keep him talking for a good hour by reminding him of another one just before he finishes the one he's telling. This one was great. I never realised he got up to all that mischief in one day.

If I could go back in time, I reckon Dad and me would get on great as kids. I'd love to be tramping around Birkenhead with him, Eddie and Gobber. If I could find a way to go back in time, I would have to make sure they'd like me. It's difficult to make friends. I'm not good at it, so I would take some cool modern weapon back for Eddie to wield. I could take American comics for Gobber and Dad, well... I'd hope Dad would like me for who I am. After all, we are family, but he couldn't know that because that might mess up the space-time continuum. I'd just have to be really cool when I get there. Surely because I'm all modern, they'd think I'm cool anyway.

We are still huddled around the gas burner; I've dried off a bit, but I haven't put my jeans on yet. We sit in silence now after laughing at Dad's story. We've drained the last of the tea from the thermos flask, and I swirl my last swallow of tea around in my tin cup and sling it out, as we always do. Tessa does the same. I stand, pulling the blanket up around me. Dad is standing on the other side of Tessa, leaning against the fallen tree trunk, looking into his last bit of tea. I wonder if he's thinking about when he was a kid. Thinking about it, If I do go back in time, he would have already met me. I have to find a way to ask if he remembers a boy like me called Billy. So far, I've never appeared in his stories, but maybe the next one he tells might have me in it.

I want to be closer to Dad, so I walk past Tessa and in front of him to stand on his other side. As I go, he absent-mindedly swirls his cup and slings out the tea. It sloshes right in my ear, and I freeze. Dad blurts out a laugh, and Tessa calls out, "What? What happened?"

"Blimey Billy," Dad says, "You're determined to get soaked one way or another!

ELEVEN

Before. Three Saturdays ago. Evening time.

Going out on a Saturday evening is rare, and Dad never seems pleased about it. Certain things indicate we are going out. Upstairs always smells entirely of Ellenett hairspray. Dad puts on a shirt and tie and sits, slumped on the sofa near the fireplace. He always takes hold of the brass shoehorn and slowly slips his feet into each slip-on shoe, easing his heels in with the horn. I like to do the same when I put shoes on, but I usually forget and stuff my feet in as fast as possible. This, I'm repeatedly told, breaks the back of the shoe. I've never seen a shoe with a back.

Whenever Mum announces we are invited out, Dad always makes the same joke. No matter what it is, he gives Mum a broad smile and says, "Well, *you* lot have a lovely time!" To which Mum responds with her wordless tight expression.

When we get to Mike and Sharon's house, there are loads of back slaps from Mike and coos of "*Oh!* It's been *too long!* Why don't we meet more often?" from Sharon.

Mike and Sharon's house is always a mystery to me. I don't think I've ever seen it in the daylight. It's way bigger than ours, and it seems to have grown since the last time we were here. We're all ushered into the kitchen. They have one of those counters in the centre of the kitchen, and everyone stands around it. There is a selection of bottles and bowls of different types of snacks, some I've never seen before.

"What can I get yah, *mate?*" Mike asks Dad, and somehow, without speaking, a beer works its way into his hand.

Whenever Dad mentions Mike, he does it the same way John does in *Dear John.* In that show, John is divorced, and his wife has remarried a man called Mike who's all big and quiffed, like our Mike. When John says Mike's name in the TV show, he does it in a deep voice and swings his arms out like a gorilla. Dad does the same about this Mike. Mike is all back slaps, handshakes and calling everyone *mate.* I'm not sure how Mum and Dad know Mike and Sharon, but we don't see them as much as we used to.

Tessa takes a glass of lemonade, and I do the same. Mike and Sharon's two sons appear.

"Here they are!" Mike says proudly, "Thought you two were a no-show."

They say their hellos but hang by the kitchen door as if they might dart away at any minute. They are both older than Tessa, and I'm never sure which one is the oldest. They go to a different set of schools than us, and they are impossibly tall and broad. They wear the same smug grin. I'm not sure if Tessa fancies one of them, or both of them, or neither of them.

They stand close and whisper to each other. I'm sure they are talking about me. They're not looking directly at me, but their gaze did move across me like the shadow of a cloud. I know that's how most people do it. They see you and then look in a different direction so as to seem interested in something else. Then they talk about you thinking you won't know that you are the topic of their conversation. As they whisper and giggle, I push closer between mum and Dad at the counter, hoping that if I'm not seen, I won't be of interest anymore.

“So, how's the old print trade then, Ray?” Mike asks dad.

Dad presents a smile, but before he answers, the conversation takes a swirl, and Mum asks, “Weren't you away recently?”

I don't know how Dad did it, but he managed to make everyone feel like he answered Mike's question when he didn't. Dad always seems to not want to be at these types of events or social gatherings. It gives him this enviable air of aloofness that I think actually draws people to him, which appears to be the opposite of what he wants. I wish I could be like that and give off that air. It's so cool to *not* want to be involved when you are. If I am ever involved in something, I'm usually too excited just to be there to be able to give off that kind of vibe. If I'm not involved, I feel jealous and wish I were. I don't think Dad feels that way. He seems to be able to take it or leave it. Most of the time, I think he would rather leave it.

We once had a party at my Grans house, and she had some friends over. One of the old men brought his harmonica, and he started to play old war songs for the rest of the group to sing along to. I really enjoyed it, and then I noticed Dad wasn't there anymore. He was stood out the back. Tessa had just joined him. He was looking up at the star-riddled sky.

"You not singing, Dad?" I asked.

He smiled and looked back up at the clear night sky. "Amazing, isn't it?" he said. "There's so much out there."

We ended up staying out there until Mum came and got us with her frown. I remember thinking then that I wish I hadn't enjoyed the sing-a-long. I wanted to be like Dad and *not* want to be there at all.

"Yah, we were. Spent a quick weekend up in the *Big Smoke*." Mike said, "Took the lads and took in a couple shows." Mike doesn't say *yes* or *yeah* anymore. He says *yah.* In fact, everyone who lives in this house says *yah.* Dad will mimic this for the next couple of days.

"Sounds lovely," Mum says, sipping at her wine.

"Yah, it really was. Fantastic place, you ever been up to the city?" Mike says, but before mum can answer, he continues. "Thinking we might buy a pad up there, y'know? Might take advantage of the slump. It'd be a great investment. Be great to have a place to crash up there, and, you never know, if one of the lads goes to

Uni up there, then their accommodation is sorted. Then it pays for itself." Mike always calls his sons *the lads,* which makes them sound like a pair of dogs he's unnaturally proud of.

Mum chokes down another sip, "I see. Yes... Well, that would be convenient, wouldn't it...." Her voice starts to trail off, "...and a good... investment."

I'm not sure what Mike does for a living. As far as I know, he just drives around in a car with electric windows and a sunroof. One time he happened to pull up next to us in his car while we were stopped at a traffic light. He let his passenger side window lazily glide down with an electric hum while Dad worked hard to wind his down with the handle. Our widow made a loud screech sound as it unevenly dropped. They exchanged a few words, and when the lights started to change, Mike's window was closed in seconds, and he shot off, leaving Dad working his window back up to the sound of car horns before we spluttered forward again.

Mike pauses while opening a bottle of red wine for Sharon and looks at Mum. He lets out a smile as if he's made of fool of himself by forgetting something.

"Oh... You mean the tan!" he says and points to his hairy forearms that are half exposed because he has his shirt sleeves rolled up twice. "Sorry!" he says as if he's been slow on the uptake. "Yah, we popped over to Spain. Wanted to keep the healthy glow a bit further into the darker season, y'know."

"Oh, that must have been lovely, mustn't it, Ray." Mums says, her eyes pleading that he get involved in the conversation.

Dad nods and holds his glass up to take a sip of his beer. He holds it in front of his mouth for a moment to hide an expression I can't see.

We usually go on a camping holiday to Cornwall or North Devon, and it rains every day. We've come to expect it now. None of us ever seem to have tans.

We've been to London once, but that was because Grandad had

to have an operation that no one else in the country could perform. We didn't *take in any shows*. While Mum was at the hospital, Dad took pictures of us in front of lots of different places. We walked everywhere, and on the few occasions we got the train underground, it was so busy I felt I would be lost.

There are lots of strange people in London, especially in the underground. Dad said not to look at them when we went past them, but it was hard not to. There was one very dirty looking woman. She was sitting on the floor with a hat in front of her. She looked sad and very thin. Her skin looked like old leather, and her eyes were like marbles. She saw me looking at her, and she held out her hand. I stepped towards her as she seemed to want to tell me something, but Dad snatched me away. I've always wondered what she might have said if she had got the chance to speak to me.

"How's Billy doing at school?" Sharon's question to Mum is not as quiet as she intended, and it wrenches me back to now. I look at *the lads* who look smugger than ever. They've ensnared Tessa into their whispering.

I glare at the kitchen counter, focussing on the three shadows cast around every object. My face starts to burn. This is a rehash of the same conversation they have every time we see them. Why do they need to do this every time? Sharon will ask how I'm doing as if I can't hear her, and mum will try to mumble a response to hide her answer from me. I'm not an idiot! I know people talk about me and my *problems.*

Why does it matter how I do at school? When have the A-Team ever managed to get out of a fix by being able to recite what seven times eight is right there on the spot? When has their spelling been able to help them get away from Colonel Decker? How will these things help me in life? And it's not just what I can do at school that they all discuss, it's *who* I know and *who* likes me. Why does it matter how many friends I have or who they are? The A-Team are outcasts. They don't care who avoids sitting next to them in assembly, and they don't care if they never get picked to play a game at lunchtime, so why does it matter to all the grownups around me.

I can feel my vision clouding over until Dad nudges me. The darkness clears, and I look up at him. He raises his big eyebrows at me. It's comical, but it's also an *are you okay/it doesn't matter* gesture. I nod at him just once and look back at the counter. There is a bowl of twig type things that have dried peas and other bits in it. I reach out to take some but pause as no one else has taken any from this bowl. I'm not sure for a moment if it's a snack or something to make the room smell nice. I look up at Dad, who nods to go ahead. But I don't.

"What is it?" I whisper up to him, and he shrugs. He reaches out and takes up a handful. He holds his closed fist over my open palm and lets some of the snack drain into my hand like birdseed. He then eats what he has left in his hand and looks down at me. His eyebrows raise to encourage me. I eat it. It's spicy but nice. Even the peas are good. I look back up at Dad to get me more, but he points his head at the bowl for me to get some myself. I shake my head. Dad repeats the move, taking a handful of the mix and sharing it between us.

“So,” Mike says, interrupting our silent dialogue, “You like the Bombay mix, eh? Little fella?”

I look at Dad, who seems to apologise with his eyes at Mike's use of the phrase *little fella*. I nod at Mike.

"Spicy, eh? Yah, they were in a restaurant we went to in London. The lads fell in love with the stuff, so I picked it up in a shop around here. Pretty pricey but del-ish, right?"

I nod and look at Dad. If you didn't know him like Tessa and I do, you would believe the fixed expression he's wearing to be a natural one. But there is just a hint, a flicker of irritation and sometimes suppressed humour across his eyes if you look deeper. Like when Mike called me *little fell* – irritation. When Mike said *delish!* – irritation, then humour. When Mike said *Oh... You mean the tan!* –flat out humour, all masked with a fixed, suppressed look.

I nod that I like them and tug at Dad's sleeve to retrieve me some more. As an alternative, he slides the bowl over to me and gives me an encouraging tilt of the head. I glance at Mike, who doesn't have the silence Dad has. He tells me, "You crack on, little fella!" Dad's fixed look masks irritation.

"Oh, you really must upgrade!" Sharon is telling Mum. I start to tune into their conversation now that they've stopped talking in code about me. "The finance deal is a steal, and you get a practically new car!"

"No practical about it," Mike chips in, "It is a new car!"

What I don't understand about Sharon is how her name has changed over the last few years. She was always Sharon to us, even Auntie Sharon, but now she talks about herself in a different way. To start with, she always says her own name when telling a story about herself. It's as if she needs to reinforce her own name change through repetition.

"So, my hairstylist says to me, 'Shazza, you really must trade that old boneshaker in and get a new toy!"

Dad's fixed look is working overtime, burying irritation and a waning sense of humour. He needs back up, so he holds his glass up to his mouth and pauses before he drinks.

"Oh, don't you already have a new car?" Mum asks, innocently taking the bait.

"That's the co car. Nice, eh?" Mike says.

"What's a co car?" Mum asks.

Mike seems as pleased as a fisherman with a big catch as he reels mum in.

"That's the company car. We don't pay for it, just abuse it, y'know what I mean?"

I look at Mum and Dad in turn. I don't know what he means, and by the look of them, neither do they.

“We run it all over the place, might as well as it’s not ours. Get a new one every couple of years. Shazza...” There that name is again. It would appear that Mike has been recruited to help the *Shazza* name change reinforcement. He continues, “...Shazza’s gonna get the nippy little run-around. Amazing, eh Ray? How the lady gets the nippy run-around, and we get the workhorse!" Mike smiles at his own joke, but we only have one car.

I can't see how his car is the workhorse. His car is amazing and goes really fast. You can hardly compare it to ours. Then I start to feel guilty as if I've betrayed our car and Mum and Dad.

Once again, Dad seems to have reacted in a way that means he didn’t have to speak, and yet Mike seems to think he has agreed with him. Mike must know how different they are, yet he keeps making comments as if they are exactly the same.

Mum shoots Dad a quick glance, and then her eyes scour the countertop in search of a change in subject.

“I must say, that’s a lovely bowl you have there, really pretty,” she says.

I inwardly groan. This is another rehashed conversation piece, a social fallback in times of emergency silence fillers. I even know the exact words that will come from Sharon... Sorry, Shazza... next.

“Oh, that...” she says. She seems to start every sentence with *Oh!* as if each topic raised were a compliment she is too humble to take. “...Yes, thanks. We picked it up in Barcelona. Beautiful city, have you been?” she asks, but she must know the answer because I know this conversation word for word. “It’s not really a bowl you use....” I have to stop myself from mouthing the next words with her, “It’s more of a statement piece.”

Silence seems to fill the kitchen for a moment. Even the *lads* and Tessa appear to quieten down. Mum saves the gap by saying, "Yes, I see, well it really is an eye-catcher." With that, the hum of the room returns.

"Why don't we move into the living space," Mike says, arms out in an ushering gesture.

The phrase *living space* draws a noticeable exchange of glances between Mum and Dad. As if the level they were expecting to play at tonight has just been raised without their agreement.

Dad thirstily takes up his glass, and on second thought, he takes the can of beer and gives it a shake to gauge how much is left. Mum looks at her half-empty glass and then longingly at the perspiring bottle of white wine on the counter. She's missed her chance of a refill because Mike has started to move us into the *living space.*

The *lads* see this as their opportunity to bail out, and they gesture to Tessa to come with them. She does, and all three of them slip out the kitchen door as we head in the other direction. Only Dad and I see them go, and his gaze lingers on the empty doorway for a moment longer than mine. He's brought back to the moment by mum's whispering voice.

“Don’t forget, you’re driving tonight,” she says.

His face returns an expressionless nod. As we follow behind Mike and Sharon, Dad quickly takes the beading bottle of wine and tops Mum’s glass up without our hosts seeing. She gives him a grateful and relieved half smile as he replaces it on the counter.

When we walk into the living room, I notice that this room, in particular, has grown. Mum lets out a sigh of approval by an “It’s really lovely, how nice, eh Ray?”

There is a soft orange glow in the room that has drawn my attention. We are directed to the sofas and armchairs. I still choose to sit on the floor next to Dads leg, despite there being plenty of places to sit. Once settled, I look around for the source of the orange glow. It is coming from a free-standing rocket-shaped thing. It has metal legs and tip, but the thing's body is clear and filled with thick orange liquid. It glows, and there, in the middle, are blobs of what look like lava floating up and down. They separate on their journeys and collide again, absorbing each other only to fall apart again in huge, shape-changing globules. It's mesmerising, and I stare at it, transfixed.

I nudge dad and point to it. "What's that?" I whisper. He's looking at it too and tries to push my finger down, but it's too late. Mike has seen us.

"Amazing, isn't it?" he says, "It just draws you in, eh?"

Mum sees it and asks for us, "What is it?"

"That, Jan, is our lava lamp," Mike says.

"A what?" Mum asks, not hiding her reaction.

"It's a lava lamp," Sharon adds.

"Is it… real lava?" I ask with quiet hesitation.

"Heavens no!" Mike says, "But it's impressive, don't you think?"

I can do nothing else but nod.

"A neighbour of ours had one. I just loved it when I saw it. Had to get one. So, we went for the biggest."

Dad's mask hides a, *of course, you did* irritation.

"You should get one, Ray. There is nothing better than coming home after a hard day's work and unwinding in front of the old lava lamp. It's incredibly relaxing, better than watching the old goggle box, right Shazza?"

"Oh, yes. It really sets the mood of the room. I think it gives us a bit of a space-age feel. Mike loves to stare at it."

"Yah," Mike says, "It's where I get most of my inspiration."

Dad holds his glass in front of his mouth, hiding a private smile.

I shuffle on the floor. My hands stroke the soft, plush carpet. I run my fingers along each thread, looking for a coarse end I can pull at, but there aren't any. I keep checking, and I shift to get more range, but Mike spots me.

"You'd rather be upstairs with the big kids? Eh, little fella?"

I wouldn't rather be with them. I'd rather be at home with the tele all to myself. I would rummage through the videos and see if I could find a grown-up film that wouldn't give me nightmares.

"It's okay. You don't have to stay here with us old fogies," Mike says.

"Oh," Sharon says, slapping Mike playfully, "You speak for yourself! Old fogies indeed! Right, Jan?"

Mum smiles and looks at me to see what I'll do.

"It's alright, little fella. The lads will take care of you. You can run upstairs if you like."

Now I'm stuck. I don't really want to go up and see the *lads* because they might just tease me, but now I have to get up and walk out of the room. Why can't Mike leave me alone? Why can't I just blend in with the room, so I can watch but not be involved or even noticed?

I give Dad a glance, but he doesn't tell me anything with his eyes. I wish he would tell me to stay, but he doesn't know that's my preference. He probably thinks I can't wait to get away from Mike. I know he would jump at the chance to leave the room.

I stand awkwardly and shuffle off to the doorway nearest the stairs in the corridor. If I had to choose, I'd go through the other doorway into the kitchen and finish off the Bombay mix, but then they will be able to see me from the living room.

I pause by the threshold. The conversation behind me has picked up but not enough to mean they are fully absorbed. If I stole across the hallway into the dining room, they would see me. I consider taking the risk and doing it anyway but then what? I'd be trapped in the dining room. What if there is nothing to do? And at some point, one of the grown-ups will go upstairs and check on *us* kids, and if I'm not there, they might think the older kids have been mean to me. And then they'll ask what's going on, and the big kids will say I never went up there in the first place, and I'll have to explain why I chose an empty dining room over company, and it will just get really awkward and... and... and! Breathe... I need to breathe.

I'm still standing in the doorway, and I realise my time is up. If I don't move, one of the adults will ask what I'm doing or what's wrong or worse... take me upstairs themselves! It's move now or be noticed. I move around the door frame and onto the first stair. These stairs are broad, wooden, and heavily varnished. They don't even creak when I step on them. These would be ideal for listening to conversations happening downstairs. I reckon I could get halfway down without being noticed and could hear everything said if I lived here. Not like our stairs, where every step has an independent creak.

I leave the voices in the living room behind me and pad up the silent staircase. The upstairs seems even bigger than the downstairs. I stand on the landing and consider retreating back to the grown-ups. I can hear the dull chuckle of the *lads,* but there are so many doors I'm not sure which one they are behind or if I really want to find them.

I move quietly down the corridor until I come to a door that is ajar with soft light spilling out onto the carpet. As I draw close, I stand on what must be the only creaking floorboard in the house, and my presence is announced with a squeak.

"Shh!" one of the boys inside says, and the door is snatched back.

Shane stands like a giant in front of me, his face in shadow.

"Oh, it's just you. I thought it was one of *them* eavesdropping." He leaves the door open, goes back into the room, and slumps on the ruffled bed. He hasn't told me to get lost, but he hasn't invited me in either, so I just linger by the door. *Lurking* is what Dad calls it when he catches me dithering in doorways.

Inside, Tessa is sitting on a chair that can spin around, and the other *lad,* Wayne, is sitting on a table, foot up and arm resting on his knee, looking nonchalant.

“You get bored with the oldies downstairs, Bill?” Shane asks.

I look at Tessa, who is looking at the floor. She seems embarrassed to have me here and unsure how this encounter will go. I noticed that Shane called me Bill. Not Billy. *Billy* sounds little. He hasn’t called me *little fella* either. *Bill* sounds big. It’s this that gives me the brief confidence to look up at him and nod and shrug at the same time.

“Yeah,” Shane says, “They can be a drag.” He looks at Wayne for a moment and then says, “Dad show you that bloody lava lamp?”

I smile and nod again.

"Man!" he says and looks at Wayne, who smirks. "He's so weirdly proud of that thing! It's creepy, man! He'd rather look at that than talk to Mum!"

“When he’s here!” Wayne adds.

I look from the two of them to Tessa. I feel like I’ve suddenly seen behind the wizard’s curtain. Tessa smiles in a coy way. Does she know this kind of stuff already?

"Your old man seems okay, though," Shane says.

I nod.

“At least he’s not obsessed with a lava dick!”

I smile but feel awkward at the word *dick*.

“Hey Billy,” Wayne says, “You got any girlfriends yet?”

Shane looks at Wayne. I get the feeling he disagrees with this line of questioning, but he says nothing. This is where it starts. I know from experience. I begin to feel accepted, and then one of the group takes the easy route and starts to put me down and push me around. I look at Tessa for support, but she isn’t looking at me. Maybe she is unsure of her standing in this group.

“Well?” Wayne asks, “You having any of the old smoocheroo?” And he puckers his lips at me.

Shane looks bored. I shake my head, hoping that’s enough to stop this where it is but knowing it's not.

"No... Really? It won't be long *little fella.* You'll soon have the ladies all over you!"

Little fella. He said it. I think he is following his Dad closer than Shane. I long for Shane or Tessa to say something.

"Don't you talk?" Wayne says.

I shrug and wonder if I can just walk away.

"I'm talking to you!" Wayne says.

My face starts to burn, and I feel stranded even though three people are close to me. I don't want to cry. I wish I could just be left at home.

"Hey!" Shane says. "Let's play a game!"

"Don't be lame, Shane!" Wayne says.

"You're lame, *Wayne,*" Shane shoots back, "C'mon, it'd be cool. You want to, don't you Bill?"

I look at Shane. I'm not sure if this is a genuine suggestion or a trap. I nod, not wanting to leave Shane hanging, but I'm fearful of how this will go. My mind screams at me to run away! Go back downstairs where it's safer.

"Let's play hide and seek," Shane says.

I look at Wayne, who has lost interest.

"C'mon. Let's do it. There are loads of places to hide up here."

Wayne seems to consider this and picks something out of his teeth. He looks at whatever it is for a moment and then flicks it away. He looks over at Shane, who gives him a *come on* look and then he shrugs.

"Yeah, okay, Tessa, are you in?"

I hear her say *yes,* but the look between Shane and Wayne has worried me. There could be some silent dialogue going on, and I start to dread this game. It could go one of two ways. They might hide and get me to look for them and then all shoot downstairs, leaving me fumbling in the dark up here alone. Alternatively, they could get me to be one of the hiders and then never find me and leave me upstairs alone. I know all the tricks they can play. I should just walk away and take the brunt of their jeers as I retreat.

"Okay, great!" Shane says. "Right, Wayne, you count, and we'll hide."

Right... so it's going to be that I hide, and they run away and leave me. I resign myself to being made a fool of and wait for the next instruction.

"Oh, man! Why do I have to seek?" Wayne whines.

"You'll get to hide next time. C'mon, don't be gay." Shane says. "Don't start yet. I'll tell you when."

Shane, Tessa and I step into the dark hallway but remain in the room's soft glow. Shane bends down to speak to us.

"Tessa, you go that way. Bill..."

Here we go. I'll be sent to the furthest corner and left there while they all have a good laugh at me.

"Bill, you hide with me. I know a great place."

My face and my feelings immediately brighten. If I hide with him, then they can't be trying to get rid of me. I look at Tessa, who seems disgruntled at having to go off on her own. Maybe she was hoping for some hide and seek smoocheroo with Shane?

"Okay, Wayne-ker!" Shane shouts, and I stifle a laugh, "Start counting!"

"Don't call me that, Shit Shane! I'll tell Dad!"

"Oooh, *I'll tell Dad!*" Shane says back in a falsetto voice. "You have to find me first!" He pats me on the shoulder, "Come on, Bill." And we slip down the hall. I'm giddy with excitement as it looks like Shane is *actually* being nice to me, not pretending to be nice just to lure me in.

We play for a while, even Wayne gets into it, and I can't help but bounce on the spot when we are all together. Sharon shouts at us at one point for thumping around as we run to hiding spaces. The house is great for hiding in, with lots of rooms, floor-length curtains and wardrobes.

"Okay," Shane says, gasping for breath after making Tessa jump when she found him amongst his Dad's suits in a wardrobe, "Let's go one more time and then get some lemonade."

We all agree, and I want to be the best hider this time. So far, Shane has gone to all the best places, but I've thought of a good one. It's in the room that we agreed was off-limits because Mike would flip if we went in there, apparently.

Wayne is counting again, and we all scat as he begins. I slip around the corner, not seeing in which direction Tessa and Shane have gone. At the end of the corridor is the off-limits room. This is going to be great, they will all take ages to find me, and then they'll say that I am the best hider they have ever seen. Or not seen in my case!

The door has one of those round handles, and my sweaty palm slips on it as I try to turn it. I use both hands, and the door opens. I push it just far enough to slip inside and then close the door behind me. The room is completely dark. I can see a crack of light between the heavy curtains and the moonlight making a line on the carpet to me. There are dense shadows on either side of me, and I start to feel a bit scared. I need to focus on the moon-light path and get to the window. I walk along it like a tightrope walker, and when I get there, I slip quickly behind the curtain, just before the hand of whatever creature my imagination has dreamt up snatches me back into the never-ending gloom.

I start to jitter. They will never find me. This is an even better hiding place than I could have hoped for.

Off in the distance, I hear Wayne finish his countdown and begin his search. He doesn't shout the *ready or not. Here I come!* I guess that's too babyish for him.

I look at the curtain directly in front of me. It's a thick and heavy curtain, the type I imagine old theatres had. I'd use this as a stage and burst out of the curtains like Eric and Ernie if I lived here. I wonder why the *lads* aren't allowed in here. This is perfect for shows.

I touch the fabric in front of me. It's ridiculously thick, and I try to think why these curtains are different from the rest of the house. I look up at the curtain rail and then try and lift some of the curtain to feel how heavy it is.

I peek around the curtain and look into the room. It's completely dark except for the streak of moonlight. I follow its path with my eyes up to the door. I can't see anything on either side. What is this room used for? It's not Shane or Wayne's bedroom or Mike and Sharon's as I've already hidden in those rooms. If any room were off-limits, surely it would be the parent's room. What goes on in here?

I stare into the darkness to try and pick out some shapes. I know it will take a few minutes until my eyes get used to the dark. I decide not to look out the window behind me as, due to the bright full moon, the garden is better lit than in here, and I don't want to delay my eyes adjustment.

In the distance, I hear Wayne find Tessa, who shouts *boo* at him as he finds her to try and scare him. I grow excited. Only Shane to find, and then I'll be the winner.

I keep my eyes fixed on one side of the black room. Shapes start to form in the gloom, but they shift the more I stare at them. I start to see the outline of something long like a bed. Maybe this is a spare room, but why the secrecy of the thick curtains?

I stare harder at the shape. No, it's not a bed, it's something similar in length, but it looks more oval than a bed. What is it?

The gloom draws back as my eyes delve into the darkness, and then I realise what it is. Startled, I jerk my head back behind the curtain. I don't want to look anymore. Is it really what I think it is? It looks just like it. What else would it be? I think about looking into the room again, but I know that I won't see well as my eyes have now been exposed to the moonlight.

I look at the curtains right before my face. Of course! That's why they have such thick curtains to keep the sunlight out during the day! I need to see if it's open or closed. I feel a cold fear creep up my back. Bloody hell! Was it really what it looked like? I look back into the room.

The coffin sits there. The lid looks like it's closed, but it's hard to tell.

I start to jitter. Why is there a coffin in here? Can I make it out of the room without the coffin opening? Is the vampire still in there waiting to come out or...? Is Mike a vampire, and this is his *real* bedroom? Oh no! Are Mum and Dad downstairs having their blood sucked? Was Mike just waiting to send me upstairs before he attacked them?

No... No...! I saw Mike's reflection in the kitchen window. If he were a vampire, I wouldn't have seen him in the night-time mirror. So that must mean they keep a vampire here, but why? Have they made some deal with the devil to give a vampire a home in return for...? For... A car with electric windows?

My head is buzzing. This is nonsense. Of course, it is. There are no such things as vampires. But that is definitely a coffin. And the room is off-limits as if it holds some secret.

I want to run across the room and back into the corridor, but my hands are sweating more than when I came in. I won't be able to grip the round door handle. In my panic and distraction, the coffin could open behind me, and I'd be a goner!

No, I'm better off staying here.

But... maybe the vampire heard me come in, and it is just waiting for the right time to sneak out and pounce on me. I think I hear a creak in the house with only one squeaky floorboard. Is that the coffin opening? I can't look. I don't want to see the grey, stooped and fanged creature coming towards me.

Stop it! Why does my brain do this to me and give me the worse images at the worse times? Hopefully, Wayne and Tessa will find Shane, and he might think to look for me in here.

I look through the window behind me and down into the garden, which looks silver and grey in the full moon's glow. The full moon! I know werewolves come out at full moons, but does it do anything to vampires?

Oh no! Oh no! I need a wee, but I'm too terrified to move! I'm gonna wet myself right here behind the curtain moments before a vampire kills me! Why did I have to show off and try and be the best hider?

There is a clunk sound, and I shrink back against the windowsill, hiding as much as I can behind the curtain.

“Billy?”

"Dad!" I cry out.

The curtain is snatched back as if it weighs nothing at all. Dad stands there looking down at me with the warm glow of the landing draped across his back, sending his face into shadow. For a moment, I think I'm in trouble, but then he crouches down, and I jump into his arms. I feel his thick, coarse hands on the flat of my back as he hugs me to him. We rarely hug, us both being boys, but this is instantly natural. He holds me tight as I try to choke back my rising tears. Tears of relief, tears of embarrassment, tears of the fear that have just dissolved.

“You're alright, Bill?”

Bill. He called me Bill, not Billy. Bill sounds even better coming from Dad. Even better than when Shane said it.

"It's okay, Bill," he says, and I relax into him. He takes my body loosening as a sign that I am okay, and he pulls away to look at me. "Did you get yourself into something you couldn't get out of?"

I nod. I look beyond his shoulder into the landing expecting to see Shane, Wayne and Tessa creeping up to see what's going on, but the landing is empty.

"They're downstairs," Dad says, "Don't worry. They said you hid so well they couldn't find you."

I start to half blub and half talk, my words coming out in punctuated gasps. "I'm not... supposed... to be... in... here!" I manage to say and then start to cry.

"It's okay," Dad says and gives me a small but discernible smile.

"Mike... will... tell... me... off...." I stutter.

"He won't say anything," Dad's voice is low, warm and knowing. I believe him.

Then I remember the coffin. I look over his shoulder at it. I can see the shape clearer in the light from the landing. It looks like a futuristic coffin or a capsule from a spaceship.

"Come on," Dad says. "You need the toilet." And the urgency of my bladder comes back to me.

Holding Dad's hand, I walk with him across the room, keeping a cautious eye on the coffin. As we draw near, I shuffle around the other side of him. He has not reacted to the coffin at all, as if it's the most natural thing in the world to keep the crypt of the undead in your spare room (if you have one). Either that or he already knows about Mike's undead house guest.

He pauses and looks down at me as I shift sides. I look up at him, and he raises his eyebrows in a question. I draw closer to his leg and grip his trousers. I whisper, "Why does Uncle Mike have a coffin in his spare room?"

Dad looks at the capsule as if seeing it for the first time, and his face brightens. He looks back at me with unmasked humour on his face.

"That's not a coffin,"

"How do you know? It looks like a coffin," I say, beginning to think that we both might be attacked if we don't get moving. "What is it?" I ask.

Dad rasps his thumb along his chin, squinting one eye.

"Well... if I had to guess, I'd say it must be Spain," he says.

I look at him, feeling a bit safer but none the wiser.

"Spain?"

"Well, it must be Spain because it's what Mike uses to keep *that healthy glow going in the darker months.*"

TWELVE

Before. Three Sundays ago. Morning.

“Stuck?” Dad says. “What d’you mean you’re stuck?”

“I’m stuck! I can’t pull my feet out,” Tessa calls back.

“What were you doing out there anyway?” he says.

She looks down and says quietly, "Well... Well... I thought I could make it all the way around."

Dad leans his elbow on the top of the brick turret and looks out across the wide and empty riverbed to the woods on the other side. For a moment, it looks as though he’d rather be over there than here.

"Why were you trying to get all the way around?" he asks, not looking down at her.

He doesn’t see her shrug.

“Good grief,” he says quietly to himself. Then he looks down at me. I’m stood close to him. “Well, at least it isn’t you this time.” to which I nod happily.

“Can you get me out?” Tessa’s voice calls out.

I peer over the top of the turret. She is below us, stuck fast in the wet mudflats of the tidal river.

“We could wait until the tide comes back in, and you could float up to us,” he says.

“Dad!” she calls. “That is not helpful!”

“Neither is getting stuck out there.”

“I thought I could make it,” Tessa says quietly.

Dad says nothing but just nods and looks back at the woods across the river.

Tessa and I *both* thought she could get around. It was only luck, my luck that is, that she tried first. Otherwise, it would be me stuck out there, but Dad didn't need to know that.

We were on our riverbank walk, the sun was still low. The mist crept wistfully across the empty riverbank, like ghost ships searching for the tide. The grass was thick with dew, and the remaining brown leaves looked heavy and ready to spiral down from the trees gnarled claws. We usually walk along the bank of the river and either picnic at the turret, which is a circular brick viewing platform that juts out into the river and looks like a lost piece of a castle, or we head into the woods to the lake. This time, once we got to the turret, Dad wanted to see if there was another path to take us back to the car rather than using the one we came on. He got out his map and poured over it, leaving us to gaze out at the mudflats. Dad can spend hours looking at a map.

To entertain ourselves, we had started by finding the biggest stones on the bank to throw out and splat into the mud. The rocks made wet slapping sounds as they hit the surface and then started to be pulled under by their own weight. Then Tessa reckoned she could wade out into the mud and get all the way around the turret and sneak up on Dad from the other side. We have waded before, but never that far. She reckoned she had figured out the way to avoid getting stuck. It was to always keep moving and not let the mud get hold of you because if it did, it would start to suck you down. I reckoned I could do it better, but she puffed out air in exasperation and set off. She did pretty well too. She managed a continuous motion that enabled her to keep pulling her boots free from the thick silt. That was until halfway around when her confidence waned, and she stopped. At which point the mudflats claimed her.

Dad couldn't seem to believe his luck. It had been going so well, especially after last Sunday when we had all turned up carrying our wet jeans with us after my upside-down dunk into the river. That Sunday night, even Mum seemed speechless. Although we couldn't see her from our perch at the top of the stairs, she sounded like she had her hands on her hips. Dad calls that pose *the double-handled teapot*. One hand on the hip (the one handled teapot) means he is in a little bit of trouble, but the situation is humorous enough to keep everyone happy. The double-handled teapot is when he really is in trouble, or Mum just can't believe what she is hearing, just like last Sunday.

“But... you were on Dartmoor?” she said, perplexed.

"That's right," Dad responded in good-natured agreement.

There was a pause as Mum seemed to take this in. “You weren’t at the coast. You weren’t racing the *bloody* tide again! You were all on dry land!" This is when the double handled teapot probably struck.

"I know, but we thought it'd be fun to swing on a rope," Dad said.

Mum was quiet for a moment. I wondered if the double handled teapot had progressed to the no-nonsense crossed arms.

“But... But...” She let out a despairing sigh and changed the approach to her questioning like they do in the interrogation scenes in police films. “So, let me get this straight. After getting Billy soaked two weeks ago at the coast. After I tell you *not* to go back there for a while because he fell into the sea... THE SEA, RAY! Within two weeks, you take the kids out and decide it’s a good idea to swing like Tarzan over a fast-flowing river? NOT a gently rope swing over DRY LAND, but over a river where he could have either cracked his head open on a rock or been swept downstream breaking all sorts of bones as he goes.”

My hand felt furiously for strands of carpet with hard ends to pull and unravel. Tessa gave me annoyed and accusing looks. The funny side of my fall had evaporated. We weren’t sure if Mum was finally going to call an end to our Sunday adventures.

“Yes... that’s right.” Dad said. “I thought they’d be okay with it.”

"I don't know, Ray," Mum said, and I could tell by the way her voice got quieter and louder again that she was shaking her head. "What is it with you three? You seem to find trouble wherever you are."

“I’m sorry. Look, next week I’ll take them somewhere quiet. No coast, no rope swings, I promise.”

There was a huff from Mum. “Oh, and don’t forget we’ve got Mike and Sharon next Saturday.”

It appeared that this time at least, Dad knew not to make his *Well, you have a lovely time,* joke.

Dad shifted his feet and leaned over the top of the turret. Tessa tried to stretch up towards him, but he held his hand up to stop her.

"Don't," his voice clipped. "Don't... move. If you overbalance, you'll be covered in mud. And I can't be having that."

I peer over the bricks and see Tessa retract her arms and then wobble. Dad and I both freeze, willing her to keep upright. She fans out her arms and claws at the air as if dragging herself up along the walls of a narrow corridor. She must have pulled too hard because next, she is bending forward, her arms wafting in front of her to fend off the pending impact of the mud. Her movements slow, and she rights herself, standing slowly to her full height.

Dad and I both let out relieved gasps. Tessa gives us a confident smile. I wonder if she was just joking. If so, that was funny. Dad has lightened a bit and lets out a short laugh. “Bloody hell, I thought you were gone then! Now, don’t move. Get it?”

“Got it.”

“Good.” He looks around for inspiration and then leans over and looks down the outside of the turret. He seems to have settled on something. He empties his pockets and hands the contents to me.

“Don’t lose this,” He says.

I place the items in my satchel, and then I take it off and lay it carefully against the opposite side of the turret. When I turn back, Dad is up and over the wall and standing on the outside of the turret. I rush back to his side and look over. A narrow brick ledge runs around the outside of the turret. Dad has his feet flat to the side and pressed against the wall. Only half of his boots fit on the ledge. He loops his arm around one of the turrets brick teeth and stretches out to Tessa.

“Don’t reach for me until I’m close enough to get a good grip,” he says, and she nods.

I grab his arm holding the turret, and he stops his lean and looks back at me.

“Don’t hold on to me. If I go, then we’ll all end up in the bank.”

I retract my hand and watch, feeling useless. He starts his stretch again. He is so close to her. His arm is out as far as it can go. I fidget and try to avoid the temptation to pick my nose.

“Can you reach me?” he asks Tessa, his voice straining.

She lifts up her arms and leans towards him. Her balance goes, and she falls towards him, but he catches her. His arm snakes around her, just under her armpits, and he hoists her up and into him. I move close as Tessa's hands slap against the bricks, and then Dad is stood straight again on the outside ledge. He helps Tessa shift around, and then she swings her legs over the wall, quickly followed by Dad.

The three of us slump together and slide down the wall, sitting in a pile on the stone floor.

“That was a close one!” Tessa says as Dad starts to rub his right shoulder with his left hand.

“You okay?” Tessa asks.

“Yes,” Dad says as he rotates his shoulder, doing what he can to hide a wince of pain.

“We might just make it out of this Sunday incident-free,” Dad says. He’s about to say something else, but his voice dries up. He’s looking at our gaggle of feet. He frowns and then hitches himself up to look over the wall at the riverbank. He sits back down and lets out a sigh.

“Tessa?”

She looks at him, her face pleasantly bright.

“Where are your wellies?”

She frowns innocently at his question and then looks at our collection of feet. Her eyes wonder over them, as do mine, and at first, she doesn't seem to notice anything. There are Dad's boots, her socks, my boots... Her eyes go back to her feet. They are mixed with mine. Out of our collective six feet, only four have boots. She wiggles her toes as if to discern if these *really* are her feet.

“Oh,” she says and then slowly lifts herself up to look over the wall. I follow, appearing just after her. There in the mud, stood proudly are two now empty wellie boots. She has been pulled free of them.

“Oh...” she says again.

"Oh," Dad says.

After getting myself stuck in Mike’ tanning room last night, I was worried everyone would know what had happened to me. I still felt unsure whether or not the whole thing had been orchestrated by the *lads.*

When Dad and I got back downstairs, after I had used the toilet, everyone seemed pleasantly surprised to see me, especially Shane.

“Whoa, man! Where were you? You got some skills. We looked

everywhere!" Shane said.

At this, Mike's face flinched with mild concern, and he looked between his two sons. "You guys been going into *all* the rooms?"

"He's like Houdini this one," Dad said, letting Mikes question and concern fall flat.

Dad had not said a word to anyone, and he maintained that I was just a good hider for the rest of the night. He explained that the only reason he had found me was that he was just as good a hider when he was a kid.

On the drive home that night, while Mum narrated her disbelief at some of the gaudy things Mike and Sharon had come out with, I looked at Dad's half profile. He was illuminated by the soft glow of the dashboard's lights and the occasional passing car's headlamps. He looked older in the half-light, the shadows accentuating the creases in his skin. He doesn't have a face as crinkled as Grandma's, but he has some deep lines across his forehead.

I wondered when or if I might be like him. He seemed to know a lot. He always seemed to know what to do, or at least have confidence that he'd figure something out. He never seemed to want to be someone else either, the way I do. If we watch a film and I really like the hero in it, I start to try and be like him. I start using the same phrases he uses in the film. Dad never does that. He must be comfortable with who he is. I wonder what that feels like.

I felt safe in the back of the car as Tessa nodded off against her window. I knew that we were all safe. Dad had found me in that room. He had got there just in time. Just before I cried out in fear or wet myself. He had found me, and now we were all going home. I remembered his promise to Mum that he'll always get us home safe. Maybe, instead of trying to be like the hero in the last film I've seen, I should try and be more like him?

The scraping rasp of Dad's thumb against his chin means he is thinking. The three of us look down from our vantage point in the turret at Tessa's wellies which stand there in brazen defiance. Dad doesn't look annoyed. He just looks as if he is concentrating. It's the same face he pulls when he's reading a book. He sits there in a dining room chair on a Saturday lunchtime, eating a sandwich and, with a slight frown, he reads.

“Could you lasso them?” I ask Dad.

Without looking away from the boots, he says, “I didn’t bring a rope.”

“What about a vine?” I say with enthusiasm.

“There aren’t any,” he says.

“What about a stick?” Tessa says.

Dad doesn’t say anything but looks at her and raises his eyebrows.

"What if we got a long stick with a branch sticking out like a hook? We could hook the boots out!"

He is silent for a moment and then barks, “C’mon then, let’s see what we can find.”

We walk down off the turret onto the wet grass, but Tessa stops at the last step and looks at her socks.

“Um, Dad?”

Dad turns and looks down at her feet. Her toes wiggle as if giving him a wave.

He opens his own bag and pulls out two rags and a couple of plastic bags, wrapping one and then the other around her feet, tying the bags off around her ankles. “There you go, that’s how Robin Hood got around.”

“They had Summerfield bags in those days?” Tessa asks.

“Smartypants.” Dads says.

Eyeing the makeshift shoes, Tessa takes one step onto the wet grass and waits to see if the water seeps through. It doesn't, and she happily trudges off into the woods that run alongside the path in search of the perfect branch. Tessa looks in a shallow part of the woods while Dad goes deeper. I stay on the path and kick about through the long grass. I don't really think the branch idea is a good one. There is no way we could prise those boots out with a long stick.

I mindlessly glance around me and then look off in the direction of Tessa and Dad. They seem deep in their search. I tramp over to the edge of the woods, and there, just beyond the grass, is a long stick with an L-shaped end. I look up to where the others are. They must have seen this stick and dismissed it already. I can't really be the one to save the day, could I?

I'm about to shout out to them, but I pause. If they had dismissed this stick, then I would look silly saying I found the perfect wellie hook. Although I was not the cause of this current situation, the way I usually am, I don't want to lose ground and look like a right wazzock. I bend down and pick the stick up. I feel its weight and its damp, flaking bark beneath my fingers. It's a decent length. I pull it free from the leaves.

Dad and Tessa are off in the distance, heads down in what seems like an endless search. I stand the stick up and look it over. It might not be long enough. I decide to test its reach before I call them back.

I stand on the bank and edge the stick out, bit by bit, towards the stubborn wellies. The stick grows heavier the further out it goes until eventually it falls just short of the boots and slaps into the mud. The silt starts to absorb the end of the stick like an alien blob monster. I pull at it, and the stick draws back across the surface of the mudflat, leaving an impression that slowly disappears like fog from your breath on a window.

I am surprised by how easy the stick is to pull out of the mud. I hold the stick upright and then drop the end into the mud in front of me. I let it sink, cupping my hands around it to ensure it doesn't fall over. When it's sunk as low as it will go, I grip the stick and pull it up and out of the silt. The stick makes a fat sucking sound as it breaks free, but it comes out easily enough.

I look at the wellies and rub my chin with my thumb the way Dad does, but without the rasping sound. I reckon Tessa's only mistake was stopping. If she had kept going, the mud wouldn't have gotten a good hold on her. The mud is easy to get free from. My stick experiment has just proven that. I must be stronger than Tessa, and I'm smaller and lighter. I could get out there, grab her boots and be back without stopping. I really could be the one to save the day. This time I will be the one to get us all home safely! Dad will be so impressed! Just imagine, they both come back, and I'm sat on the edge of the bank, looking across the riverbed nonchalantly, the boots by my side. "Oh, these?" I will say, "Well, you know, I just went out and got them. It was a piece of cake!" But I wouldn't brag too much. That would be too much like Mike and his bomb-day mix and volcano lamp. I will just be all quiet and cool about it.

Yeah! This is a great idea!

*

"Stuck?" Dad says. "What d'you mean you're stuck?"

I look down, my face flushes red.

"What the bloody hell did you think you were doing?" he says, scratching his head with his chin rubbing thumb.

"I... I thought I could get all the way around," I say, recognising the exact words Tessa used. As soon as I say them, and wishing I could claw them back into my mouth.

Dad and Tessa are standing in the turret. They are leaning through the gaps on either side of one of its brick teeth. They have the same baffled look on their faces.

"But..." Tessa starts saying and then stops, looking genuinely confused. "But... you saw me... get stuck out there."

I am standing a foot beyond the abandoned wellies, stranded in the mud flats facing the turret. I know how stupid this looks. Dad and Tessa didn't see my stick experiment! They don't know the scientific thought I had put into this decision before I set off on my expedition! I search my mind, but I can't find the words to explain that my stick experiment made me believe I could replicate her trip with a very different result.

"Oh boy... And I thought I was stupid," Tessa says and rolls her eyes towards Dad. He looks back at her and doesn't disagree. They both turn back to me, sharing the exact same frown. I can't bear to look at their bewildered faces.

The problem came when I neared the wellies. I realised as I approached them that I would have to stop to pull them free, and by doing so, I would become stranded. Up to that point, I was doing well. I kept a continuous movement, not spending too much time on either foot, pulling each free as I strode with awkward, boot sucking determination. As I drew close, the problem dawned on me. In order to buy some time to come up with a new plan, I circled the boots a few times. In hindsight, I should have just marched back to the grass bank, and no one would be any the wiser. But I wanted to save the day, I had come this far, and so I stopped as briefly as I could to snatch up the wellies. Unfortunately, I stopped too far away to reach them, and the mud claimed me. Dad and Tessa arrived back at the turret just as the reality of my situation, and the humiliation, dawned on me.

Now, under Dad's and Tessa's disbelieving gaze, I am slowly sinking. The mud must be deeper here because it feels like I'm sinking further than Tessa did.

"Dad," I say

"Yes?" he replies, his expression that of a condemned man who has accepted his fate.

"I'm still sinking."

"I can see that."

"Dad," I say.

"Yes?"

"The mud is getting to the top of my wellies!"

I'm not wearing the tall type boots like Tessa. I watch with increasing panic as the mud seems to bubble up as it slowly consumes me. It lets out a fat burp that splats my jeans as the silt reaches the top of my boots and starts to pour inside. I feel its cold wetness ooze around my ankles and creep down towards my toes.

"DAD!"

"Hey, Dad! Look at this!" Tessa shouts.

She has left the turret, as if my predicament has started to bore her, and is standing on the bank. She proudly holds up the stick *that I found* and brandishes it above her head like a trophy.

"That's perfect!" Dad says as if he, too, has forgotten me. "Bring it up here."

"DAD!" I shout. I can't believe that they are going to leave me here and use *MY STICK*.

"Hang on, Billy," he says as he takes the stick from Tessa. He holds it up, assessing its weight and then grips it in both hands and tries to bend it to test its strength.

In a quiet tone, he says to Tessa, "This is great. Where did you find it?"

Tessa gives an '*it was nothing*' kind of shrug, "Just over there, by the edge of the bank", she says with quick, false modesty.

"I must have walked right past it. Great find, Tessa."

I fold my arms in protest and put on my biggest frown, but no one notices. In my slow sinking, I lose balance and start to fan my arms out to steady myself, resuming a pathetic scarecrow stance.

Dad edges the branch out over the turret and down towards the wellies. To my amazement, from the turret, the stick reaches.

Dad slots the L-shaped end of the stick into the boot and tries to lift it out, but it doesn't move. For a moment, I am pleased by this failure.

He considers this for a moment. Then, with the end of the stick still deep within the boot, he angles his end up and starts to slide the boot towards him like the oar of a gondola. I watch the top of the boot as Dad slides through the mud, like a sharks fin, to the base of the turret. Once there, Dad retracts the branch and drops the boot behind him in the turret.

"THAT'S NOT FAIR!" I shout, "I found that stick first!"

Dad is halfway through sending the stick out to get the last boot when he stops, the branch hovering above the mud.

"You found this stick?" he asks with disbelief.

I nod, a satisfied smile on my face. I wait for the praise.

"And yet... you still went out there in the mud?" Dad's tone is that of someone who has discovered some kind of natural miracle. The natural miracle of my stupidity.

Tessa slaps her face with her palm and shakes her head. My smug expression slips from my face and joins the mud pooling into my boots.

Dad continues his fishing out of Tessa's last boot. She puts them on and does a little jig, clumping her boots on the stone floor.

"DAD!" I shout. "What about me?"

"I'm hungry," Tessa says, "Can we have our picnic?"

I can't believe they might have their picnic without me. "What about me?" I shout.

Dad looks at his watch and then at Tessa. "Well," he muses, "It is lunchtime and," he nods his head at me, "he's not going anywhere."

"Except down!" Tessa says.

They both laugh, and he gets out the sandwiches from his bag.

They start to eat, looking out at me as if I am a programme on the television.

"I'm hungry too," I say, quietly.

Before Dad can stop her, Tessa launches a square of sandwich in my direction. I lift my arms, desperate to catch it before the mud monster can claim it. I am so preoccupied with not losing my sandwich I forget my restrictions and try to leap for it as it spins in a seemingly slow arc. My leap is short-lived as my boots weigh me to the ground, and I tip beyond the point of balance and fall forward. My arms flail out to my sides in a pointless attempt right myself, and I face plant the cold mud with a hard, thick smack. I pull my face free of the mud's sloppy embrace, just in time to see the sandwich plop next to me.

I can't call out because I'm afraid the mud will pour into my mouth. I start to feel my whole body begin to sink. Panic fills me, and I think I'm about to drown in the mud bank when I feel the back of my jacket wrench up. With a thick and slow movement, I am hauled onto my back. The mud slides down my neck, pressing greedily against my bare back, doing all it can to keep hold of me. I am dragged in slow, short bursts towards the bank. I look helplessly at the long impression I leave in the mud as I am pulled along. I watch as the imprint slowly lifts and disappear as if I were never there.

Dad drags me by my collar all the way back to the grass bank, never stopping so as not to get stuck himself. My arms and legs feel glued as the mud feels like it is mummifying me. With great effort, I hear him strain as he slops me onto the grass like an oversized slug. I can now see him as he hauls himself up from the ever-hungry flats and collapses next to me on the grass.

I feel like I am more mud than human as the brown gloop blobs onto the grass around me. My hearing seems to return and fade as mud drains from my ears. The sound of my breathing is drowned out by Tessa's high-pitched hoots of laughter. I can't open my eyes as the lids feel heavy, but I don't have to see her to know she is clutching her belly, doubled over in hysterics. Next, I hear her let out a shriek of despair laced with hilarity as she shouts out, "I'm gonna wet myself!" And I hear her run into the woods to relieve herself.

In the distance, there is a panicked rustling followed by a scream as Tessa has not made it in time to get her jeans and knickers down. Despite my own situation, a laugh bursts forth from me and pops through the mud around my mouth. I hear Dad laughing next to me, and then I feel him shove my leg with his boot.

“Puddin ‘Head.

THIRTEEN

Before. Three Sundays ago. Past bedtime.

Tonight, I'm sitting at the top of the stairs on my own. Tessa was mortified by her "accident" and was in a grump all afternoon, or as Eddie, Gobber, and Dad would have said when they were kids, *she had a right cob on.*

I feel tired, but I don't want to sleep. If I sleep, it will be Monday morning a lot sooner than if I stay awake. I will have to go through all the faff of getting ready for school in the morning, and the weekend will feel like a year away. I hate Mondays. I hate all the weekdays apart from Friday, from 3:30 pm onwards.

Mum and Dad are downstairs, and I try to listen to what they are saying to each other. Sitting here at the end of the weekend has quickly become yet another Sunday tradition.

When we got to our front door, Dad made us stand in single file behind him, just like at lunchtime in school, so as try to relieve the initial shock for Mum. When she opened the door (we had to knock because we couldn't very well tramp in spreading mud everywhere), she cocked an eyebrow at Dad. He held his hands up in a calming motion and said, "Now... Nobody got hurt," and Mum quickly escalated to a one handled teapot stance. At which point Tessa and I poked our heads out on either side of Dad, and Mum shifted to a double handled teapot.

"Bloody hell, Ray!" she barked in a raised whisper, "Get inside, all of you!"

Tessa had to wash first, and Dad and I were not allowed to leave the front porch, not even to step foot on the matt inside the front door. Mum left the door open so we could see her nip up and down the stairs and hear her huffs and puffs. Dad and I stood there, not exchanging a word, like strangers in a lift occasionally smiling at each other. At one point, when Mum walked towards us only to veer right at the last minute and stamp up the stairs, Dad looked from her scowl down to me and raised his eyebrows. This almost made me laugh out loud, but Dad shook his head. I swallowed it down. He was right. He knew what was best for both of us.

When I was carried upstairs and plonked into a steaming bath, I was fascinated by how quickly the water turned brown. At one point, Mum made me stand up to drain the tub down. She gave the tub a wipe around and then refilled it.

Dad's voice drifted up from the front porch, "Everything alright, Jan?" he asked with caution.

"I'll deal with you later!" Mum shouted back down and slammed the bathroom door. I winced in sympathy for Dad. This was going to be quite the Sunday night conversation to eavesdrop.

As Mum scrubbed behind one of my ears, I thought I saw a trace of a tight-lipped smirk on her face. Each time I tried to look at her face, she moved it away. There was a definite smile suppressed there. This became a sort of game, me trying to look into Mum's face and her turning away at the last minute to hide her expression. So much so that this made her laugh, and I felt the air lighten.

She maintained her scowl as best she could for the remainder of the day, but there were times when everything fell quiet, and she would snort out a laugh and then clap her hand over her mouth or jump up and bolt out the room, slamming the door behind her. Our doors weren't that thick, as my time at the top of the stairs has shown, and in the distance, the three of us could hear muffled laughter with the occasionally whispered self-instruction, *"C'mon now Jan. Stop it!"* From over the top of his book, Dad looked at the two of us and raised his eyebrows. I think he was as relieved as we were.

Sitting here alone, I can hear the distant soft snore of Tessa, and I edge forward as the voices start from downstairs.

"Bloody hell, Ray! I wasted four bathtubs of water on you lot today. I had use two on Billy. That mud got everywhere!"

“I wish you could have seen him when he fell. God love him! The noise he made when he hit the mud was like something from *Tom & Jerry*!” Dad says.

“Don’t!” Mum says, snorting back a laugh. “But honestly, how do the three of you get into these messes?”

“I’m not sure. I used to think it was all down to Billy, but now I think it’s a combination of the three of us.”

“How were you planning to get him out?” Mum says.

“I hadn’t figured that out. I was still working on it when Tessa lobbed a sandwich at him.”

Mum laughed. “I’m surprised you didn’t get stuck.”

“I didn’t stop moving. I ran out to get him. He looked terrified. Well, at least he had a soft landing.”

“You and your bloody Sunday adventures,” Mum says, but her tone suggests that she’s not calling a stop to them yet.

“We’d probably be safer back on the coast,” Dad says, with an air of trepidation in his voice, testing the waters.

"Hmm..." Mum says, not convinced. "Not yet. I told you, a few weeks more, please. I just have a bad feeling, that's all. I can't explain it, Ray. I'm sorry."

“Okay,” Dad says, agreeably, “They miss it, but we’ve had fun in the other places.”

They go into the living room, and I hear the television come on. They'll sit and watch one of their grown-up shows. They like the one about some builders, but I don't know what's so grown up about builders. I say ‘*they*’ but it'll be Mum who watches it. Dad will be asleep within the first ten minutes.

It's funny, he never complains about being tired but put him in front of the tele, and he will always drift off. Mum gave up waking him to go to bed years ago. Now she just leaves him to sleep through it. We'll all be glued to the T.V, and then we will hear the snores coming from Dad, slumped to one side of his armchair, his face locked in a sleep frown. If he snores really loud, we all end up watching him because we know, at some point, he'll let out a bone-jangling snort that will wake him up. When he wakes up, he stays exactly where he is and looks at each of us from under his eyebrows to see if we noticed he had fallen asleep, as if we could ignore it. When he does this, he looks like a gorilla. You almost can't see his eyes beneath his eyebrows when he frows like that.

The funny thing is, he always denies he's been asleep. He can be snoring to high heaven, and if your eyes meet his once he has snorted himself awake, and you say something like, *"Did you enjoy your sleep,"* he'll deny it.

"I wasn't asleep," he'll say, and then look at the other two to confirm if he's right. Then he'll look at the T.V, and there will be a new character on the screen whose introduction he's missed. He'll point them out and ask, "Who's dat den?" Amongst sideways glances and smirks, one of us will tell him, and he'll pretend he knew them all along.

We've watched him try and stay awake by sitting on the edge of his seat, and he tipped forward, sprawling onto the floor when he nodded off. We've watched him stand in the living room doorway, determined not to miss any of the film, and he began to snore standing up. He slipped off the door frame once and stumbled into the room *and* still claimed to have been awake the whole time.

One time, Mum watched him fall asleep with a mug of tea in his hand, and he dropped the whole thing into his lap. He bolted upright from a dream where his thighs were on fire.

Sure enough, in less than ten minutes, I can hear him snoring.

The noise drowns out the dull sound from the television. With exaggerated irritation, Mum huffs and clunks about, making a show of deciding it's pointless trying to watch the T.V. show over his snores. I hear her slippers slap louder than usual, going the long way around to the stairs. Out of the living room to the dining room, clacking across the hard kitchen floor and into the hall. She walks past the other living room door, which would have been easier to take if she wasn't trying to make a point, and to the stairs. Dad snores on in blissful ignorance.

Usually, he'll wake up in the dark, the white snow on the television being his only light. He'll no doubt look around, wondering where everyone has gone, as if some thief has stolen time and he's woken up in a future he wasn't prepared for.

I hear Mum enter the hall, heading for the stairs. I steal away, back into my bedroom using Mum's creaks on the stairs as cover for my retreat. I slip into bed, leaving my door open, as is the rule and listen to Mum as she runs through her night-time routine. I hear her gargling, and at some point, I must fall asleep because the next thing I know, she's gone quiet. I listen as I curse myself for submitting to my tiredness. Now I'm even closer to Monday morning!

The house, at first, appears to be silent, but then I hear Dad's snores from downstairs. I must have woken in a break in his snoring, as now it rattles through the house as if he were next to me. I lie there and wonder how he can sleep through his own noise. It must be the equivalent of shouting as loud as you can when you're asleep. Whenever I try to imitate his snoring, I can only do so for a few seconds before my throat gets sore. How can he make this much noise all night and still be able to talk in the morning?

I push back my duvet and peer down the landing. Mum's light is off, which means she'll have her earplugs in. Despite knowing she can't hear anything over the wax balls she stuffs into her ears every night, I creep down the landing and return to my spot at the top of the stairs. I can't stay here because when Mum gets up for one of her countless night-time wees, she'll catch me.

I start to walk down the stairs taking care to avoid every individual creaky spot. I reckon that if I still live here in thirty years, when I'm *really, really old,* I'll still have the stairs creaks mapped out perfectly in my head. That's not to say that I can get up or down the stairs without making any sound at all. Our stairs have far too many creaks for that, but I know where to place my feet to make the least amount of noise.

I know that step four, if you are counting from the bottom of the stairs upwards, is one the only one with almost no creaks. With stealth, I zig-zag my way down to stair number four. I ease myself onto the bannister side and sit down.

This must be the latest I've ever been awake. I have no idea what time it is, but it feels really, *really* late. I rest my head on the bannister railings. Within a few seconds, I've nodded off again. My head slips from the railing I'm leant against and smacks into the one next to it. I sit up straight, startled as the dull throb of the impact edges across my forehead.

I can't fall asleep. I don't *want* to fall asleep! I stand and slip down the last three stairs, avoiding the final one that has no silent part at all. The living room door nearest the stairs is closed, but I can still hear Dad snoring like a troll through it. If I didn't know him or this house, I would be terrified to be down here alone. I walk into the kitchen. I need to stay awake. I need to eat. Mum always says I get a burst of energy after I've eaten.

With slow caution, I lift a bowl from the draining board and get a box of cereal from the bottom cupboard. When I open the fridge door for the milk, its hum suddenly gets louder. It makes me jump. I look in every direction to see if anyone has heard me. I'm still alone. I close the door, and the hum lowers to a night-time pitch. After I pour the milk into my bowl, I leave it out, not wanting the fridge to make that loud noise again.

I walk slowly through the dining room and stand in the living room doorway. Dad is slumped in his armchair next to the wall. His elbow is on the wooden armrest, and his cheek is squished up against the ball of his fist. I don't know how he is comfortable sleeping like that on his knuckles.

I take a sloppy spoon full of cereal and watch as his mouth closes and drops open again to let out a horrendously loud snore. If this were a cartoon, I'm sure my hair would have been blown back with the force of his roar.

The room is lit by the snow on the television, which gives everything a grey old movie tinge. I turn from the television back to Dad just in time to see his elbow slip off the armrest and drop down the side of the chair. His head, which was previously supported by his closed fist, smacks against the wall. I snort milk through my nose and barely stop myself from coughing out my mouthful of cereal.

His eyes pop open, startled, and he looks right at me. I consider acting like it's still evening time, and I haven't gone to bed yet. Dad glances quickly about the room and then looks back at me as the confusion starts to melt from his face.

“You okay?” he says and yawns, covering his mouth with his hand.

I don't answer. Instead, I just look into my bowl.

“Can’t sleep?” he asks off the back of his yawn

I shrug.

He cocks his head and says, “Don’t want to?”

I look deep into my cereal now. I feel hot tears boil up and brim at my eyes. The thought of him knowing how I *really* feel makes me want to cry. It makes all the dread of tomorrow real. I start to breathe deeply with increasing speed. I don’t want to cry. I *don’t want to cry!* I *don’t want to cry!*

"C'mon," Dad says as if he hasn't noticed my dry sobs, and he nods his head towards the armchair next to his.

I shuffle to the seat. Dad holds my bowl as I climb onto it. Once I'm settled, he hands it back. He gets up and stands in front of the TV. "Let's see if anything is still on, shall we?" He snaps through the four channels, but the screen flicks between different pictures of snow and one little girl standing in front of the blackboard. He switches it back to snow and then sits down again. I'm pleased he's left this on. It makes this moment more like a film, more false and real at the same time.

"You'll be tired tomorrow."

I shrug, and then the feeling of Monday creeps back to me. I start to feel the fears, and the tears crowd in. I breathe hard again to try and keep them under control, but I know I'm too late. I can feel Dad looking at me.

"Is it as bad as all that?" His voice is low and soft.

Without looking up at him, I nod. I hunch over, wishing I could climb into the bowl on my lap. Tears quietly track down my cheeks.

"I know."

I chug in some desperate gasps and then lean over again. I can see the wet marks my tears have made on my pale blue pyjamas, which look grey in this light.

"You know, Bill," There it is again. He called me Bill, not Billy. I feel like it's just the two of us in the house right now. Maybe it's just the two of us in the whole entire world. "There will always be something you don't like or don't want to do."

"I *hate* it," I manage to say.

"I know, but even in the worst things, you can find something good or fun."

"It's all ... rubbish," I say, and then wait to be told off for calling school rubbish.

"Well, you'll never see anything good if you think like that."

He pauses and looks at me. Slowly, I lift my face to look at him.

“There’s good bits and bad bits to everything,” he says, “But, things are changing all the time. It may not seem like it, but it is.”

"It doesn't change," I say.

“It’ll seem that way. There’ll be times when things aren’t changing fast enough for you, and there’ll be times when you like something just as it is, but that will change too.”

"I wish school would change," I say.

He turns his head and looks at the T.V. The fuzz on the screen constantly evolves, and I think I see a shape in it before it vanishes again.

“It’ll all change fast enough. If you’re smart, you’ll go with the change. If you’re really strong, you’ll make things change.”

“Did you like school?” I ask.

“Me?” he says and shifts in his seat, indulging in a short stretch, “No. But school was different back then. Besides, you don’t want to be like me.”

“Why not?”

He tilts his head back and scratches his neck. “Well, I didn’t look for the good bits when I was in school. Now I’m in a trade I don’t like.”

This was true. Whenever I ask him how his day was, he always says, with a comical burst, "RUBBISH!" Like Eric from Morecambe & Wise. But I still wouldn't mind being like him instead of being me.

"School is tough, I know. In some ways, it can be tougher than work, but you'll get through it. If you do your best, then you might enjoy what you end up doing."

“Dad?” I ask.

He gives me his upward nod, which is his way of telling me to continue.

“The stories you tell us, about when you were a kid, you always seemed to have had fun."

"Well, I only tell you the good bits."

"There were bad bits?" I ask.

He nods once.

"I don't have stories like that," I say.

"Course you do," he says, "Look at today. When you look back, you'll have loads of stories to tell."

"But, in our stories, I'm the Uncle Bertie," I say. "I don't like being the Uncle Bertie."

He looks at me for what seems like a long time. "You're not Bertie."

"I am."

"Bertie was forced on me. I had to take my little brother everywhere. That's why... That's why I wasn't very nice to him."

"But I'm always doing stupid stuff like he did," I say.

Dad fixes me with a warm smile. He leans in close and whispers, "You, Bill... You... are what make our stories great."

FOURTEEN

Before. Two Sundays ago. Picnic time.

The man knew he had no way to escape. He could hear the creature on its two hooved feet, thumping on the grass somewhere behind him. Exhausted, he pushed on through the dense fog. He could only hope he didn't run into a bog because then the creature, whatever the creature was, would have him.

He thought that the monastery would be his saviour, his salvation from the rain and wind of the Moors. How could he have known that it was home to this thing that they set free upon him? Maybe he should have stuck to the road when he bolted from the heavy wooden doors that kept people out and this thing, this devil-like creature, within.

There was no time to think about that now. His only hope was to keep moving. He may not be able to outrun the hooved beast, but maybe, just maybe, it would get lost in the fog, just like he was.

He stopped for a moment, catching his breath. Had he lost it? Had it got lost as he had hoped? He turned in the direction he last heard the hooves, but there was no noise now. He bent over with his hands on his knees and gulped in the air, trying to listen and pick out shapes in the swirling fog. Was that something moving out there or just the moonlight catching wisps of the mist that had been disturbed as he had run through?

Nothing. Silence.

No... Wait!

... Thump!

... Thump!

The beast had slowed to a walking pace. One hoof struck the ground with an angry and persistent thump. Could it see him? Could it smell him?

He heard an animal snort.

He turned and ran as fast as he could away from the noise. He heard the thump of its hooves increase in speed as it seemed to gallop on all fours now.

Suddenly the ground tilted up in front of him, and he fell forward. It was a hill! He scrabbled up the steep and damp slope as fast as he could. As he neared the top, he saw the fog begin to thin. He was climbing out of the mist!

As he got to the top, he could see out over the moors. The fog lay low, and there were other mounds and hilltops he could see in the distance, lit by the eerie moonlight. If only he could pick out a landmark, something he recognised that would lead him back to the village he passed through before he got a flat tyre!

He heard the snort of the beast as it approached the base of the hill. Its hooves slowed, and, from the sound of its step, it must have returned to standing on its hind legs. It thumped the base of the hill angrily, and he heard it sniff the air. It was trying to track him! He looked down from his hilltop at the dens, billowing sea of fog below, like an aeroplane pilot looking down at the clouds covering the earth.

It wouldn't be long until the beast figured out where he was. He spun around to see if he could spot the village, or at least the spire of its church. The wind blew, and the fog drifted away from around the hill in front of him. Just beyond it, he could see the tops of turrets. He recognised the old structure; it was... it was... Oh no! OH NO! How could this have happened? It was the monastery! He must have got turned around out here on the moors. In his confusion, the monastery of the evil, devil-worshipping monks was in front of him, and behind him, slowly pacing at the bottom of the hill, was the devil they worshipped.

Then, just on the hill in front of him, coming straight for him, he saw...

... Tessa and I grip each other with one hand, our sandwiches halfway to our mouths in the other. Dad looks just beyond us and takes a swig of his tea.

"What! What did he see, Dad?" shouts Tessa.

He swirls the last slug of tea in his cup and tosses it out.

"Dad! What did he see?"

"Who?" he asks.

Tessa and I exchange a look.

"The man! The man on the run from the beast and the evil monks?" Tessa says in disbelief that he could have lost track of the story he was telling.

We are sitting on a rock eating our picnic. Dad is standing opposite us. The weather is typical for the Moors. Cold, windswept and grey. We had trekked up over a tor and had rock hopped down the other side. We came to a clearing where there was an old abandoned concrete building with a steel door. The old rusty door had, what looked like, stab marks in it. Dad had said it was the claw of the hooved beast. *The beast that followed, the beast that chased.* It had been let loose by a group of evil monks who lived in a monastery nearby, and it would stop at nothing until it claimed its victim. It would walk in an unrelenting straight line, even walk straight over a building to catch its prey and leave its claw mark where it went.

I fingered the claw mark, and it was sharp. I felt a sudden fear that touching the door and the mark it left, meant that it would come for me next. I asked to go, and so we hiked up to the crest of the next hill and sat to have our picnic. Tessa had pleaded with Dad to tell us more about the *beast that follows,* and so he started to tell us a ghost story he had read in the paper when he first moved down here. The type of story Mum would not approve of.

So here we are, sitting on the cold, hard rock. Our obliviousness to our numb bums has begun to evaporate as Dad's story abruptly stops. I shift from buttock to buttock, and life painfully seeps back into each cheek only to ebb away again as I sit straight.

"WHAT DID HE SEE?" Tessa pleads.

"Oh, yes..." Dad says, gearing up to tell us what happens next.

Without anywhere to discard my crusts, I stuff them into my mouth. Tessa and I grab hold of each other, eyes wide with fear and excitement.

"Where was I?" Dad says.

"HE'S ON THE HILL, AND HE SEES...?" Tessa and I shout.

"Oh yes... Then, just on the hill in front of him, coming straight for him, he saw... The *hooded Monks* walking in a line over the hill, carrying an open coffin, to bury him in!"

Tessa and I gasp and almost climb into each other's coats with fear.

"They sort of looked like that," Dad says, and he points to the hill behind us.

Tessa and I slowly turn towards each other, exchanging a brief terrified glance, and then continue our turn to look at the hilltop behind us. There, cresting the brow of the hill is a line of shadowy hooded figures. Heads keep popping up from behind the hill to join the continuously moving line of shrouded monks.

"The MONKS!" Tessa and I yell, my crusts falling out my mouth onto the rock. Our scream is cut short when we realise that they aren't just walking over the hill, they are heading towards us and carrying something very large and long.

"AND THEY'VE GOT A COFFIN!!!" I shout, pointing wildly.

I slip off the rock, pulling Tessa with me, and we scramble to our feet and try to run, but our bums are so numb we can't keep upright. I fall and pull her with me. We try to scrabble to our feet again when Dad shouts out, "WAIT!" He waves his hands at us to come back. He is holding his stomach as if he's in pain, and then I realise that he's laughing.

"DAD!" I say, "They're coming!"

He roars with laughter again and waves us toward him, unable to speak. We glance at each other. With trepidation, we move back to the rock where Dad is slowly getting his breath back.

"It's okay, kids. It's okay! They're not monks," he says, and then to himself, "Oh my God, that was well timed!" He pulls out his binoculars and passes them to Tessa. "Here, look for yourself," and wipes his eyes. "Oh... I can't believe that! That was classic. Wait until I tell Jan."

I look towards the monks. They are getting closer to us. Tessa takes the binoculars from him with a scowl and looks through them in the direction Dad points. Tears of laughter are still rolling down his cheeks. I tug at Dad's sleeve, pleading that we run before they see us.

"It's okay, Billy Boy, it's okay," he says.

Tessa, elbows resting on the rock, frowns into the binoculars. "Who are they?" she asks. "They look like... Soldiers?"

"What?" I say, not believing I could mistake the military for monks.

Dad nudges Tessa, "Give him a look."

The binoculars get passed to me, and I look through them. I never understand how in films when you see through binoculars, they always have a figure of eight outline, but in real life, when you look through them, it's just a circle, the same as a telescope.

I blink, seeing my eyelashes flutter before me, and then I see them. I jolt back as they appear so close but then see that Dad is right. They aren't wearing brown hooded cloaks. They are wearing waterproofs. Their hoods are up against the rain, they're carrying backpacks, and a group in the middle are carrying a large metal box on their shoulders.

I scan the line and then catch the grass on the hill just in front of us, and as I do, a hooded head pops up, making me reel backwards. Dad catches me and takes the binoculars away. The man I saw through them is right in front of us and makes his way over. He has on the same heavy-looking backpack but is way ahead of the others.

"Afternoon," he says.

"Afternoon," Dad says.

The man draws parallel to us and stops, looking back at the line of figures trudging his way. He looks back at us, Tessa and I stare at him, wide-eyed.

"Not the best day for a picnic," he calls, noticing our thermos flask on the rock.

"We don't mind the drizzle," Dad says back with a smile.

I look from Dad to the man and back again. This man seems twitchy and edgy. He keeps looking him over as if assessing him in some way. I feel uncomfortable. If I were Spider-man, I'm sure my spider-sense would be tingling. The man is acting like one of the kids on my list at school. Maybe he is a modern kind of Monk, and he's keeping us talking until his friends catch up and then they'll summon the *Beast that Follows!*

I tug at Dad's sleeve, but he placates me with a nod that says, *it's alright.* The man looks back toward the snaking line of monks, judging their distance.

I can't hold it in any longer.

"ARE YOU A MONK?" I shout at the soldier.

The man whips around to look at Dad. He starts to twitch his head. Dad glares down at me. Tessa keeps quiet. I think she's not sure either way.

"Am I a what?" the man asks, wiggling his finger in his ear as if to check that it still works.

Dad gives me the *why do you do these things* look. I scowl at the ground, my neck burning hot red.

Dad clears his throat, and with a slight strain in his voice, he says, “He asked if you were a Monk.”

The man seems to inflate and starts to walk over to us. His shoulders swing as if they are so big he needs their momentum to move. “A what, now?” The man’s voice is crisp and icy. “You called me a what?” He has taken offence. It dawns on me that he thinks Dad has said what I said. Does he know we are on to him and his evil monk friends?

“Oh shit!” Tessa says.

Dad turns from the approaching hulk, whose true size establishes itself as he draws near us and gives Tessa a parentally disapproving look.

"Oh, God!" I shout, "He is a monk!"

"Pipe down, Billy," Dad says and turns back to the man who's now just a few paces away. With a clear and calm tone, Dad says, "It's the hood. The *hood* you’re wearing. From a distance, it makes you look like a Monk, y’know, like from a monastery.”

The man stops. He looks at each of us. "A monk?" he says as if tasting the word for the first time.

“I was telling them a Dartmoor ghost story, involving monks, and then we saw you all coming over the hill. They got a fright.

The man takes a moment to let the words sink past his scowl, and then his face cracks into a smile. "Oh! A Monk! With the brown dressing gowns?"

Dad’s relief is clear, but his face sours when he glances at Tessa for her swearing.

"I thought you called me a punk!" The soldier says and lets out a short but false sounding laugh. It's tempered with an edginess that could run cold at any point.

"Oh, no. Christ no," Dad says. "I was just telling them a ghost. You couldn't have turned up at a better time"

The soldier looks back towards the men who have now crested the hill. The soldier gives us a fake smile. "Yeah, I guess we do look a bit like monks," He turns to look at us, "But we ain't no punks."

Dad leans against the rock and gives him a nod. The soldier stares at us for a bit longer and then, not being able to find something else to start an argument about, turns and trots away. The line of soldiers following him trudge past without looking our way. We watch them go, our heads moving left to right simultaneously as if we were all watching a tennis match or had trackside seats at the Grand Prix until the last man appears. He looks smaller than the others and is jogging to catch up. I can't help but think that he is the runt of the litter, trying to prove he is one of the big boys. I feel sorry for him because he is just like me. He just wants to belong. I make a plan then and there to never join the army.

He is also the only one he looks over to us as he waddles past. He gives us an exhausted but good nature smile and a brief wave of his hand. Then he hunkers down and tries to increase his pace, but his burst of energy, possibly put on for our benefit, doesn't last long, and he falls back to his painful looking jog.

Once he's gone from view, I feel Dad's eyes on me. I slowly turn to look at him, knowing the expression that'll be on his face.

"Are...you... a... monk?" he says with an exasperated smile and a shake of his head.

I shrug my shoulders. He turns to Tessa, who's sat crossed-legged on the rock. His soft smile slides from his face. "And you. Where'd you hear words like that?"

Tessa looks at him with that knowing innocence that only she can get away with. "You said it yesterday, Daddy."

I note the strategic use of the word *Daddy* to appeal to his softer side.

"When you scrapped your knuckles on the concrete when you were loosening the nuts on the car's wheel." She flashes her smile at him.

I look from Tessa back to Dad, who has a vague warning in his eyes. He *had* said something yesterday when we were helping him with the car. Tessa had let out a giggle, and he had told her to pipe down. I had asked what he had said, and he kept saying loudly over Tessa, "NOTHING! It was nothing!" No matter how many times I had asked, Tessa hadn't let me in on the secret.

"Well," he said, looking from one to the other of us, "That's not a word a little one should be using."

He turns to glance over the moors, and Tessa gives me smug *got out of that one* grin.

"Come on. Let's get back to the car before those punks circle back."

FIFTEEN

Before. Two Sundays ago. Afternoon.

As we tramped down the slope towards the small gravel car park. I can see our cream coloured car sat there on its own. Dad and Tessa are ahead of me. I would try to keep up with them, but I have restricted myself to step only on the spongey tufts of grass. These are green nobbles that pepper the moor landscape. I like them because they are springy. I'm sure that I can jump higher and further if I bounce from one to the other. It doesn't always work, admittedly. Sometimes they are too far apart, and I have to take a quick step in between or, when I jump, I don't land on the centre of the nobble, and my foot slips off the side. This runs the risk of spraining my ankle, which I have done previously. Oddly, the threat of this happening again doesn't dissuade me from doing this. I know if I sprain my ankle, I will get *the look* from Dad, but I just *have* to try and get all the way to the car using only these tufts.

Up ahead, I can pick out parts of Dad and Tessa's conversation as I leap.

"What was he going to do?" Tessa asks.

"I don't know, but he was *that* sort of person," Dad says.

"What sort is that?"

"The type that looks for an argument or tries to find offence in anything they can." Dad glances back in my direction, and I quickly step down from my current tuft and walk normally. As soon as he turns away, I start leaping again.

"Why would someone want to have an argument?" Tessa asks.

"Some people do," he says.

"But," Tessa starts and turns to look at him as they walk, "That doesn't make any sense."

"It doesn't. And it won't make any sense to them either. They are just angry,"

"At what?"

"At everything, at anything."

"I don't get it," Tessa says.

"Well, you wouldn't because you're not like that," He shoots her a sideways glance. "D'you know anyone at school like that?"

"No," she says,

"Really? Aren't there any bullies at your school?"

"Sure, but they don't bother me."

She is so lucky. What's so different about her? We're from the same family. Why is she not bullied like me? Why am I the only one who gets picked on at school?

My jumping takes on a more determined and irritated tone.

"Are they angry a lot of the time?" Dad asks.

"Sure, they pick on a group of nerds."

"Well, they are the type of people we're talking about."

"They just don't like them, is all," Tessa says, kicking one of the grassy nobbles.

"They don't like anyone, and they want to show it. Bullies don't change. They just get older." He stops walking and turns to face her. "People like them, people like that *Monk* we saw, they can't find a way to be happy, and so they want to ruin it for everyone else. They only feel involved if they can play the one role they know. The Bully. So, they will do anything they can to carve that part out for themselves."

Tessa scratches her head beneath her woolly hat. I stand deathly still, balanced on a tuft and riveted by what Dad is saying. I wish

I was in the conversation or that he was talking to me.

"I know people like that," she says.

"We all do," and he shoots me a sideways glance. "It's not just bullies, it's people who don't know how else to be, it's not always their fault. Some people only know how to act if they're in an argument... or showing off."

"Like Uncle Mike," Tessa says.

Dad resumes walking. "You said that, not me."

"But he does. He's always showing off," Tessa says.

I look at the ground beneath my nobble of spongy grass and consider abandoning my leaping to keep up with the conversation. Instead, I decide to jump faster and further.

"Well..." Dad says as he starts to pat his pockets, "He's the same but in a different way. He only knows how to act if he has more than you do."

"How do you act?" Tessa asks.

I abandon my nobble jumping and, putting on a short jog to catch up, fall in step alongside him.

"Me?" He pauses and thinks for a moment. "I'm very lucky with my lot in life. From now on, it's anything for an easy life," he says and stops again, patting his jacket pockets and looking back the way we came.

"So, how do you know this?" Tessa says, following his gaze.

I start to think that the Monk may have followed us, and I turn and look back as well. When I look forward again, Dad has resumed his walk towards the car, still rummaging in his pockets, Tessa at his side.

"There are only so many types of people. When you get to my age, chances are you met most of them, and so whoever you meet, they are a bit like someone you met before." He says and pulls a bag of fisherman's friends out of his pocket only to glare at it and put it back.

“You ever meet anyone who’s not one of those types?” Tessa says, trying to run around in front of him and walk backwards so she can watch him as they talk.

“Where the hell is... Hmm?” He looks at Tessa and then continues. “Occasionally, yes.”

“Who?”

“Your Mum,” he says and pulls his jeans pockets inside out, “That’s one of the reasons I married her. She surprised me.” He stuffs the pockets back into his jeans and then stops and rubs his chin.

“Anyone else?” Tessa asks.

Absently now, as if something important has dawned on him, “Well… There’s you two, of course. You two always surprise me… Where the hell is it?” he says, irritation creeping into his voice.

“Where’s what?” I say.

“The car keys, I could have sworn I had them,” he says.

I shoot a look at Tessa, whose face is blank. I know what happened to them. When we first set out, Tessa had forgotten her bag when we left the car, and Dad gave her the keys to run back and get it. I didn’t see her give them back to him. I wait for her to admit this, but she doesn’t.

We exchange glances. I wonder if I should say something. If it were the other way around, Tessa would tell Dad, but I'm never that sure of myself. I'm never that sure of anything. For example, I can do something a hundred times over, check it and recheck it again and again, but if someone tells me it wasn't what I thought, I'd be more inclined to believe them rather than myself. So, I say nothing in this case of the missing car keys.

"Come on," Dad says.

When we get to the car, Dad squats down to rummage through his bag. I kick at the gravel dust of the car park and then press my face against the car's rear window. There, on the back seat, are the keys.

I would know Dads car keys anywhere. He has so many on his bunch, and his keyring is one of those double-sided picture frames that slot into a brown cover. If you take it out of its cover, you'll find a school picture of me on one side and Tessa on the other. Whenever he comes home from work, the first thing he does is hang them on the key rack in the kitchen. It signifies the end of his working day, which he always seems pleased about. I also think he hangs them there because if he doesn't. he will lose them.

I look down at Dad, who has started to mutter to himself. He stands and goes through all of his pockets again. Tessa is balancing on one of the boulders dotted around the small car park's edge, marking its perimeter. I look back inside the car and wonder if I should say something or just let things find their way without my involvement. Dad glances in the direction we came from again, possibly contemplating retracing our steps to see if he dropped the keys somewhere, when he catches sight of me by the car window. I must have a worried look on my face.

His expression doesn't change. Without looking back through the window, I raise a finger and point to where I know the keys are. He walks over to me, rearranging his pockets and cups his hands against his face as he looks in the car. He expels a breath and looks down at the gravel.

He looks at me and says, "Well, that's a problem, isn't it?"

I nod and, without meaning to implicate Tessa, I look over at her. She's stood on the boulder but is now looking off over the moors.

Something about her back or the way she's standing makes me think she is living out some dramatic girly daydream in her head. As if she's waiting expectantly for some weather-beaten figure, who has travelled miles just for her, to come striding across the windswept moors.

Dad follows my stare and is now leaning against the car, his elbow on its roof. He looks like he's standing in the pint of beer shop having a chat. Relaxed despite the problem.

"Tessa!" he calls.

Jolted from her daydream, she spins around to look at us. Dad points a finger at the car window and waggles it. Her face pales. She begrudgingly climbs down and trudges over. When she joins us, she looks first at Dad, then down at me. For me, she reserves a petulant scowl that Dad can't see. She looks in through the car window. Her mouth drops open.

"It was Billy," she says in a flash.

If I knew the right words, I would have expressed my outrage. But I don't. I just gasp a bit and shake my head. I hate the way she never wants to be seen as anything less than perfect in Dad's eyes. Even if that means selling me out at every turn. I look wildly at Dad and do all I can not to boot Tessa on her shin. The traitor!

"It wasn't Billy," Dad says, re-cupping his face and looking through the window again. He doesn't sound angry or annoyed, which I find really unfair. If I had left the keys in the car and blamed someone else, I would have been in *so* much trouble.

"We got us a challenge," Dad says.

He looks around the car and then moves to the boot to check if that too is locked. It is. I look at the back seat. The keys seem impossibly close. It doesn't seem fair that they can be this close, and we can't reach them. I look at the door's lock pin standing to attention from the interior of the door's plastic casing. We are always told to make sure we clunk them down when we leave the car and then check the door to make sure it's locked. They never disappear completely within the door because then you couldn't unlock the door from the inside. I look at the pin, arrogantly sticking up at me like a rude gesture with a middle finger. Maybe it's not as far down as the 'locked' position?

I pull at the door handle, and, unfortunately, there is no relieving sound of the mechanism releasing. Dad has been watching me. He tests all the other doors, but they are locked. He looks over at me and gives me a confirming head shake. He leans down and looks in through the window at the lock pin. He comes back and stands next to us both.

"Right. What would MacGyver do?" he says. This is another of his catchphrases, reserved for when you are facing a problem. The last in his catchphrase repertoire is usually reserved for me when I have done something particularly foolish. I get the *look* and then told *You'll never get in the A-Team.*

He rummages through his bag, looking for inspiration. He looks up at us both and says, "What have you got in your bags?"

We both start to mimic Dad's rummaging, but I only have my penknife and a stick from our riverside walk last weekend. Tessa has the remnants of our picnic, and from her pocket, she pulls some stupid plastic card thing she's recently taken to carrying around everywhere. She picked it up when we were in one of those coastal gift shops that sell loads of stuff you want but only ever use once. Things like seashells, postcards, kid's buckets for making sandcastles and nets on sticks for fishing in rock pools. They always have those turn display towers with postcards or fridge magnets. Tessa found one that had bookmarks that displayed the meaning of different names. In the same tower were these little cards that had poems or advice on them. She had taken a particular interest in one that told the story of a man walking on the beach with Jesus. She kept it with her because she thought it was "meaningful".

Mum had read it to me once, and it was just about this man whose life is a beach that he has walked with Jesus by his side. When he is about to die, or something, and he looks back at their footprints sprawling out across the sand, and at some point, he sees only his footprints and not Jesus's next to them. He moans at Jesus and says that he left him during the difficult times in his life, but Jesus says that during those times, he carried him. I thought it was pretty stupid because surely the man would have remembered being carried, especially by Jesus.

Dad looks at the card in her hand. It is made of plastic. He then walks over to her and looks in her bag. It contains the rubbish leftover from our picnic. Three empty crisp bags, crumpled cling film that our sandwiches had been wrapped in, and the empty KitKat wrappers.

Dad pulls out the cling film and looks at it closely, then he looks at the car. I watch him intently, trying to guess what he is going to do next. I wish I could think the same way he does but I can't figure out what he intends to do. As if deciding something, he takes the 'Footprints' card from Tessa's still outstretched hand and goes to the car.

He uncurls the balled-up cling film and stretches it out so it is more like a plastic string. He places the end of Tessa's card in the middle of the cling film and folds either side down each side of the card. He slides the card, with the cling film string hooped around it, through the side crack of the window. I see it appear on the other side of the glass, inside the car.

"What are you doing?" Tessa asks.

Dad doesn't respond. He has his tongue gripped between his teeth as he wiggles the card in through the window and then slowly draws it back, leaving the loop of the cling film on the inside. Its two ends are still on the outside. Dad pushes more of the cling film loop into the car with the card.

I look at him, then the loop, and then back at him. He glances at me and gives me a frowning smile.

"So," he says, including Tessa in this. "I'm not sure this will work but let's give it a go."

"Give what a go?" Tessa asks.

Dad holds up a finger as if to say, *Ah... just wait.* He is now left with a large loop of cling film on the inside and the two ends outside. He slides the card in again and starts to push the loop towards the lock pin. With his other hand takes the two ends of the loop on our side and pulls the whole thing down to the base of the window. The loop slips over the lock pin.

"Did you mean to do that?" Tessa asks.

Dad gives her a frown and then rubs his forefingers against his thumbs and takes hold of the two ends of the cling film jutting out on our side. He slowly pulls them towards him until the make-shift loop fits snug against the lock pin. Then he rubs his thumb and forefingers together again and grips the ends. He pulls them tight against the lock pin and slowly pulls the cling film up.

"Come on... Come on..." he whispers to himself.

Nothing happens. He lets go and looks off over the top of the car.

"Dad...? Dad...?" Tessa asks, and I wish she would just shut up, but I say nothing.

He hunches down again and pulls at the cling film, pulling it tight and upward. I think, for a moment, that the lock pin might snap, but Dad gives the cling film a hard yank up, and the lock pin pops up.

"No... Way...!" I say and look at Tessa, whose mouth is wide open.

Dad holds up a hand to tell me to wait. He lifts the door handle, and the mechanism clunks, and he pulls the door open.

"NO WAY!!!" I say.

"That was amazing!" Tessa says.

Dad allows himself a wry smile and hands Tessa her 'footprints' card.

"Can you break into any car?" I ask.

"Never tried until now," he says, reaching around to the back door and unlocking it.

He opens it and leans in to get the keys. He stands straight and points the keys at Tessa.

“Be more careful,” he says.

She nods, and he leaves it at that.

I’m annoyed because I’m sure I would have been in so much trouble if this were my fault.

The roads on Dartmoor sweep and arch across the landscape. The car glides along the deserted road. I can feel every rise and fall in my tummy as we go. I lean and look out the front window between the two front seats. By doing this, I should be able to avoid feeling car sick. My annoyance at Tessa getting off scot-free from such a mistake has faded. I'm left with a feeling of excitement at how Dad did a real-life MacGyver and unlocked the car door.

I don’t really know what to do with myself, so I just shout out, “Dad! That was soooooo cooool!”

I see his eyes in the rear-view mirror. He quickly raises his eyebrows in what I think is a smile.

“What would you have done if I wasn’t there?” he asks us both.

“Eh?” Tessa asks.

“If I wasn’t there, what would you have done?”

“I don’t know,” she says and looks back at me. I just give her a shrug.

“Come on,” he says, and I catch his eyes in the mirror. “You’ll never get in the A-Team like that! Think about it.”

“Maybe smash a window with a rock?” I offer.

"Um... That wasn't quite what I was thinking," Dad says, "Besides, neither of you can drive, so there's no point getting into the car."

“D’you mean, if you weren’t there at all?” Tessa asks.

"Yes, let's say I've fallen down and hurt myself, or I've gotten lost somewhere. What would you do?"

"Make sure you were okay?" Tessa suggests.

"Yes, but think of it as an adventure. What would you do?"

"Um... Well, we'd could go and find those soldiers and ask for help?" Tessa says.

"Yep. That's a good one. But they were going at some speed in the other direction. You may not catch them." He shifts down a gear as we drive up a hill.

"We could stop a passing car?"

"Another good one." He slows the car at the junction. His hand is on the gear stick, which is in neutral, and I can hear his ring rattle against it. "But," he says as he swings the car onto the main road, "There aren't many cars around."

I push myself up and look out the back window and then out the front. He is right. We haven't seen a car since we left the car park.

"What else?"

"Ummm... Come on, Billy Boy, help out!" Tessa says, sneaking a look back at me.

"Call Mum?" I blurt.

"There you go!" Dad says.

"Oh yeah!" Tessa says, her face changing from what was potentially about to be an eye roll to an excited smile. "There was a phone box in the village we passed through. Bit of a walk, though."

"True, but at least she could get a cab out and bring the spare set of keys. You always have phone money on you, don't you?" he says.

Tessa and I look at each other and then shake our heads. Mum tried that once. She gave us phone money for emergencies. Tessa and I promptly bought all the misshape sweets we could afford.

"Oh... Well, you know how to reverse the charges, don't you?"

"I do!" Says Tessa, and I'm pleased the conversation has moved on before Dad can explore what happened to the emergency phone money.

"There you go then!" he says.

"But where would you be?" I ask, some concern in my voice.

"Oh, don't worry, it's just a hypothetical question."

I frown. "What's a hyper-dermic question?" I ask.

Dad spurts out a laugh that sprays the windscreen with saliva.

"Yuck!" says Tessa.

"Sorry!" he says and points to the cloth in the compartment on Tessa's side. "Can you pass me that?"

She does, and he wipes the window clean, then he looks at me in the mirror, "A *hyper-dermic* question is a question about something that hasn't happened yet. A 'What if' question."

I nod and say the word over and over to myself. I want to use that word again, but I can't think of a time when I would ask a 'what if question' instead of an 'I want question'.

Tessa becomes absorbed in her door and plays the lock pin, flicking it with her forefinger. She looks sideways at Dad and then back at the door.

"Dad?"

"Yes," he says, slowing the car down to rattle across a cattle grid. I always like the feeling I get when we drive over cattle grids.

"When... when can we go back to our coast?"

He turns his head to look at her for just a moment too long before he looks back at the road. She stays absorbed in the lock pin. Then I see his eyes in the rear-view mirror as if to check if Tessa is asking on my behalf as well. I don't know how to react. I want to know the answer to this question, so I just look blankly at him.

"Well," he says, eyes shifting back to the road, "We'll have to see. Soon I reckon."

He looks at us both again and doesn't get a reaction. This is unusual. On Sundays, he is the leader of our gang. He always gets a response from us.

"Well, just look at us."

I look myself over in case I missed something.

"No cuts, no bruises, we're not soaking wet or covered in mud. I'd say we've done pretty well this week!" He pauses for a moment. "True, we almost got throttled by a marine and had to break into our own car, but..." he waves a dismissive hand, "What does that matter."

We both smile. He has us back on side, and I feel happy. I feel that we will be going back soon. I want to go back. I miss the place when we don't go. More importantly, I miss the adventure. I miss the freedom. I don't feel small when we run the tide. I feel like I can do and be anything. No one else does this. Everyone makes rope swings, everyone goes for hikes on the moors, but no one has the adventures we have at our ragged, weather-worn stretch of coast.

SIXTEEN

Our Coast.

Most people go to the beach to stretch out on the handful of sunny days we have in the summer. They like to go to beaches that have far-reaching soft, white sand, a sea that gently laps against the shore and is warm enough to entice them deeper than a gentle paddle. They sit and read their books. They occasionally let their eyes drift across their children as they entertain themselves by building sandcastles or writing their names in the wet sand.

This is not the sort of beach we go to. I have never seen Dad stretch out on a towel and do nothing but soak up the sun. In fact, I've never seen Dad in shorts, let alone swimming shorts. He's not like Mike, who likes to expose as much deeply tanned flesh as possible. He doesn't wear sandals or have his shirt unbuttoned to expose chest hair that erupts through in dark curls. If I had to choose a word for Dad, it would be modest. He won't talk about how he managed to get us into our car with only Tessa's stupid card and cling film. It won't come out in conversation the next time he's dragged around to Mike and Sharon's. He seems to know himself and does not need any further validation. I wish I were like that.

Our stretch of coast is not soft and lazy. It's rough and ragged, and we love it. Our Sundays always start early, so we never see anyone when we go out. We always have the coast to ourselves. I guess that's why we have a sense of propriety about it. On the rare occasion we see someone, usually, when we are about to leave, I feel that our magic has been invaded and that *they,* the latecomers, don't belong.

Our stretch of coast is accessed by a steep and rickety iron staircase bolted into the rock face. It brings you down into the first of a series of coves. When the tide is high, the first two coves are as far as you can go. There must be some people who have come to that cove at high tide and have never discovered the excitement and adventure that lies beyond it.

When the tide is going out, you can walk around that first outstretch of rock, scrabble over some fallen parts of the cliff and jump down into the next and largest of the coves. This is when you know it's all about to begin. I feel a prickle up the back of my neck every time we are there. We run across the cove to the next rock face that juts out from the cliff. The tide is on its way out, but it has not gone out completely. The sea still churns at the end of the coves jagged wall. If you count the waves correctly, you can run around the end of the rock and into the next cove as the sea swells back, drawing in its breath, before it thrashes in, closing the brief doorway between coves.

This stretch of coast is made up of a series of coves. The rocks bordering them are all different. Some reach out far towards the sea, so you risk getting soaked when running around them in the small gap in the waves. If you can't get around them, there are others that you can get far enough out between waves and reach a part that you can climb over. The whole coast is like a series of ragged fingers reaching out to the sea, clawing at it as if reluctant to let it go. The coves are the webbing between the fingers, where we catch our breath before running around the next slice of headland.

It is the Sunday that offers the most thrilling of our adventures. True, we are never in any real danger. The worse that can happen is that we miss count the waves and get licked up our backs by the tide as we run into the next cove. These trips are timed well. They are only when the tide is retreating.

I love the sea. Not the clear blue expanse you see in the holiday billboards or the magazines stapled into the middle of the

Christmas edition of the Radio Times. I love the grey, flinty sea. The sea that is the same colour as the jagged rocks that tumble towards it, holding hands when the tide is high, pointing at it when the tide is low. The sea we know is a tumultuous and angry beast. It froths and writhes with such power that I never tire of looking at it. It is an unforgiving but thrilling playmate that we know and respect, and we only have fun with it when it's in a good mood.

SEVENTEEN

Before. Two Sundays ago. Late.

Dad snorts himself awake, his mouth making a loud clump sound as he shuts it abruptly. He glares at me for a moment and then looks around the living room for the ever-elusive time thief. The room seems to change shape as the shadows expand and contract with the changing image on the TV screen. He looks back at me and, to delay having to respond to a question he may ask, I take a mouthful of cereal.

"Again?" he asks.

I nod. He tilts his head in the direction of the armchair next to him and holds out his hand to take the bowl from me as I clamber up, just like last time. I settle down and take back my cereal. On the television is a black and white film. The sound is low. Mum must have lowered it before she went to bed. I wonder why she didn't just turn it off? Maybe to make Dad feel like he still had company when he woke up. If he woke before the channel's programming stopped.

"What's this?" he asks, frowning at the grey haunted-looking house on the screen. The image cuts to the interior of the house, a grand and stately room with rugs and an enormous fireplace. Wood panelling and animal heads decorate the walls. Two men in suits with solid jawlines talk to each other, each holding a cigarette. They stand stiffly as everyone does in these old films. One of them glances about in mock nervousness and runs his hands through his inky jet-black hair. Then he reacts as if he's heard something from behind a curtain. He walks towards the large drapes that look more like carpets than curtains, not dissimilar to the curtains in Mike's tanning room.

Even though there is hardly any sound coming from the T.V, I'm instantly gripped by the old film. I don't want to take my eyes away from the screen in case I miss what happens next. It's like when I was watching the snake eating an egg, but this is more of a fun fear, if there is such a thing. I don't look at Dad, but I assume he is just as gripped as I am.

The man on the tele looks at his friend and then pulls back the drape. In the window is the pale and floating face of a ghostly woman. He bites his knuckle and turns back to his companion, who does not appear to have seen the woman at the window. The first man gestures, but the second one shrugs and lights another cigarette.

I look at Dad.

"Spooky, eh?" he says.

"Have you seen this before?" I ask.

"I believe I may have slept through it at least once before.".

"Is it scary?" I say, glancing back at the tele.

"Some bits are, some bits aren't."

I look at the screen. The man has now gone out through the heavy wooden front door and is looking around the outside of the mansion in the wind and rain. He's shouting someone's name and looking dashingly windswept and terrified all at the same time.

"What's the best ghost story you've heard?" I ask.

He considers, "Well... That one about the monks today was pretty good."

I smile, but that was not the answer I wanted. I want him to tell me another ghost story.

"Are ghosts real?" I ask.

"Um..." He rubs his neck, stalling for time, considering how far to answer this question. "Some people believe they are."

“Have you ever seen one?”

“Um… Well, possibly.”

I look at him and frown. “What do you mean?”

“Well, have you ever seen someone you thought was real, but then when you look back, they’ve suddenly gone, or they couldn’t have been there in the first place?”

I think on this, “I’m not sure… I mean…” I stop, not finishing my sentence, as is my bad habit.

Dad shifts around slightly in his chair to half look at me. “Well, you’re young, you’ve not known anyone who’s died.”

“Nanna died,” I say.

“True, have you ever thought you’ve seen Nanna after she died?”

I shake my head. I have thought of her a lot. After she died, I started to fantasise… well, at least imagine what it would be like if Mum and Dad died, but then I felt really guilty and sad. We were driving home and just turned into our estate. I had gotten so far into thinking through my fantasy that I started to cry in the back seat. I didn't dare tell Mum and Dad why I was crying because I felt bad for wishing them dead. I tried to take it back in my head again and again, and then I was scared that just by thinking it, I might actually make it happen.

"I don't believe in ghosts like in these types of stories," Dad says, pointing at the screen. Now the man is being tended to in his four-poster bed. "Not the scary hauntings. But I think there is something out there."

This comment yanks my eyes from the screen to look at him. “You believe in ghosts?”

He scratches his throat with the back of his fingers. “Some people believe in God and Jesus and all that, but I don’t believe in that.”

“Why not?”

"I was brought up in Catholic school!" he says with a smile, which seems like enough of an explanation for him, but I don't get it. I thought that Catholics believed in God. I want to ask what he means, but I don't want him to get distracted from what we're talking about.

"Everyone sees things differently. For example, if I lost something and couldn't find it, I would l keep looking for it. Someone who believes in God, like Auntie Flo, would not look for it but pray for help, and when she finds it, she'd think God helped her find it. I would say that she found it on her own. I just can't believe in all that, but it's fine that Flo thinks that. That makes her happy.

"Anyway, some people believe in God, some people don't. If you believe in God, you will see what happens in life in one way, and those of us who don't will have a different explanation for what happens."

"But you *do* believe in ghosts?" I ask.

"I think so. I mean, there are certain things I can't explain. I'd rather believe that there is something out there, yes. Some people believe that when you die, there is nothing after that."

"Not even dreaming?"

"Nope. They think that is all over when you die."

This thought jars me, and Dad seems to notice.

"But I don't think that," he says quickly.

"Why?"

"Well, if you look at it scientifically... You'll do this in a bigger, bigger school... a famous scientist once said that energy can never be created or destroyed. It just changes form. Well, we – you, me, Mum and Tessa, every living thing, are made of energy."

I find myself frowning again.

"For example, if you rub your hands together, that takes energy, and that movement transforms into heat because when you rub your hands together, they get warm."

I nod.

"So rather than that energy from you disappearing, it is transformed into warmth. So, when we die, that energy in us *has* to go somewhere. Maybe it stays around and comforts those of us who are still here."

"Is that why you believe in ghosts?" I ask.

"Well, there's that and something else."

"What is it?"

"It was a long time ago, and I may have remembered it wrong. But I thought I saw someone who couldn't have been there."

I am gripped, despite my eyes feeling dry and heavy. "Who? What?"

"Do you remember I told you that me and my friends used to play a lot down on the docks in Birkenhead?"

I nod, feeling that I am about to be told a story that no one else has *ever* been told.

"Well, we used to go down there a lot, sneak on the boats and have a poke about. Sometimes we used to go down there in the evening or at night when all the dock workers had gone home. They would leave lots of different tools and equipment around. We were terrible little kids really, when I think back. We were into everything.

"One evening, a group of us were out late. Bertie was at home, and I was with Gobber and Eddie. We were out with a bunch of other kids. There must have been about ten of us. The sun had gone down, and the dark was creeping in, and with it came a low mist that rolled up the river and into the dock. It lay over the ships that were moored there and started to spill out onto the streets. Someone had the idea of using the mist as cover to get on to the ships and explore them.

"So, we climbed over the railings and dropped down into the

dockyard. We clambered over trucks, cranes and stole into the cabins. We must have been everywhere, but you could hardly see each other through the fog. It was so thick. A couple of the boys were inside one of the open-top storage units on a ship. There must have been a crane above it for lifting things out. Anyway, one of the other boys had gotten into the crane's cab and was messing around with the controls, just playing, like you do when we are in the car when it's parked. Playing at driving.

"He must have pressed something or pulled some leaver because the next thing we all know, there is a sudden metallic rattling sound as if something had been set free, and then there was an almighty crash. We all pegged it out of there, knowing that the noise would bring the dockyard security running. We couldn't see each other very well, but in the dim mist, I could see the shadows of the other boys scurrying over the piles of rubble, up the gangplanks and over the fences and railings. It was like a swarm of giant rats fleeing back to the streets.

“Eddie, Gobber and I ran out of the dockyard together, but we didn't even say goodbye to each other. We ran like hell to the lamppost where our streets met and went off in different directions. We separated without breaking our pace. I knew the metal studs on my shoes were making an almighty racket as I ran down Price Street, but I just kept running all the way home. I was afraid some copper, or worse, a dockyard hand would grab me.

“I got a clout from my Nan for being home late and was slung into my room. It wasn’t until the next day, when I was out again with Eddie and Gobber, that we heard that one of the boys never made it home that night. But it still took a few days to find out what really happened.

"It was late autumn then, just like it is now, so it was getting dark earlier. For the next few nights, I took the long way home when leaving Eddie and Gobber at the lamppost. I would circle back to the dockyard on my own, just out of curiosity to see if I could find out what had happened. The mist remained for the next few nights and hung over the part of the shipyard we had been in.

"Each of these nights, when I walked past the docks, from a distance, I thought I saw a boy standing just next to the railings in the mist. He looked like one of the dim shadows I had seen when we all legged it that night. On the first night I saw him, I shouted out to him, thinking he would be one of the boys I knew, just snooping around like me. It was hard to make out in the fog, but the figure looked around at the sound of my voice, but he couldn't seem to locate me. I shouted out a few names of the lads I knew, just in case it was one of them. I waded into the mist, but I couldn't seem to get any closer to the figure. He always seemed to be the same distance away from me, and then I lost sight of him.

"The next night, I went down to the docks again. The fog was still there, and the whole place seemed deathly silent. I was alone, so I just kicked around, and then there he was, off in the distance. He looked more like a shadow than a real person. At least, that was how the fog made him appear. Just like the night before, I tried to get closer, but I couldn't. With every step I took, he seemed to drift further away. I shouted out again because he just looked lost like he was looking for something or someone or just searching for a way out of the fog. As I drew close to the edge of the dock, I lost him again. By the time I got to where I had thought he had been standing, he wasn't there anymore. I looked across the docks, and I could have sworn I could see a boy disappearing back into the fog, back into the dockyard.

"The next night, Eddie's mum came around. She said that one of the boys we were with that night had been killed, crushed under a falling crane. When I heard this, I instantly went cold. There was an investigation to find out what went wrong and why the crane fell, but the locals were all told to keep their kids away from the docks, especially at night. I wasn't allowed out for a few nights, but I just had this feeling that the boy I saw lost in the mist was the one that died. The next time I could get out, the fog had lifted, and I never saw the figure again."

“You really think it was him?” I ask. “The boy that died?”

“Maybe. I can’t explain it.”

I felt sad for the little, lost boy, not knowing where all his mates had gone. Not being able to go any further and leave the fog and having to go back to the place where he died each night.

"That's spooky," I say.

“It is, but it’s not scary. Not like these types of stories,” he says, pointing at the film still rolling on the television.

“So, you believe there is something after people die,” I ask, looking for confirmation.

“I’m not sure, but I would like to think so. I tell you what,” he says, changing his tone and turning to me. “I’ll make the same deal with you that I made with your Mum.” His face is bright and fun now. “I told your Mum that if I go first, and there is anything out there after death, I’ll find a way to let you know. How’s that?”

I smile. I know that Mum would have told him off for saying this to her, let alone how she would react to him telling me. She always tells him off for joking about stuff like this. She calls him morbid. It might seem strange, but I like it. I feel an odd sense of comfort at what he’s just said.

“Mum will tell you off for saying that,” I say.

“True,” he says, smiling, “maybe it’s best we keep it to ourselves.”

“Don’t worry, Dad,” I say with a growing feeling of confidence, “It’s just a... it’s just... A... A... hyper-dermic question."

EIGHTEEN

Before. Last Sunday. Morning.

Were things better back then? I'm not sure. They were different, that's for sure. Everything is cleaner now than it was back then. Back in those days, everything was grey. No matter what colour they were when they were made, all the steam trains soon became a uniform black. Thick with soot. The Liverbirds were black, not clean like they are now. You don't have the same smog that hung everywhere, and there aren't all the bombed out buildings. I guess that is for the better.

Things are more convenient now. We have more machines to do things for us. We'll probably all evolve into creatures with just one eyeball and a finger because that's all we'll need to do, to look at a screen and press a button.

You have everything you want now. You have a TV in your house, tape decks in your rooms, ones that you can put batteries in and take with you wherever you go, like when we recorded that pirate story. Back then, when it rained, you couldn't just turn on the television. You didn't have one. You had to make up things to do. You had to play or read comics or torment the cat.

We had a radio. We called it the wireless, but that wasn't on all the time, and the signal wasn't always very good, not like it is in the house now. You'd have your favourite shows, the way you have on television now. It might be a serial of Buck Rodgers, and we'd all race home in time to listen to it and then talk about it the next day. If you wanted to watch something on a screen, you had to go to the cinema, the pictures as we called it back then. We couldn't always afford to all go in, so we'd scrape enough money together to pay for one of us to go in. Then that one would shoot down the aisle and open the door in the back to let the rest of us in.

The pictures were great back then. That's something that hasn't improved over the last forty years. It's got worse, and more expensive. Back then, you used to have a whole afternoon at the pictures. There'd be the news because you didn't have the news on tele at home, then some cartoons, then your B- movie, that was normally a western, like the ones with Randolph Scott. Then, you'd have the big picture. In the fifties, we had Cinema-scope and technicolour. The screen was massive and would arc around you. You'd have to turn your head to see what was happening on either side of the screen.

You could go in at any time during the show. We'd all sneak in and sit amongst all the blokes out with their Judy's. It didn't matter if you came in halfway through one of the films because they would show the whole thing on a loop. You'd watch it until the point where you came in and then leave.

Now, what do you get? Trailers and a film? And it's so expensive! The pictures were definitely better back then. Over the next forty years, you'll probably have a cinema in your own living room, you won't even need to leave the house.

Everyone has a car now. Well, most people do. Back then, if you had a car, you were rich, especially in our area. If a car ever pulled up, we'd be all over it, asking the driver to give us a ride and jumping up and down on the footplates. I guess that's one of the reasons no one ever brought a car down our way.

Back then, you still had horses and carts. The rag n' bone man had one. The coalman had one to deliver his coal. We used to try and run along the back of him, hoping some would drop off the back of the cart and then we'd snatch it up and race home. The milkman delivered with a horse and cart. There used to be a lot of horse muck. Horse muck was like gold. If you saw some, you'd scoop that up as well and race that home. It was good fertiliser for whatever your family was growing in the yard,

There'd be smears and remnants of horse's dung. If it was wet, we'd shove a stick in it and chase each other around with it. If it were dry, we'd kick it at each other. There was a lot of airborne donkey dunk back then, and you'd constantly be getting flecks of it in your eyes.

I'm not sure if you'd say it was better back then, but we made the most of it alright.

NINETEEN

Back when the world was black & white.

I never liked the cat. It looked evil and stupid, all at the same time. When it rained, it stayed indoors just like we had to. Whenever it came near me, I tried to give it a boot. It hated me and would try to scratch me any chance it had. Our relationship was one of mutual disdain.

It loved string. It would chase string all around the house. I would always get in trouble for using up all the packing string playing with that divey of a cat.

At the bottom of our spiral staircase, I saw it. Padding out from the living room, having warmed itself up in the range.

"There it is!" shouted Bertie from next to me at the top of the stairs.

"Shut up, yah eejit! You'll scare it off!"

You know, thinking back now, we never referred to that cat as a *he* or a *she*. It was always an *it*.

Bertie settled down again on his knees next to me and waited. I tugged on the string. Just a bit to make the end at the bottom of the stairs wiggle. That cat caught sight of the movement and froze, waiting to pounce.

This was a delicate operation. If the cat caught the string straight away, it would never let go. It would just gnaw on it. The game would be over before it started. I had weaved the string in and out of the bannister's railings. The last time I did this, I ran the string just up to the first floor. The cat had only made it halfway up before it slipped off the stairs completely. It tried to follow the end of the string that I had weaved in and out of the railings. That was funny, but I had gone for the ultimate obstacle course this time. I had run the longest piece of string I could find right up to the fourth floor. I had threaded it not only in and out of the railings but across the stairs and around pieces of furniture on the landings.

Admittedly, I was being overly optimistic about the cat's ability to chase this piece of string, especially considering its last failed attempt, but the truth was, I was bored. It had rained for two days straight, and I couldn't think of anything else to do.

Across these days of weather enforced confinement, I had stood on the top floor and dropped different things down the centre of the spiral staircase, just to watch them fall and hit the floor. I had even got Bertie to stand at the bottom of the stairs to catch them. That had ended badly when I only told him the stuffed doll was coming moments before it landed on him. Like a right wally, he looked up and then jerked his head away, smacking it on the circular swirl that marked the end of the bannister. That had won him a black eye from the bannister and me a belted arse from Dad when he got home.

We had exhausted the bannister slides. When Nan came out of a room on the second floor as I slid, bum first, past her on the curling wooden, she had hitched up her dress and ruffled petticoats and bolted after me. She was faster than was possible for a woman of her size and age, not to mention how she was dressed. Knowing what was coming, when I got to the bottom of the bannister, I slid straight off and into a sprint toward the kitchen. I don't know how she did it, but she caught me by the lug hole before I even made it to the kitchen door. In mid-stride, I was wrenched off my feet by my earlobe and swung round and backhanded across the tops of my legs in one swift movement.

"He's going for it!" Bertie said, nudging me and pointing down at the cat.

"I know, I know!" I said, slowly retracting the string to tantalise the cat.

The cat tried to paw at the string, but I had pulled it just beyond its reach to the first step. The cat cocked its head, almost in recognition. Did it remember the fall from the stairs the other day? Nah, surely not. This cat was the dumbest cat I'd ever seen.

It was about to lose interest and lick itself when I gave the string a sharp tug, making it jump up two steps. The cat jumped at the sudden movement, and then the chase was on. I pulled the string back, wrapping it around my hand to take up the slack. The cat shot up the first few stairs, and then the string snaked out around a railing. I pulled it slowly as I didn't want to lose the cat over the edge of the stairs too early. To my surprise, the cat slipped effortlessly around the railing, its body mirroring the shape of the string as it bent around and back on itself.

I was struck by a slight sense of concern as it looked like I had underestimated my opponent. I shifted onto my knees and focussed. I pulled the string with more speed. The cat rose to the challenge. It pounced towards the end of the string and just narrowly missed it. The string slithered back out around the railing, and this time I pulled it faster. The cat shot out and almost slipped off the edge of the stairs completely. Its paws scrabbled at the wood digging its claws into the railing and just managing to spin itself back inside the stairs.

“This cat is sooo dumb!” Bertie said, but I wasn't so sure anymore.

"It's smarter than you are," I said, and from the corner of my eye, I saw Bertie stick his tongue out at me.

The cat sprang after the string, unperturbed by its near-death fall. I started to pull the string frantically as the cat leapt up the stairs, three at a time. It shot up the second flight of stairs, and I panicked, pulling the string fast so that it whipped in and out of the railings too quickly for the cat to follow. It paused, paw half in the air, its head twitching back and forth, watching the string wiggle in and out of the railings. Once the string was back on the inside of the stairs, the cat resumed its pursuit. This little kitty had learnt a trick or two.

“It's gonna catch it!” Bertie whined, and he tugged at my arm.

“Gerroff!” I said, shouldering him away.

The next stretch was a clear run. I pulled the string quickly up the third flight of stairs, and the cat scampered close behind. I shuffled around to get a better view of the third-floor landing. That was where the trap lay. The cat wouldn't get me on this stretch. Not on this stretch, it wouldn't.

It was as if the cat could sense all was not as it should be. At the top of the third flight of stairs, it paused. I let the string come to a stop in the middle of the landing.

"Come on, little kitty, come on...." I said like an evil mastermind toying with the hero, tugging gently on the string.

The cat cocked its head with each twitch of the string. Suddenly it dove forward, claws bared, and let out a hiss. This scared me, and I rattled the string back. My plan had been for the cat to try and get the string as it circled around the leg of the sideboard, bonking its head against either the wall or the wooden leg. To my ear ringing despair, this was not what happened.

The cat barged its way behind the sideboard, knocking it so hard that the whole unit began to wobble. On top of the sideboard was Nan's favourite vase. It had been with her for years. It had withstood the time when her own house was bombed in the war, and it had not received so much as a scratch when Dad dropped it by accident two years ago. Now, it seesawed back and forth, its base making a bowel-loosening rolling sound against the wood as teetered this way and that.

The air felt like it was sucked out of the landing as Bertie and I froze. I hoped that if we stopped moving, so would the vase.

“No, no, no, no, no, no, no, no, no, no, no, NO!” we both screamed.

The cat was now wedged behind the sideboard, stuck between its wooden leg and the wall. It kept still for a moment as it listened to the rattle of the vase above it. The cat appeared to look up in my direction, slowly tilting its head to the side. Then it bucked like a wild horse in a cowboy film and broke free of the sideboard making the whole thing tip forward.

"NOOOOOOOO!" I shouted, but it was too late. The cat had scrabbled free, and the vase fell, erupting into fragments as it hit the floor.

Bertie was soundless, but I could see his mouth drop open. The cat tore up the last flight of stairs like it had been kicked by the sound of the shattering vase.

"Oh jeez! Here it comes!" blurted Bertie, and I saw the devil in the cat's eyes. Was it chasing us now?

I whipped the string back up. The cat swerved back to pursue the string, and I jumped to my feet.

"Come on, Squirty!" I yelled, scooping up the spools of string and running across the landing, the last part of the string slithering behind me.

The cat was almost at the top, but I'm sure I saw a glint in its eye as I looked back. The kind of glint that suggested it wanted to scratch *my* eyes out.

We ran into Mum and Dad's bedroom and slammed the door. The last part of the string was still in the corridor. I heard the cat reach the top of the stairs and its paws went at double speed as it raced in our direction. I pulled the string under the door as fast as I could. The cat's paws thumped on the landing floor towards the bedroom door. I snatched the last part of the string in, and then the door shook in its frame as we heard a huge thunk sound from the other side. The cat had ploughed headfirst into the door. A meek sounding meow followed, and Bertie and I looked from the closed door to each other.

"Jesus Ray!" Bertie said.

I looked from him back to the door. We listened, but only silence spilt into the room from beneath the door.

“Oh, God! I think you killed it.”

“It was your idea!” I said without hesitation.

"No, it wasn't! And don't you dare tell Mum that!"

I moved to the door and put my ear against it. I was hoping to be able to hear the cat breathing, or purring, or something.

“Did you kill it?” Bertie asked. I waved him quiet.

There was no sound. Nothing at all.

“I think you might have,” I said.

“Me? Me!” Bertie said. “It was your idea! And the vase! Nan’s gonna kill you!”

I had forgotten about that. I felt the colour drain out of me. It wouldn’t be long until that was discovered. She’d be home soon, and so would Mum. I looked out the window. Thank God the rain had stopped, and the streets glinted as the sun broke through the clouds.

“She’s gonna throttle you,” Bertie said again, and he was about to say more, but I silenced him with a glare.

First things first, I thought and went over to the door. I gripped the door handle and turned it.

“No!” shouted Bertie, covering his eyes, not wanting to see the dead cat in a heap on the other side.

I opened the door a crack and peeked out. I couldn’t see the floor directly in front of the door, so I opened it a bit further.

“Is it there?” Bertie asked from behind his hands.

It wasn’t. I let the door swing wide. The landing was empty. The cat had gone.

“Jesus,” I said, “Where the hell is it?”

Bertie came out from behind his hands and started to act all brave now. “It’s gonna get you! It’s gonna scratch your eyes out…” but I silenced him with another glare.

As I went to creep out of the room, Bertie said, "Look at that!"

I spun around, expecting the cat to be in mid hissing flight towards my face, but he was pointing at the bottom of the bedroom door. There was a dent in the wood panelling, right where the cat's head must have hit the door. I crouched down and rubbed my fingers across the mark.

From the bottom of the stairs, I heard the latch click and Nan's mumbling and irritated voice fluttered up the stairwell. Both Bertie and I jumped and looked at each other for inspiration. We held our breath and listened. It sounded as though Nan and gone into the kitchen. I ran to the staircase and looked down to the bottom floor. She *had* gone into the kitchen. It was now or never.

I slipped onto the bannister and slid down the spiral, past the destruction on the third floor to the second floor, where our bedroom was.

"Wait for me!" called Bertie, but I ignored him. He could get caught if he wanted, but I was gonna peg it! I put my boots on, jamming my toes against the newspaper, scrunched inside them to make them fit, and bolted back out to the landing. Bertie had just run down the two flights of stairs, and we passed in our doorway as he ran to get his boots.

I looked down the stairwell and listened. Nan was still in the kitchen. I mounted the bannister again and slid down to the ground floor. I heard Bertie thumping down the stairs behind me as I struggled with the front door latch.

"Wait for me, Ray!" he called.

"Shut up, Squirt!" I hissed, just as I felt the air shift. Nan was standing in the kitchen doorway. I didn't need to look. I *knew. I felt* she was there.

"What the feck is all this thumping and shouting!" she yelled.

I managed to snap the latch up and flung the door wide. Jumping down the four steps onto the pavement, I sprinted down Price Street. I heard Nan scream for me to come back, and in the distance, I could hear Bertie's boots clumping behind me.

As her voice retreated, I heard her shout, *"AND WHERE ARE YOU GOING SQUIRTY?"*

Eddie and Gobber were leant against our lamp post. Gobber had on strange squint. He had one eyebrow raised, and he kept flipping a coin in the air and trying to snatch it back into his fist as it came down. I recognised this. It was what the Private Investigator had done in the film we saw in the pictures the last week. Gobber wasn't very good at it. He was trying to do it while glancing, as nonchalantly as he could, up and down the street. The problem was that he kept missing the coin and batting it across the road. Then, he abandoned any attempt at looking cool as he desperately chased the coin, trying to snatch it up before anyone else could grab it. He did this at least three times as we approached, and each time he would resume his lean and squint and toss the coin again as if he hadn't just looked like a right pleb.

Eddie, as good-natured as ever, was watching this charade with a look of puzzled amusement. He leant on the other side of the lamppost, and his hand was resting on something metal, clipped to the string that held up his shorts.

As we got closer, Gobber saw us but pretended he hadn't. He made a show of looking the other way and squinting his hardest.

Eddie looked over and waved at us energetically. "Y'alright, our kid!"

"Y'alright, Eds," I said and looked at Gobber. "What'smatter with yer eyes?"

He turned to me and was about to give me some Yankee slag insult when he realised Bertie was coming up behind me. His hand twitched and covered his groin.

"Wha's he doing here?" he said.

"S'matter Gobs? You scared of me little brudder?"

“He is!” Eddie said, shoving Gobber, “Look at him! He’s worried about his nut bag!”

Gobber shouldered Eddie off the lamppost, and he stumbled. Gobber seemed pleased with Eddie’s fall but kept his hand over his groin all the same. Eddie resumed his place against the lamppost and rested his hand on the thing clipped to his trousers.

“What’s that?” Bertie asked, pointing to the metal thing attached to Eddie.

“You like it?” Eddie asked.

“What is it?” I said.

"It's me ray gun," he said and looked off into the distance as if the street was the cosmic world of Buck Rogers.

"That's not Ray's," Bertie said, looking at me as if Eddie were an idiot.

Eddie shifted his faraway look to Bertie, “Not Ray’s gun, you pleb, a *ray gun.*”

“Yer wha’?” Bertie said.

“A *ray gun.* Like they have in Buck Rogers!" He unsnapped it from his trouser string and held it like a gun, making *pew, pew, pew* noises as he shot at the other kids on the street.

“Where’d you get it?” I asked.

“In was in some pile of junk left out for the ragman,” Eddie said.

At the mention of the ragman, Gobber’s other hand involuntarily cover his bum.

“It looks like something Mum sticks in her hair to make it go all bouncy,” Bertie said.

I snorted a laugh through my nose. “Yer right, it does.”

“No! No! It’s not a lady thing. It’s me *raaaay gun,*” Eddie said.

“Yeah, right,” I said, “You doing yer Mam’s hair tonight?” This made Bertie and Gobber laugh,

“Up yer bum, Ray," Eddie said and re-clipped the thing on his trouser string.

Gobber looked us over, “Wha yer saying then, boys?"

I shrugged, “I dunno, can’t go home for ages. Bertie made a right mess.”

“It wasn’t me!” he shouted.

At Bertie’s raised voice, both Gobbers hands shot to cover his crotch.

“You got any dosh?” Eddie asked us, and we all shook our heads. We had no money at all. Then our heads turned to look at Gobber’s closed fist protecting his nuts.

“How much is dat?” Eddie asked him.

Gobber looked at his coin, “It’s nowt. Nowt to you anyway.” he said.

“We can’t even go pictures,” Eddie said.

"Why don't we sell that girl thing you've got to some old biddy," I asked.

“Stick it up yer bloody arse, Raymond!” Eddie said, “This thing is great, you wait, my ray gun will save us one day.”

“Do you even know what it is?” I asked.

“It’s mine is all.” he said, “Anyway, what we gonna do?”

We shrugged at each other, and Gobber looked at his closed fist. “We could go and nick a couple of bottles from Misty’s place, get some money that way.”

“It’s hardly worth the risk,” I said, “If Misty gets hold of you yer dead.”

Misty ran the pub and the shop. It was common for a shop to be attached to a pub back then. He ran the place pretty much on his own. The thick wooden and highly polished bar in the pub snaked around to the front and disappeared through a hatch into the shop next door, where it arced back on itself, mirroring the pub's layout. The whole bar was like a huge wooden horseshoe. From his post behind the bar, Misty could walk from the pub right around to the shop depending on where the next customer was. Customers couldn't walk from the pub to the shop, they had to go outside and back in through the shop door.

During the day, Misty would mainly be in the shop, keeping a watchful eye on the customers, especially kids. He seemed to hate kids. He'd saunter round to the pub now and again to make sure the day drinkers weren't helping themselves. None of them would dare. Misty was just as mean to thieving grown-ups as he was to thieving kids.

You didn't have plastic bottles for pop and fizzy drinks in those days. You only had glass bottles which, if you returned them to the shop, you'd get a bit of money back. Not enough to buy a whole other drink, but if you returned a few, you'd get the price of a new one. Some of us used to sneak into Misty's backyard and swipe a few empty bottles that he kept in piles of crates for refilling. Then we'd go back into the shop and return them for money.

Misty wasn't dumb, though, and as I said, he was mean. He caught a kid in his backyard once. Caught him red-handed. The poor sod was stood there with an empty bottle in each hand, reaching up to pass them over the wall to his mate. The rumour was that Misty broke the kid's fingers and stole his soul with his dead eye. His eye was the reason he had the nickname Misty. He couldn't see through it. All the kids said it was because he got shot in the head in WWI, but the bullet ricocheted off his temple because he was so mean. He was fine apart from losing the sight in his left eye, but it left him meaner than ever. The eye was all grey, and if you looked at it hard enough, you could see little clouds in there swirling around. If you ever made him angry, the clouds swirled faster, and his eye would start to glow.

That's what they all reckoned happened to the kid he caught thieving in his yard. He glared at him with his cloudy eye so that the kid was hypnotised and couldn't run away. He drew his soul into his eye, which started to swirl faster and glowed and then, for good measure, broke all his fingers.

Misty terrified all the kids in our neighbourhood. He wasn't massively tall like the cowboys in the pictures, but he was impossibly broad. His forearms, which were always exposed because he had his shirt sleeves rolled up, were thick and coarse looking. He had faded tattoos on them that had no real form or shape. He was bald apart from a tufty, wiry band of hair that snaked from his temples around the back of his head in the same shape as his horseshoe bar.

He eyed every kid in the shop or newcomer to the pub with suspicion. He would look you over and rub his hands on his stained white apron, probably wondering how best to throttle you if you put a foot wrong. Ever since we heard about the boy with a lost soul and broken fingers, no one had ever tried to steal his bottles again.

"You scared, ya rat?" Gobber said, adopting his squint again.

"Yes!" I said, "You'd be a fool if you weren't!"

"Y'know..." Eddie said, while investigating a stain on the elbow of his jumper, "Misty hasn't been hit for a long time. He'd never expect anyone to steal from his backyard again."

"That's because he'll bury anyone who even tries!" I said.

Gobber looked at Eddie, "I think you're right. I think he's gotten lazy. I reckon it's the perfect time to hit him."

"No way. You two are nuts. No one does that to Misty anymore for a very good reason."

"C'mon, Ray," said Eddie, "Where's your sense of adventure?"

I was tempted. I could feel it. The thought of getting one over on Misty, the grumpy old git, was pulling at me.

"Besides, we'd need you to be able to pull it off."

I shook my head, but I knew I was in, "I dunno, it's not worth it for just a couple of bottles,"

Eddie took the bait, "Then we go late, and we steal a whole crate! That would keep us in pop and sweets... and the pictures for ages!"

Still looking in the other direction, Gobber said, "You'd need more than one crate for all dat."

"Then two or three crates." Eddie said, "What d'you reckon, Ray?"

I rubbed my chin with my thumb, mulling it over. Bertie was looking at me open-mouthed. He couldn't believe I was even considering it. He tried to give me an almost imperceptible shake of the head to warn me off, but I ignored him.

"We'd need something to carry them in. Something big enough for more than one crate," I said, now pacing back and forth in front of Eddie and Gobber.

Eddie ran his palm up his nose and gave a loud sniff. "I've got that covered, Ray."

"Okay, when should we do it?" I asked.

"Tonight," Gobber said. "We should hit the old git tonight."

"No way! *Nooo way!*" Bertie said.

"No one asked you to join!" Gobber said and crossed one leg in front of the other.

"Why don't you go home, Squirty," I said. I heard Eddie and Gobber smirk.

Bertie looked at the two of them, and they fell silent. Bertie was getting a bit tougher these days.

"I can't go home, can I?" he said, irritated. "I'll get clobbered for the mess and killing the cat!"

Gobbers voice came out with a choke of fear. He pointed to Bertie, "You... killed yer cat?"

Bertie shrugged the question off, "He did," and pointed to me.

"We don't know that it's dead yet." I said, "Anyway, just blame it on me. But don't tell Ma what we're up to."

"I ain't going home. No way," Bertie said and folded his arms.

"Well, if you come with us, you shut up, okay?" I said

Bertie eyed me and then gave a reluctant nod.

"Right, let's meet at the back of Misty's yard at sunset," I said, and Eddie and Gobber darted off.

TWENTY

Back when the world was black & white.
The back of Misty's yard.

The sun had disappeared over the top of the houses, and the streets were plunged into a chilly shadow. You could hear the mam's calling their kids in for their tea, and I started to wonder if Eddie and Gobber would show.

We didn't want to wait for them right at the back of Misty's place because he might catch sight of us and grow suspicious. So, we stationed ourselves down the alley just off Misty's and kept peeking out to see if Eddie and Gobber had turned up yet.

"Y'reckon they'll come?" Bertie said to the back of my head as I took another look down the cobbled alley.

"Course they will," I said.

"Y'reckon they'll bring some food. I'm starving."

So was I, but I didn't want to moan like Bertie, so I just rolled my eyes at him and turned back to scan the alley.

"I hope they bring some food with them," he said to himself.

I heard a rustling sound, and I looked at Bertie, who froze under my stare. "What's that noise?" I asked.

Bertie looked at his boots. He was wearing the ones that were too big for him. "I just did what you did," he said, "I stuffed some newspaper in them."

"Those are way too big for you. Why didn't you wear your old ones?"

"I like these ones," he said indignantly.

“I’m surprised you were able to get away from Nan in those clown shoes. They’re almost twice the size of yer feet!”

“Nan says I’ll grow into them.”

“If yer ever grow," I said. "You've been that size since you were five.”

“Shut up! It’s not my fault you got the growing side of the family.”

“Ere, you better take that newspaper out if we’re gonna be sneaking around Misty’s yard. He’ll hear you a mile off,” I said.

“No way!” said Bertie, “They might fall off.”

“Better that than having yer soul sucked out of you by Misty’s eyeball," I said.

Bertie looked from me to his boots and then back at me, unconvinced. So, I added, “And all yer fingers broken.”

He looked at his hands, then at me, and then at his boots again. Slowly he took them off and pulled out all the newspaper. There was loads of it.

“Bloody hell, Bertie. You got cod n’ chips in there as well?”

I heard a rattle, and I shot a look down the alley. Good old Eddie was pulling a wooden cart behind him piled with towels and sheets.

“Psst! Over ere’ Ed’s!”

“Y’alright, boys?” he said, wheeling his cart down the alley.

“You doing yer Mam’s laundry or wha?” I asked, pointing at the sheets and towels in his trolley.

“Don’t you worry,” he said, tapping the side of his nose. “Just trust in old Ed’s.”

He looked at Bertie dumping all the newspaper from his shoes in a nearby metal bin. Eddie looked at Bertie’s massive shoes as he slopped back to us. He was making more noise now than when he had the paper in them.

Eddie cocked his head and asked, “Have you shrunk, Bertie?”

“Nah,” I said, not giving Bertie a chance to respond, “He just grabbed the wrong pair.”

“Well, better than being too big for them, eh, like Gobber,” he said.

"What you saying, hairdresser boy?" Gobber said. He was now leaning against the corner of the alley, looking off into the distance, still flicking that bloody coin.

“Whatcha, Gobber," Eddie said as if he hadn't just been insulted.

“Still wearing your hair clip?” Gobber said, pointing his chin at the thing still clipped to Eddie’s trousers.

“Gerraway will yah,” Eddie said.

“Curl yer Mam’s hair wid dat, did ya?”

“Pack it in yous two,” I said. The sun was sinking fast. “We need to see the lay of the land before it’s too dark.”

Leaving the cart where it was, we all snuck round to Misty's backyard wall. We piled some empty crates up, and Eddie and I climbed up to peek over. The yard was small and cobbled. It had stacks of crates full of empty bottles all around the walls. A few loose bottles were strewn around here and there. There were two metal posts at either end of the yard with a washing line in between them. There were some sheets and one of Misty's aprons hanging from it.

"I didn't realise he actually washed his aprons. Look at dat, they’re still filthy," Eddie said.

I stared at him, “Are you here to check his whites or make some dosh?”

He sniffed in response.

In the gaps between the laundry, I could make out the crates of empty pop bottles on the far side of the yard. To the back of the yard, there was a wooden door that led out to the labyrinth of alleys. I looked down at Bertie. "Test the yard door, will yah, just in case," I said and looked back over the wall.

“You test it,” I heard him say.

“Just do it, will yah Squirty!” I hissed without looking at him.

Bertie kicked the crates we were on, and we gripped the wall to steady ourselves as the makeshift tower wobbled.

“Whasermater with you!” I said in a hushed shout.

He disappeared around the corner and then slopped back in his oversized boots. “It’s locked.”

“Did you *really* try it?” I whispered.

“Yesss!”

“You better had.”

From our vantage point, you couldn't see into the pub. There was a back door, but it had frosted glass. There was a dim rectangle of light on the yard floor from the door's window. The rectangle got larger at the furthest end. Misty's unmistakable shadow flashed across the frosted window. His head reared up and looked distortedly huge in the shadow that was briefly cast across the cobbled floor. We ducked back down, gripping the top of the crate we were balanced on, our knuckles white.

“What! What!? Is he coming?” Bertie asked.

I glared down at him and then looked at Gobber, who was standing next to him, looking all casual as if he were waiting for a bus.

“Would you shut him up!” I said to Gobber.

“I ain’t touching him,” he said.

We climbed back down to the alley.

“Right,” I said, rubbing my hands together. “There’s a whole stack of bottles in crates, but the pop bottles are on the other side of the yard behind his washing line.”

I looked up at the darkening sky. “We should do it now before it gets too dark to see anything over there."

Against his sulking protest, we lowered Bertie first over the wall onto one of the piles of crates. Terrified, he quickly slipped down and disappeared into a dark space between two stacks of crates. Eddie and I hunkered down again behind the wall, waiting to hear if we had been spotted.

"Shall we just leave him in there and scarper?" Eddie said.

This made us both laugh, and we clapped our hands over our mouths.

"I can still hear you!" Bertie whispered back.

Eddie laughed and snorted out a huge greeny over his hand. This made me want to burst out laughing, but I clenched my eyes shut and tried to think of the trouble I was in with Nan. That soon calmed me down.

"Come on, you schmucks!" Gobber whispered up from the bottom of our crates. "Just get over there, will you!"

Eddie lowered me down, and I felt my feet touch the top of a wooden box. As Eddie let go of me, I realised I was coming to rest too close to one side of the crate. I felt the tower of boxes tip over to the right, and I grabbed hold of the wall. The crate fell to the side and thudded against the stack next to it where, luckily, it stayed, wedged above the small gap where Bertie was hiding.

I hung from the wall, my legs scrabbling against the bricks. If Misty came into the yard now, my soul would be in his eye faster than Nan's backhander.

Eddie's head reappeared over the wall and looked at the back door. Then he gave me a smile. "That was close," he said.

My boots were still scraping against the wall, trying to get a foothold. Eddie looked down past me and smiled. "Just let go," he whispered.

I looked down and realised that I was less than an inch above the next crate. I dropped down and then slid onto the cobbles and slipped into the gap with Bertie.

"Find yer own hiding space!" he said and elbowed me in the ribs.

"Pack it in you div'ead!"

Then, I saw the hulking shadow of Misty, growing large across the rectangle of light cast across the cobbles. He was coming to the back door. The light from the pub made his shadow look like a giant. I shoved myself further back into the dark gap, squashing Bertie against the wall. My feet slipped and skidded against the cobbles as I tried to get back far enough to pull my legs out of view. The giant shadow was a perfect outline of him. I could see the wisps and individual strands of his grey hair corkscrewing out from behind his ears. His shadow grew until it filled the light from the door. He paused. I could almost hear him breathing. In my mind, I could see the misty glass fog up even more under his hot breath. I could feel Bertie trembling behind me.

"I think I'm gonna have a *movement,*" he hissed in my ear.

I closed my eyes and waited for the sound of the door opening and the smell of Bertie's fear induced *movement*.

Neither came. I opened my eyes. The shadow had gone. I eased away from Bertie, who wheezed like an old organ as the air went back into him. I peeked out from our hiding space. The coast was clear. I looked up at the wall and saw Gobber's bum appear, and then he dropped onto a crate and down into the yard.

It was dark now, but luckily there was enough light coming from Misty's back door and from the windows of the neighbouring building. I glanced at the billowing sheets on the washing line. Like a rippling cinema screen, the light from next door caught it and, for a split second, I thought I saw the shadow of a cat slinking across its ballooning surface. I blinked, and it was gone.

"D'you see that?" I said to Gobber.

"Yeah, he almost caught you. Come on!" He slapped my chest and beckoned me to follow him.

“No. I meant the cat.” I said.

But Gobber had already swatted the ballooning sheets out of the way and disappeared behind them. There was a scraping sound next to me, and Bertie appeared from his dark hiding space, looking flatter than when he went in. He gathered himself to his feet and looked around as if he were on a ghost train.

“Come on, Bertie, get to the door,” I said.

“Get stuffed!” he said.

“C’mon Bert! We need you as our lookout!” I said.

Bertie was meant to look through the keyhole into the pub and let us know if Misty was heading for the yard.

“No way! If he comes, I’ll be the first one to get caught!”

“Ray, I need your help,” Gobber whispered from behind the sheets.

"We need you, Bertie!" I pleaded. "Besides, if he comes towards the door, you'll be the first to know and the first to scat."

I could see Bertie mulling this over, and then he scuffed over to the door and got down on his knees, putting his eye to the keyhole.

“It’s really smokey in there,” he said. “Maybe something is on fire?”

I pushed past the sheets and found Gobber restacking crates.

“You not looking for a job!” I said.

“The pop bottles are at the bottom,” he said, straining as he pulled another box and placed it on the floor. “We can’t return beer bottles to Misty, can we.”

“There is a lady with big nellies in there,” whispered Bertie.

Gobber and I lifted the last box, revealing the pop crates.

“Who’s got big nellies?” Eddie called from the top of the wall.

“I dunno who she is. She's the only lady in there," Bertie said.

Gobber looked over at Bertie.

“C’mon Gobs, help me with the crate,” I said.

“She’s pretty,” Bertie said.

“What’s her bum like,” Eddie asked.

“Can’t really see. Some man has his hands all over it,”

“Gobber!” I said, “Grab a crate!”

Gobber looked at me and then pushed past the sheets on the washing line and shoved Bertie out of the way, taking his place at the keyhole.

“It’s Marge, from Hamilton Square. The one who stands by the corner all night!” Gobber said. “She’s got massive tits!”

“Why does she stand on a corner? Is it a bus stop?” Bertie asked.

“She’s a right tart, my Mam says!” Eddie called, and then as an afterthought, said, “Dad always stops to talk to her, though.”

“No way, she just grabbed her own boob!” Gobber said.

“OI! Gobber! *Help me with the crate*.” I pleaded.

“What is she doing now?” Eddie called to Gobber.

“She’s sat on some fellas lap… wait, hang on…is that me Da?”

“Let me see,” said Bertie.

“Gerraway,” Gobber shoved Bertie, who slipped off the doorstep and fell into the crates next to the back door. The tower of crates fell back against the wall then toppled forward, falling across the backdoor step.

“Watch out!” Eddie shouted.

Gobber jumped back, and the crates collapsed on the door-step, making a tremendous splintering and shattering sound. I pushed through the laundry and pulled Bertie out from under the mess of broken wood and glass.

“Quick, hide!” Eddie said. “Someone’s in the top window,” and he dipped his head down behind the wall.

Gobber pressed himself flat against the wall next to the back door, and I swung Bertie into a gap between two crate towers, pushing myself back in against him.

In a strangled voice, Bertie said, “Not too tight. My movement is coming back!”

A new square of light appeared on the yard floor. Someone had pulled back a curtain upstairs and was looking out.

“It’s Mrs Misty!” Eddie said in a hushed voice from behind the wall.

I pushed further back into our hiding place, ignoring the squeak of air that came from Bertie. I wasn’t sure which end of Bertie the squeak came from.

The square of light disappeared, and Eddie’s voice called out, “All clear!”

I peeked out. Gobber peeled the top part of his body away from the wall and looked up at the now curtained window. We could see the drapes still lightly swishing after being dropped back into place.

“Quick!” Eddie said, “She’s probably on her way to tell Misty!”

“Let’s grab a crate!” Gobber said.

“Are you nuts?” wheezed Bertie from behind me.

“We’re already in for it. Let’s grab one!”

Gobber and I grabbed a crate and shuffled to Eddie's side of the yard. We slid it onto a box and climbed up, passing it over to Eddie, who took it and placed it on his cart. From the top of the wall, we saw him lace the sheets and towels around the bottle tops to stop them from clanking against each other.

Gobber elbowed me. “Let’s get one more!”

Knowing this was a mistake, I nodded. We slipped back down into the yard.

“What are you doing!” hissed Bertie.

"Just check the keyhole!" Gobber spat, and Bertie, amazingly, did what he was told.

Gobber and I lifted a crate between us and sidled across the yard. I felt the sheet slip up and over my face as we pushed through it.

"Oh, Jesus!" Bertie said, his eye pressed to the keyhole, "Some old biddy is saying something to Misty!"

We balanced the crate on a box next to the wall, and Gobber climbed up.

“She’s pointing this way!” Bertie said.

“Come on! Come on!” Eddie said, waving us up towards him.

“He’s coming!” said Bertie.

“Come on!” I said to Bertie, “Let’s go!”

“Oh jeez! He’s massive!” Bertie said.

“C’mon!” I called.

“Leave him!” said Gobber, passing the crate over to Eddie, who disappeared to stack it on his cart.

I stood on the edge of the broken wood and waved frantically at Bertie, “Come on! He’ll catch you!” I said.

Bertie pulled his eye from the keyhole and looked at me blankly. Then I saw that terror had paralysed him. I caught his hand and swung him to the base of the crates just as Gobber’s bum vanished over the top of the wall. Eddie leant, reaching for Bertie. I pushed him up onto the box, and then I saw Misty’s shadow at the door, his broad frame all but blocking out the light from the pub. I heard the lock rattle as Misty was trying to open the door.

Bertie was reaching up for Eddie’s hand when the lock clunked, and the door started to open. There was a scraping sound as the door caught against the splintered wood and glass debris on the back step. Misty muttered as he shoved the door harder.

“Hide!” Eddie said to me.

Bertie turned to look at the door from his box and flattened himself against the wall. I stepped back into the yard and let the sheets balloon over me. I slid against the wall on the far side and stood as close as I could against a stack of crates behind the washing. Between the sheets, I could see Bertie, stranded on top of the tower of crates.

The door finally shoved open, and there was Misty. Broad and in silhouette, the light and the smoke from the pub spilling out around him. The door had opened wide and coved Bertie, but from my vantage point, I could still see him. If Misty had looked through the frosted glass of his back door, he could probably see Bertie's outline quaking against the bricks. If the sheets blew at the wrong moment, Misty would catch sight of me too.

Misty looked bigger than he did during the day. He looked down at the mess of wood and glass.

"What the feck..?" he said to himself.

From behind the door, Bertie was trying to point at something without moving. He was sticking his chin out towards me. Finally, he built up enough courage to take one flattened palm away from the wall and pointed his finger to something on top of the wall behind me.

I craned my neck, reluctant to take my eyes away from Misty's in case he saw me, and I looked above me. There, on top of the wall, looking straight down at me, was a cat. I could see its outline, and its head had a curious and almost recognisable tilt to it. It seemed to be saying, "Well, well well, so here you are...."

Misty stepped into the yard and more light flooded into the yard. It lit my corner, but I was still hidden by the sheets, which, thankfully, hung flat from the line. I looked back at Bertie, who was trying to say something silently with his face. It looked like he was trying to stifle a sneeze.

There was a *thunk* of paws against wood as the cat jumped onto the box above me. It looked at me again, and I glared back at it. Then I realised what Bertie had been trying to signal to me. This cat looked exactly like Nan's cat. I froze as it locked me in a smug, unflinching stare. It couldn't be her cat, could it?

I looked at Bertie, whose face was pale. He gave me a nod as if to say, *It is! It is her cat!* Misty kicked at some of the debris and went to turn to go back into the pub. The cat looked from me to Misty's back and then let out a *Meow!*

I shushed at the cat as quietly as I could. Misty paused, looking back over his shoulder. The cat meowed again, and Misty looked straight at it.

"Ah," he said to the cat. "So, you made this mess, did yah?"

Oh, thank god, I thought. He thinks the cat made all this noise. He could see the cat on the crate but not me hiding behind it.

That cat looked from him to me, and I shrank down against the wall, wishing I could slide between the stack of crates and the wall. I willed the cat to not make another sound. Misty gave the yard another quick glance and stepped back inside, pulling the door slowly behind him.

Bertie almost slid like water down the wall with relief. He turned as silently as he could to reach for Eddie's blind hand that was reaching over for him. I looked at the cat and stuck my tongue out at it.

The cat turned from me to the closing door and then looked at a loose bottle standing upright next to it. It rested a paw against the bottle and looked at me.

I shook my head.

The cat looked at the door that was now a crack away from being closed. The thin light shone through. This sliver of light was the gap I had to cross to make it out of this yard alive.

The cat looked at me again, head tilted to an almost impossible angle.

"Don't. Please!" I whispered to the cat, "Pleaaaassssee!"

The cat gave one last *meow* and then batted the bottle over the edge of the box. It shattered on the floor, and the cat hissed to add dramatic effect. Bertie froze in mid-climb. He was half over the wall, his bum facing the yard. The door paused. Then the crack of light grew wider. The cat let out a shriek and glared in my direction.

This was it; we were done for. Misty flung the door open, and it bashed against Bertie's protruding legs. Misty swung the door closed and saw Bertie's rump and his legs flailing, trying to get over the wall.

“Why, you little *bastards!*” Misty spat and hefted his bulk up onto a crate and grabbed one of Bertie’s boots.

"You wait till I get my hands round your neck!" he sneered as Bertie's foot writhed in his grip.

It looked like Misty was fighting with two short and stumpy snakes. He had the head of one while the other struck blindly out, catching his shoulders and suddenly, by pure fluke, Bertie's free foot smacked Misty in his sightless eye. Misty let out a yelp, fell back off the crates, and collapsed into the wood and glass debris on the ground. He let out a howl as he landed and immediately sprang back up. He had a shard of splintered wood sticking out of one of his bum cheeks. He looked, as best he could, over his shoulder and his rear bulk at the piece of wood that jutted out from his tweed cover arse.

“Little shits!” he shouted.

Bertie was gone. Over the wall and free from Misty, the soul catcher. I almost let out a victory cheer, and then I realised my own predicament. I was still trapped in Misty's backyard with only a thin sheet of laundry between him and me. I slapped my back against the wall. Between the crack in the washing, I saw Misty reach round to pull out the wood only to realise that he still had one of Bertie's boots in his hand. He looked at it for a dull moment. He seemed dumbfounded how he had come by it. Then he turned back to the wall and shouted,

"I got yer boot, you little thieving git! I'll find you! Old Misty will find you!"

With that, he reached around and yanked out the piece of wood without so much as a sound. I held my breath. With any luck, he would go back inside and tend to his punctured bum.

"Little feckers," he said to himself.

He looked at the mess on the floor, and then the cat started to hiss again. I glared at it, willing it to shut up. I heard Misty grunt and look up at the cat. I pressed my back to the wall so hard I could feel the brickwork imprint its pattern onto my clothes and my skin beneath.

If there was another gust of wind, the sheets would billow up, and there I'd be, a terrified alley rat, ripe to have his soul wrenched out by Misty's devil eye.

"Who's back there?" he said.

I looked at the cat. Pleased with itself, it settled down to enjoy whatever mayhem that was about to ensue.

"Come on out," Misty sneered, "It's just you and me kiddo, yer friends have high tailed it."

I slid away from the cat, which had adopted a look that seemed to say *what? Going so soon?* I hit the rear wall of the yard. I couldn't see Misty anymore, but his shadow was cast up in a slant against the white sheet. He was getting closer, his wonky shadow growing with each step.

"Come out. There's no escape. Come and talk to old Misty, come and look into my eye," he said.

I almost lost control of my bowels. I followed the feel of the rear wall, edging little by little to... where? There was nowhere to go!

He must have been two feet from the sheets. I could even see the shadow of his breath as it plumed out of his mouth as he spoke. I hadn't realised how cold it was, yet I was sweating.

"Here, ratty, ratty, ratty!" he said as if coaxing out a scared animal.

I felt the wall change texture behind me, and a dull object pressed to my back. I was against the yard door, but it was locked. Bertie had already tried it, hadn't he? Misty's shadow loomed large on the sheet. All he had to do was reach out and snatch the sheet off the line.

It was hopeless. I was trapped. Knowing my young life was about to end, I reached my hand around my back and gripped the doorknob...

You know, it's funny, but I regret not being there to see Misty's face. For months afterwards, I liked to imagine how he looked once he snatched the sheet off the line and realised he had been throwing threats to the wall and a closed, and as far as he knew, locked yard door.

I slipped out the *unlocked door*, closing it silently behind me, leaving Misty looking at an empty yard. I wish I could have seen him scratching his head and feeling like a right div.

Out in the alley, I continued to slide against the wall as if I were on a high building. I turned the corner and then bolted back to the alley where we had hidden before. I heard a roar from Misty.

"YOU MARK MY WORDS! I'LL GET YOU! I GOT YER BOOT!!!!"

The alley seemed empty except for the rubbish bins, and then I saw three heads pop up from behind three different bins like a smack the rat game. Eddie had hidden the cart behind another two. Without speaking, we took the cart, which was ingeniously insulated by Eddies Mam's laundry, and jogged as quietly as possible through the criss-cross alleys until we got to a safe distance. Once we were clear, Eddie erupted into hysterics.

"RAY! THAT WAS AMAZING! How did you get out?" he said.

"Did you pick the lock?" Gobber said.

"No," I shrugged, with what I thought was a modest charm, "The door was unlocked," I said. I turned and cuffed Bertie on the back of the head. "I thought you said you tested it."

"Good job, I didn't," he said, limping with one shoe, "Otherwise, you'd still be stuck there."

"Did it ever occur to you, Squirty, that if we knew the door was unlocked, we could have gone in that way to start with!" Gobber said but silenced quickly when Bertie stopped and clenched his fists.

We started walking again.

"Ray?" asked Bertie, "Was that really Nan's cat?" his voice seemed to go up and down with his limp.

"What? Back from the dead?!" Eddie said, "I thought you killed it?"

"I think it was, little git. Next time I see it, I will kill it!" I said.

Bertie stopped and gasped.

"Oh, c'mon Bertie, I won't really kill it. Maybe just kick it up its pooh hole."

"No, I'm not worried about the cat. It's my boot! *Misty has my boot!* He'll know it's me by my boot." Bertie sobbed.

At the time, we were all worried about Misty, but we needn't have been. Bertie and I got in more trouble for losing his bloody boot with Mam and for the mess on the landing. We both sported throbbing ears for the broken vase from Nan and sore bums from Mam for the lost boot. We couldn't sit down or hear for the next couple of days.

We laid low around Misty's place for a week. Finally, we drew straws to see who was going to be the first to take a couple of bottles back. We had stashed them in Gobber's backyard and had a plan that if his Da discovered them, we would threaten to snitch that we saw Old Marge sitting on his lap in the pub.

I drew the short straw. I took the bottles in, trying to act cool. Somehow, I convinced Bertie to come with me, and when we got inside the door, we stopped dead. There on the counter was Bertie's boot.

Misty eyed us. We had to keep moving and show no fear. I put the bottles on the varnished counter next to the boot. Bertie, his legs shaking, stood close next to me, his eyes fixed on the floor. Misty leant over the bar and looked at my boots and Bertie's scuffed old shoes. A bead of sweat trickled down Bertie's temple. Misty grunted as if satisfied and took the bottles and fetched my change from the till.

"You two know anyone missing a boot?" he said, not looking at us.

Bertie looked desperately at me. I swallowed hard. "No, Sir," I paused, unsure whether to say anymore. "Why?"

"I'm after the owner of that there boot," he said, leaning on the bar which creaked under his bulk. He looked us both over again. "It's not a tall'en like you," he said glaring at me, "or a little'un like him," he said and nodded his head in Bertie's direction, "It's some kid in the middle."

"Oh," I said and gave another dry swallow.

"And he hangs out with girls. Know anyone like that?" he asked, his good eye fixed on me.

"Girls?" I said with honest disgust.

"Yup," he said, and he held up Eddie's ray gun. "I found this with the boot."

"Oh," I said, "Wha...What is that?"

He snapped it away and put it back in the till. "It's some hair curler the lasses use."

But when he turned back, we were gone, running up the street to tell the others we were in the clear and that Eddie's ray gun *really was* a girly hair thing.

TWENTY-ONE

Before. Last Sunday. Picnic Time.

We are huddled against a rock halfway up the wooded bank. We are surrounded by trees and massive mossy rocks that, across time, have tumbled down the valley. It's as though these huge rocks were kicked down the hill by giants. I always feel like we are in the land of giants when we are here.

In the distance, we can hear the roar of the water as it erupts in unrestrained white, frothing sheets, pouring out from the reservoir and down into the valley's river. When we were up close, I couldn't believe that this overflow of collected water was meant to happen. It looked like one of those disaster movies when the reservoir cracks open and floods everything in its wake. The noise was deafening, and the air was filled with mist from the waters churn. The light caught the spray giving the autumnal woods a sparkle that, at certain angles, reflected the colours of the rainbow.

Dad looks off from our spot back up to the reservoir. For just a moment, he looks like his mind is still back when the world was black and white, and he is still scuffing along the streets with Bertie, Eddie and Gobber.

"Enjoy being kids," he says at last, "It all goes too quickly. Time is relentless."

Then he turns and takes our empty metal mugs from us, placing them in his bag. He seems distant and wistful as he tells us, "Enjoy what's around you when it's there, don't make the mistake of wishing your life away. Even the toughest times hold a nostalgia when you look back."

He takes in a lungful of air and looks around. He seems to come back to us, "And enjoy that country air!"

We replicate his deep breath and filter the pure, crisp air into our bodies.

"Rightiho." Dad says, "If I've worked this out correctly, the car should be just at the top of this hill."

I look up. The sun spears through the thick branches and reaming leaves. There are boulders to clamber over and trees to weave through. It's a perfect obstacle course.

"Let's go," Dad says.

We shoulder our bags, and Dad gives each of us a shove up and over the first boulder. These woods look like the jungle Indy treks through at the start of *Raiders of the Lost Ark.* I look around for a cave that might contain a rolling boulder to chase us.

Dad climbs up and over the bolder and joins us. He gestures up the valley's slope, "Come on, let's get a move on."

I start to run up the bank, my feet occasionally slipping on the damp accumulation of leaves and twigs. I catch myself now and then by placing my hands into the soft soil.

"Go steady," Dad calls after me, but I'm on a roll. I'm at the next collection of rocks. I climb onto the smallest one and then scrabble up the large one next to it. Once I get clear of this, I will be close to the top of the hill. Then I'll be the winner. The rock face is slanted, so, like a monkey, I scale up the mossy surface on all fours.

"Billy! Slow down!" Dad shouts.

I get to a flattened part and pause to look back down, just to gauge how far I am ahead of Tessa. I'm about to turn when Tessa shoots up the rock beside me, taking the lead. I stand upright for a moment, my surprise mixed with irritation. I launch forward to climb the next part of the rock, but my foot slips on the moss. I see the rock move away from me as I fall backwards. The tree trunks reach up to the clear blue sky. Their branches seem to curl over as they watch me fall. My head falls back, and, in a flash, I see in my mind the small rock I jumped from to climb onto this boulder. I brace myself knowing that the back of my head will be dashed against the surface of the jagged rock. I feel pale with the image of my crushed skull. This is it; I should have listened to Dad; I should have slowed down.

Suddenly I seem to bounce in mid-air. I am suspended by something that has stopped my head from hitting the rock. Has an alien frozen me in time and space with a ray gun? Or has a guardian angel surrounded me in a protective bubble? It is a strange feeling. Whatever has hold of me is not solid as I seem to quiver in its grip.

I'm still looking up at the trees, their branches crisscrossing the sky like a blue jigsaw puzzle. I see Tessa's face peer over the top of the rock from a distance. I try to look behind me by looking up, and see the top of Dad's head very close to me. I see his hair, his forehead and eyes beneath his eyebrows. His eyes are filled with relief. He raises his eyebrows to ask if I'm okay.

I realise that the thing that caught me was Dads' hand. I thought he was a long way behind me, but he must have sprinted up the hill. He must have only just reached me in time because I realise that his arm is fully outstretched.

My feet slide sideways off the large rock, and Dad raises my head, bringing me to a sitting position. I had been falling straight for the small, sharp rock. I have an image of a monkey we saw in a zoo, bashing a coconut against a rock embedded in the grass of his enclosure. I wince, seeing my head splitting open just as the coconut had. Dad slumps next to me. His face is pale and sweaty.

"I'm... I'm sorry, Dad," I say. I know how close I just came to death. I don't know how Dad did it. I don't know how he got from where he was down the bank, up the slope over the slippery and uneven ground to reach out and just, by the length of one hand, catch me a moment before I hit the rock.

He wipes a hand across his face. "Jesus. I... I thought..." He looks away from me up the valley toward the soft roar of the reservoir, "I thought you were a goner."

I want to look at him, to see that he is not angry with me, but he won't show me his face.

"You *have* to be more careful, Billy. Please," he says, still not meeting my eye.

The word *please* cuts deep into me. He does not sound angry. He sounds more sad or disappointed or some emotion in-between. I don't know what to say, so I just settle for. "I'm sorry, Dad."

"I know," he says.

Tessa slides down the slope in a flurry of leaves. "Whoa! I saw that! Dad saved your head from being split open, Billy boy! You'd have been mashed potato if it wasn't -"

"Okay." Dad says, "Let's leave it alone." He stands up and dusts away the leaves that stick to his trousers. Finally, he looks at me. His face is grim and set like granite.

"Come on, let's go."

I stand.

"Billy." his voice is flat. "You stick with me."

I nod.

Tessa walks with us as we start a zig-zag route up the hill. I want her to go ahead so I can just be with Dad for a moment. Eventually, as we near the top, she sprints off. There are no more rocks to climb. She is safe. I try to slow down, but Dad doesn't seem to notice and keeps hiking up the slope. I speed up to fall in alongside him.

My voice comes out weak. "I'm sorry, Dad," I say again.

As he walks, he looks up to the top of the hill. "I know," he says.

"Thank you," I say. It sounds strangely formal. If this were a film, we would have a long and profound talk, but Dad doesn't break his stride. He looks towards me, not directly at me, just in my direction. I'm not sure if he nods, but I know he has heard me.

TWENTY-TWO

Now. This Sunday. Morning time.

The salt wind ruffles its hands through my hair and stings my cheeks as we walk down the hill. This feeling is electric. The seagulls soar above us and cry out to mark our return. Are they glad that we are back or warning us that the sea is in a particularly playful mood? Beyond their caws, I can hear the roar of the tide. It sounds like the cheer of a crowd, only continuous and naturally powerful. This is the start; this is where our adventure begins.

In the car, when Dad parked in the deserted gravel car park, Tessa and I exchanged cautious glances. Neither of us wanted to say anything just in case Dad changed his mind or took us on the clifftop walk instead. He turned in his seat, so he could look at us both.

“Right. We are here.” He looked at Tessa and then me. “We are going to play it safe, okay?” We nodded. “No jumping ahead,” he pointed at me. “Pay attention at all times. And count the waves.”

I nodded enthusiastically. He was about to pull the handle on the inside of the door when he paused. His eyes flicked up to the rear-view mirror.

“Did you bring it?” he asked.

I nodded and pulled the timetable from my satchel. Dad took it and fanned it open to this month. His finger slid down the page and stopped. He breathed out and handed it back to me.

"The tide is on its way out. Let's go." He popped the door handle. I tossed the timetable onto the seat next to me and got out of the car.

Now, here we are. We walked past the old red phone box, past the seasonal shop that is boarded up for the winter. We walked past all the holiday caravans, the big ones that never get towed anywhere, all of them deserted. The fair-weather occupants are home, tucked up and warm in their everyday houses. They don't know that this is when the sea really comes to life. Not when the weather is fine when the sea sits idyllically calm and placid. That is not the real sea. Not the mischievous and sometimes ferocious beast we know and play with.

Dad walks down the iron staircase first. I hear the *dom, dom, dom* of his boots on the ridged metal steps. I stand on the first or the last step, depending on which way you are going, and watch Tessa as she follows Dad. Like the vibrations of the car's gear stick when I rest my hand on it, I can feel them walking down to the beach. I breathe in the air and look out across the first and safest cove. Beyond that, our adventure will begin.

At the bottom of the steps, we stop to look out at the tide. It's grey and endless and merges seamlessly with the bleak horizon. The grey of the sea is broken by tufts of white. We can see a boat crossing the cove. White tufts smash against the hull as the whole boat is driven up and down over the sea mountains.

"Looks choppy today," Dad says.

We all turn and walk around the first rock, our wellies smacking on the compressed, wet sand, the tide still out of reach.

In the second cove, we have to scramble up and over rocks that used to be part of the cliff. I always feel like the cliff doesn't want anyone else to explore the coves beyond this point, so it's shed its rock skin to block the way. But it knows us and lets us scramble over unharmed.

Tessa goes first, and Dad gives me an *after you, I insist,* gesture with his hand. I know that this is because I fell last weekend, and Dad is taking no chances. I reach up and grab the first good hand-hold on the sloped rock and pull myself up. Beyond that, I scramble on all fours up the collection of rocks and join Tessa standing at the peak. Getting down the other side is easy; you just slide on your bum all the way to the soft sand. This part of the beach is always out of the sea's reach. No matter how angry or stormy it gets, the tide can never get in this far.

Tessa and I stand for a moment together and look out at this, the widest of the coves. Usually, we slide straight down and run as fast as possible to the next piece of headland that points out towards the retreating tide, like a slice of cake. This time we both have stopped to take in this stretch of coast. It really does have a rough beauty. The rocks dividing the coves are jagged and sharp.

A whole neighbourhood of seagulls has made their nests in this cliff. This seems like a crazy and dangerous place to build your home. We look up and watch a gull try to land in its nest against the wind and drizzle. From where we stand, its nest just looks like a few spikes and twigs surrounded by white bird poo.

I feel Dad nudge up against us. He stops for a second, takes in a deep breath, and then slides down the rock into the sand, making a little crater as he lands. We slide down and fall into step on either side of him.

"How come we're allowed to come here today?" Tessa asks. I shoot her a *shut up* look, so she doesn't jeopardise our Sunday.

"It's okay. It's been a long time since we've been here. Besides, I've missed it, haven't you?"

We both nod and tramp on through the thick fluffy sand. The small boat out at sea is struggling its way across the mid-horizon. It seems to be pitching higher and deeper into the churning grey. At certain points, it vanishes completely within the swells. The first time I see it disappear, my heart lurches and then relief floods back over me when it surfaces again. I realise now that I am strangely on edge. I'm not sure if it's because I don't trust myself to stay out of trouble, or maybe I'm a bit scared. What if I do something stupid that gets us all soaking wet or hurt? I've been on a stupidity streak lately. I just hope I don't do something to ruin today for all of us, and we can never come back here again.

We draw close to the next bit of headland jutting out and separating us from the next cove. We look down its reach to the tide that froths and rolls at its end. We need to wait for a break in the waves to run around the rock and into the next cove.

"Okay," Dad says, "Let's count the waves."

There are always three big waves when the sea rolls in, and then it draws back, and there are three little waves. It's in this lull that we run to the water's edge and around into the next cove.

"One... Two... Three!"

We run, our boots slap against the compact wet sand. Dad has us both by the hand. The sea draws back for its three resting waves, and we slip around the end of the rock and then run as fast as we can to get up to the dry part of the cove. As if annoyed that it missed us, the sea roars and I feel its spray on the back of my neck as it tries to grab us, or at least soak us.

When it seems like it's given up and stretched itself as far as it can, we stop and look back at it, victors to the challenge. Deep in the wet sand, our rushed footprints are washed and eroded by the tide's white froth. It's like watching a speeded-up passage of time, the type you get in nature programmes showing how the seasons change.

"That was easy!" I say, not convinced the sea is a worthy opponent today.

"Don't get too big for yer boots," Dad says, "That was only the first one."

Dad seems a bit more relaxed now that we have done the first run. I feel less threatened by the sea and the day. This is all how it is meant to feel. We cross the narrow cove and look at the next challenge. Water drips down the rock, and Dad lets it pool in his hand. He rubs it on the back of his neck.

"Billy?"

"Yes?"

"Have you still got the walkie-talkies?" Dad asks.

I rummage in my satchel and pull out the two clear plastic bags with them inside. He takes them and switches them both on. He listens to the crackle and hiss of static from each for a moment.

"Okay, Tessa, keep this in your bag. If we get separated, then get it out and turn it on. I'll radio you. Get it?"

"Got it."

"Good," He turns to me, "You stick with Tessa or me. Do you understand?"

I nod.

"Okay. Let's count the waves.

TWENTY-THREE

Now. This Sunday. Picnic Time.

We made it around all the coves with no accidents, well, almost.

There is one section where the rock face has a V-shaped gap. That is the only way through as the rock runs too far out into the sea. I don't think it ever fully emerges, even at the lowest tide. You have to run to the V in the lull, climb a foot up the rock and jump through the gap, down to the other side and sprint away from the tide. All in the time it takes the sea to breathe its three small waves. Because the crack in the crag is only big enough for one person, we have to take it in turns. I usually get either too eager or too scared. I miss count or run too late and get caught up the backside as I've cleared the split, and I'm trying to run to safety.

The tide seemed higher than usual today on that part. I always go second. Dad is first to check that it's safe to run. He disappeared through the rift with his customary ease. Tessa and I counted the three large waves, and then she slapped me on the back, pushing me forward towards the surf.

I felt mildly irritated by her forceful shove and took a second to shoulder her away to show that I knew what I was doing. Then I sprinted to the gap, but my moment of sullen rebellion had cost me too much time. As I climbed the rock to the gap, I realised the first of the big waves was about to roll in. I panicked and threw myself through the crack, falling onto my knees in the sand on the other side.

I heard Dad shouting for me to run. The sea was coiled back like a snake moments before striking. I stumbled to my feet and ran as hard as I could up the beach. The sea frothed around my boots and up to my knees. I could not ruin today. I had to stay dry! My heart pounding, I pushed harder and got to Dad. He gave me an almost *puddin'Ead* look which melted into a relieved smile.

"You had me going there for a moment, Billy Boy," he said.

I grinned back at him, my heart thudding against my ribs. All of a sudden, I felt the fried bread and bacon churn like a wave in my stomach. My face changed, and Dad frowned. I convulsed and bent over with my hands on my knees. I vomited a mix of bacon rind and bread onto Dad's boot.

"Oh! You dirty little beggar!" he said, and I felt the flat of his hand slap me on the back. "You okay? Any more *oopty floop?*" he asked.

I shook my head and saw Tessa's boots appear next to mine.

"That was great!" she said and then sniffed. "Corr! I can still smell breakfast."

I stood up, spittle hanging from my chin. She looked down at me and then down at Dad's boot, which he bobbed, making the bacon rind flop off. She looked back at me.

"Oh! You dirty little beggar!"

The only other mildly embarrassing thing was getting into the last cove. That rock snaggles out too far into the sea as well, and so the only way around, no matter what the tide, is to climb. The rock has rows of sharp layers, like grey teeth waiting to cut a misplaced hand. You can get your boots stuck in them really easily. I lost a boot once, and had to hop to the top to call Dad back to get it for me.

This time I went over first and was climbing down the other side. I turned around and started climbing down with my bum against the rock. I felt the swell of bacon rind in my stomach again and gripped my tummy. My foot slipped and I slid partially down the rock until my jeans got hitched on one of the rock's teeth. I dangled there, my jeans wedging right up my bum and squashing my bits.

I tried to push myself up and off the spiked tooth that had bitten my jeans, but I didn't have the strength in my arms. I knew what was coming. Tessa would be over next, and she would tease me nonstop, laughing at me hanging there like washing on a line. I gave one last attempt to free myself and flapped like a beached fish. I stopped as soon as I heard the slight sound of fabric ripping. I let myself hang there and just hoped that the jeans would hold and that the damage to them so far was minimal. These jeans were new, just a few weeks old. I didn't want to get in trouble for ripping yet another pair and face the boredom of Trago Mills again.

I heard Tessa's boot clump on the rock next to me. She was climbing down facing into the rock. That was the better way to do it. She drew alongside me and gave me a smile.

"You look like one of those talking puppets," she said and thought for a moment. "Dummies!" she exclaimed, her face showing how pleased she was with herself for getting the right word.

"That's it," she said, "You look like a right dummy!"

I heard Dad's boots climb down the other side of me.

"Alright, Billy Boy," he said. "What are you hanging around here for?" He smiled at his own joke and looked at Tessa, then looked behind me to see how I was snagged. "You better not have torn another pair of jeans."

"Oh no," Tessa groaned with genuine despair, "Not Trago Mills again."

"Let's hope not," Dad said.

He put his boot under my foot and told me to step on it. Holding my hand and my elbow, he helped me as I started to lift myself up.

"Don't just watch him, Tessa," Dad said.

She looked back at Dad with a blank expression.

"Do you *want* to go to Trago again?"

She looked at how Dad had hold of me, and she did the same on her side.

"Take it easy, Billy Boy," he said.

I lifted myself up. Tessa peered behind me to check how the rear of my jeans were doing. Dad had his face intent on mine. I moved up a fraction more, and we heard another *ripping* sound. The three of us froze.

"Easy does it," Dad said. "Tessa, can you reach behind and free him?"

She let go of my elbow and started tugging at my jeans. She wrenched them up even higher, and I thought I would be split in two.

"Ouch!" I cried, "My goolies!"

Tessa chuckled and then gave one more eyewatering jerk, and I felt myself slip down. Dad steadied me and lowered me to the next foothold.

I jumped down to the beach. I looked out at the sea that billowed like a rippling parachute in the games we sometimes play in the school sports hall. But this parachute looked like it was being shaken by the bullies on my list because it thrashed violently. Dad has always told us of the mighty power of the sea, and today it seems like the sea is showing me how strong and bad-tempered it could be.

Dad and Tessa landed next to me. Dad spun me around and bent me over to look at the bum of my jeans. He gave a few parts a prod here and there.

"Hmmm, just there... I reckon an iron patch will do it."

He slapped my bum, and I stood up. I tried to look back over myself at my jeans. When I couldn't see, I felt the back of my jeans with my fingers. Just a small hole.

"It's alright, Billy. It's not your worst.".

*

We sit now inside the cave in the last cove. We can't go further around the coast because it's all rock and unclimbable. We always come this far, have our picnic and turn back. The journey back is never as exciting as the journey here because the tide is out. We can easily walk around the cake shaped slices of rock, apart from this last one and the one with the crack in it. We still have to climb those. When we do walk back, we very rarely see anybody else. If we do, it always feels like the real day has started or at least caught up with us. They are the markers that the rest of the world has woken up and missed out on our adventure.

In the cave, Tessa and I sit on the sand and Dad is sat on a rock. We are at the back of the cave, but it's well-lit as there is a large, jagged hole high above us. The grey light of the late morning strikes through the darkness at an angle. Water drips down from the hole above, leaving streaks of moss across the rock. There is more water than usual today due to the rain that has picked up since we've been in here.

We call it the smuggler's cave. Dad has told us countless stories of pirates smuggling in goods by rowing their small boats from the main ship, right into this cave at high tide. They have to hold the boat steady in the swell of the water and attach their crates to a rope lowered by the land pirates, who are the sea pirate's landlubber friends. The land pirates hoist the goods up through the hole and drag them with donkeys up the cliff.

Dad told us about Captain Saw. He was a Pirate captain who serrated the blade of his sword so when he stabbed someone, he would make sure the wound was ripped open as he pulled his sword out. This meant there was no chance of the person being saved or stitched up. They would die, and anyone who found the body would know they were slain by the infamous Captain Saw.

Captain Saw and his crew rowed into the cave one night with jewels they had stolen from a passenger ship. They were due to be met by his land partner, who owned a tavern nearby. His land partner hauled the crate of treasure up and dropped an explosive down the hole to blow Captain Saw and his men to pieces. Dad said it was because the tavern owner was sick of not getting what he thought was a fair share of the booty.

Captain Saw's rowboat was blown up, and so were his men, but he remained alive. He shouted that he would get the tavern owner, in this life or the next. The swell of the sea smashed his body against the rock, but it wasn't the rock that killed him. It was his own serrated sword. He was impaled upon it as the sea hit him against the inside the cave. The sea drew back and hit him again, driving the sword deeper, and then the sea ripped the sword out of him, just the way he had done to all the people he had killed. His ghost still haunts the cave, calling for the tavern owner.

Captain Saw haunts this cave. He waits to murder the tavern owner or anyone that crosses his path. In the dead of night, when the moon casts a silvery streak across the sea, you can hear the tap, tap, tap of his sword against the rock as his ghost grows impatient for vengeance.

The first time Dad told us that story, we looked around the cave at the shadows that could hide the ghost of Captain Saw. We heard the tap, tap, tap of metal against rock. Tessa and I were about to run screaming from the cave when Tessa saw Dad tapping his empty metal tea mug against the rock.

Now, he tells us the story again and finishes by tapping his mug against the rock and looking about as if it's the sound of the real Captain Saw.

"Does the sea really come all the way into the cave?" I ask.

Dad starts putting the empty cups and the thermos into his bag. "Yup. This bit of coastline stretches out into the sea. This cove is at the tip. The tide comes right in here. Perfect for smugglers."

I look around the cave, "So all this is underwater at high tide?"

"Yes. On the way back, each cove is set back a bit further than the one next to it. Most of them get filled at high tide. That's why the big cove at the start is never completely submerged." he says. "It's the furthest from the sea's reach."

He shoulders his bag and pauses to listen for a moment.

"The sea sounds loud. The weather must have gotten worse. Come on, let's get back. We'll be drenched by the time we get home."

Tessa and I pad along next to him. We head towards the slab of grey light that is the mouth of the cave. As we get closer, the sea sounds louder and angrier. The wind whips past us as we push on. It must whistle up the hole in the cave's roof because the cave lets out a moan. We pause and look back. I turn slowly, half expecting to see a tri-cornered hat wearing spectre with a ragged cutlass in his hand. The wind thrusts against our backs, trying to push us deeper into the cave, back to the place where Captain Saw was impaled. As the wind picks up, the moan from the back of the cave becomes a howl. We look at each other.

"That… is… creepy," Tessa says. She turns to Dad, "You just made up that story about Captain Saw, didn't you?" she asks, uncertainty slipping into her voice. "He wasn't real, was he?"

"Well, I certainly didn't make up that noise, that's for sure," he says.

The wind dies down a fraction, and the howl reduces to a low moan.

"Come on," he says, "Let's go before we start hearing a tapping sound."

We turn back to the mouth of the cave, and the wind whips up again. Our coats flap like sails in a storm. We have to lean into the wind to walk out into the cove. When we emerge from the cave, I'm not quite sure what I am looking at. This cove looks different to how it looked before we went into the cave. For a moment, I wonder if we have gone through some gateway to a different reality or we've somehow travelled in time.

The sky looks blackened now. Like piles of coal tumbling across each other, the way it does when you open Grandma's coal scuttle too quickly. The sea is in full storm and looks like the swirling wild animal you see in old pirate movies. There is a crack of thunder, and the tide roars in return. The rain stings against my face and mixes with the spray from the sea. It's like a ghostly slap across my face. The sea hasn't gone out. It's raged closer in toward the cave. The stretch of beach we walked up earlier after I was freed from the rock's teeth has gotten smaller. Fear drenches through me. My heart drops, and I step closer to Dad, pulling his arm across my face and pressing myself into his side.

"Dad?" Tessa shouts above the whipping wind.

I look up at him. His mouth is open. He looks as though he really has just seen Captain Saw or some kind of ghost.

"Dad! What's happening?" Tessa shouts again, her hand sheltering her face from the attacking rain.

"The tide..." he says, almost too low for us to hear over the mix of thundering sea and the snarling wind. He realises we are looking at him, and then he shouts over the noise, "The tide. It's coming in!"

"What?" Tessa yells.

Dad pulls us back just inside the cave and crouches down to look at us. The sea is quieter here, but only barely. He wipes the mix of rain and sea spray from his face.

"The tide," he says again, "It's coming in. I don't know how." he looks out at the sea, mystified. "I checked the timetable. It said it was going out. I don't know what...."

There is an awful sinking feeling deep within my stomach. He lets his voice trail off as he looks back at us. He must see the terror in our faces. I swallow hard. I don't want to cry, but I want to go home. I've never seen the sea as horrifying as this. I look at it, and it looks like a swirling, thrashing sea monster, just itching to swarm around us and drag us out into its hungry depths.

Dad is looking back into the cave.

“We can’t stay in here,” he says, “It won’t be long until the tide is high enough to flood this whole place.”

“I’m scared, Dad!” Tessa says.

He pulls us both to him and squeezes us tight to his chest. I feel his lips against the top of my head, and then his cheek presses against my hair. He pushes us away and looks straight at us.

“It’ll be ok. I’ll get you home. I promise. This is just another adventure,” he says, “But we can’t stay here. We need to try and get back.”

I feel my chest tighten. “NO!” I hear myself shout. “I don’t want to go out there!”

Dad lets go of Tessa and holds both my shoulders.

“I know, Billy. I know. But we have to try. This whole cave will be flooded. This part of the coast is the furthest out. We need to move across the coves before the sea comes all the way in. We can make it, but we need to move now.”

I sniff back the tears that burn against my eyes. Dad takes hold of my chin. “All adventures are a bit scary. I’ll be with you both every step of the way. I promise. We just need to keep counting the waves and keep moving.”

I look down and away from him. He dips his head to catch my eyes again, the way I did with Mum when I wanted to make her laugh when she was washing the mud from me.

“Come on,” he says, patting both our cheeks.

I look up at him, and he gives me one of his firm nods.

"Okay. We need to check the next cove!" he shouts over the wind that has started its moan through the cave again.

He takes our hands and leads us to the edge of the cave mouth. The sea has come further up the beach already. The froth of the wash is now rolling just inside the cave mouth. It wants to come in. It wants to drown everything it can reach. It spills and swirls around our boots as we stand and look out, arms up to cover our faces from the biting rain. Dad points up to the top of the rock, which cuts this cove off from the next.

"WE NEED TO CLIMB. UP AND OVER!" he shouts.

The sea roars in protest. Dad doesn't wait for us to agree. He grabs our hands and runs us to the base of the rock. Our wellies splash in the water, and I can feel the tug of this shallow part of the sea as it starts to draw back. This beast is hungry.

"Come on! Climb!" Dad shouts

I grip the serrated rock teeth that bite like fangs against my fingers and pull myself up and out of the water's grip. We are on either side of Dad, and he takes a step up and then checks on us both, making sure we don't slip as we climb. We are near the top when the wind flares up and catches Tessa. It snatches one of her hands away, and she is flung around, her back smacking against the uneven rock. I stop and look over at her. She is on the outside, nearest the sea and has borne the brunt of the storm's assault. She tries to scream out, but the wind swipes her voice away, drowning it within its own shriek.

Dad drops down a step and comes up under her failing arm, the storm tugging, yanking at her to let go of the rock with her other hand. Dad turns her and steps to cover her with his own body as she faces back into the slate grey rock. He is battered by the wind, his body jolting and straining as the wind shifts its focus on to him. It wants *him* now. It rattles around his body and his clothes. His coat and trousers flutter as he hangs on, protecting Tessa long enough for her to regain her grip. His flapping clothes make him look like a skydiver in a movie.

He tilts his head down and shouts something to Tessa. Then he nods and looks at me, gesturing with his head for me to keep climbing. He shifts to the outside of Tessa, and we begin to climb again. When we reach the top, we peak over, and it feels like the wind punches us in the face. The three of us are almost blown off the rock, back into the last cove that is filling rapidly with the bitter, ice grey sea.

We crouch down, using the top row of the rock's jaw as protection. Dad tries to shout something over the crushing noise, but we can't hear him. He points at his mouth and exaggeratedly mouths the words "*Wait here!*"

We both shake our heads, and Tessa grabs hold of his arm. He holds up his hand, trying to placate us, and then he mouths the words again, "*Wait here!*"

He stands up, and his body is hit with the full force of the wind. He wobbles back for a moment and then forces his head down to reduce his size and the storm's target. He pushes forward and leans over the rock's ridge, swinging one leg over. He looks like a cowboy under enemy fire trying to mount his horse and escape. He slips out of view over the other side.

I stare at the ridge, waiting for him to reappear. I feel the shunt and shove of the wind, and Tessa loops an arm around me, trying her best to steady herself as she does so. I fold myself tightly into her. I can feel my own body shaking, and at the same time, I can feel the tremors of fear coming from her. She shouts something into my ear, but I can't hear. I look up. Dad is leaning over the rock with his hand outstretched. His body seems to pulse as the rain and wind rhythmically beat against him.

I shift a little, feeling the spiked rock scrape beneath my boots, and I stretch out my hand. Tessa tries her best to steady me. Dad catches me by the arm, then the elbow, and finally, he holds me around my ribs. I push with my feet, and he drags me over the rock awkwardly. We crouch down on the other side, and he points. The rock is wider on this side before the next cove, and there is a low ridge, big enough to hide behind. It will provide some shelter from the wind blowing this way. He pulls me into him and shouts in my ear, "*STAY LOW!*" I can barely hear him, but I nod, and he pushes me toward the ridge.

I stay in a squat position and shuffle across the snaggled surface and huddle down behind the ridge. As I do, the noise dies down, and I look back at Dad. He has stood again and is leaning over to reach Tessa. He spares one glance back at me to make sure I made it and then hauls Tessa over. They hunker down, and he does the same with her, pointing towards the ridge and shouting in her ear. She makes her way across, closely followed by Dad.

Beneath the ridge, we can hear each other, but we still have to shout.

"Are you okay?" Dad asks us both.

We nod, but he checks our faces, arms, and hands, with particular attention to our fingers. He looks up over the ridge, and his hair is blown back. He squints and then ducks down again.

"The next cove is filling, but it's not full yet!" he shouts.

He holds each of our faces in turn and tells us, "We have to keep moving! Stay close behind me."

He shuffles out from behind the ridge and acts as a windbreak as we follow behind him. Dad turns to face us and drops down to the first foothold, and helps each of us down. The sea has almost filled this cove. We edge along the ridge towards the cliff face where the water is shallow. We usually climb up this section further down, nearer the sea, but the tide is too deep and violent there now. We reach the back of the cove and look down. There are no other footholds to use to climb down. Each of the three large waves that pound in flood this entire section. As the three small waves churn over the same ground, I can just make out the sand beneath it. It's not deep, not yet.

Dad, who is still on the outside, turns and faces us, blocking the tide and wind as best he can.

"We have to count the waves!" he shouts. "We jump and run to the other side in the three small waves!"

I feel tears spill from my eyes, but they are lost in the rain that streaks my face. I want to wipe the snot from my nose, but I am too afraid to let go of the rock, even for a moment.

Dad holds up his hand and counts down the three large waves

with his fingers. When the last one retreats, like an animal, reluctantly pulled back from a fight, I hear Dad shout, "JUMP!"

He and Tessa jump, but I don't. I can't. They hit the shallow wash. Tessa splashes down on all fours. The water is up to her elbows. It is deeper than it looks. I try to follow but fear grips tight. It won't let me take my fingers away from the rock teeth I'm clinging to.

Dad jerks Tessa up onto her feet. He looks wildly around for me and then snaps his head up to where I stand, stranded and frozen. The second small wave has already washed around their legs. He looks out at the tide that builds, waiting for its chance to be unleashed and throw its full strength at them. He turns and pushes Tessa towards the rock face on the other side. She blindly stumbles forward and then launches into a sprint.

Dad looks up at me. He can't climb up to get me because the rock face is sheer beneath my feet. He cups his hands around his mouth and shouts, "STAY THERE!" And then he turns and runs to the other side of the cove.

He climbs the craggy teeth, helping Tessa get higher up just before the first of the three powerful waves crashes in. The fuming surf surges around, throwing up a froth, spew as we call it, like some rabid animal.

I look across the now filled void between us, and Dad holds up three fingers. He wants me to count the waves. He wants me to count the waves *with him*. I fix my eyes on his hand as he drops one at a time until he is left with only a fist in the air. I can't look down. I'm *too scared* to look down.

I see Dad jump, and so I close my eyes and push myself away from the rock. I slap hard into the water. Somehow, I've landed on my back, and all I can see is grey-brown sand mixed with the swirling grey and white froth of the sea. It feels like an icy fist has gripped my heart and is pulling me away. It spins me around in its mass and floods my mouth and nose. Salt hits the back of my throat, and if I were above water, I'm sure I would vomit. I don't know which way is up. I feel like I am in a washing machine. I reach out with my hands to protect my face as I am rolled, and my fingers connect with wet, slipping sand. Then I feel the suck and draw of the tide. It pulls me like a water slide I've suddenly become too scared to ride and want to turn back, but it's too late. I'm slipping.

The undertow has me in its watery clutch, pulling me out. I swallow more water as I try to scream, and it feels like one of the tides multiple hands has thrust down my throat to deaden my protests. I dig my fingers into the shifting silt to try and claw myself out of its pull, but wet sand spills into my claw marks like I was never there. It wants to wash away this crime, this drowning.

I feel the back of my sodden jeans heave up, and an arm loops around my throat and under my armpit. I can feel and hear the suck of the water as Dad fights against the undertow to pull me free. I am lifted, vomiting saltwater onto feet that don't hold me for long. I fall forward. I can't see anything but grey. I am caught and dragged. I feel my boots almost come off as the sea reluctantly relents its grip. There is the hard, sharp feel of the rock against my front, and I blindly feel for something to hold on to. I step up only to slip down again, scraping my knees against the slicing slate. I am heaved up, and I reach out. I feel a smaller hand snatch mine. Tessa has hold of me. There is a shove on my bottom, and then I feel Tessa hugging me into her. I swipe my hands across my face and open my eyes. They instantly sting, and in my blurry vision, I see Dad's shape rise up next to me as he climbs to join us.

He presses us both back with his arms, flat against the rock. My back is spiked and stabbed by its uneven and wicked teeth. The sea roars into the cove, the first of the big waves pushing against the slate, dead-end corridor. Its white froth spraying up at our boots. We are just beyond its sweep, and it seems annoyed by this.

We turn to face the rock and climb. Dad puts his arm around me to help me with every foothold we take. We reach the top, and I lie over the rung of jagged rock, ignoring the blast of cold air that hits me. I vomit out more water. I feel the salt sting the back of my throat, and the inner depths of my nose as the water uses every avenue to eject itself from my body. Dad slaps me hard on the back. I look up, my eyes raw, and he hugs me. In my ear, I hear his voice.

"You're okay, Billy boy. I've got you. I've got you."

He looks at the next cove. Reluctantly, I do the same. It is set further back than the last two, but the sea is high within it, trying but not yet powerful enough to reach the base of the cliff. Dad straddles the rock in front of me and rubs my back as I look down again. He gives me a few brief moments to recover.

He must have said something to Tessa because she is clambering down to the cove when I raise my head again. She stops a safe distance from the bottom. If she moves further in, she will be above a thin strip of sand at the base of the cliff. It is wet but not flooded. The sea has not pushed its full force in yet. She waves her arm at us both to follow her. I feel Dad looking at me. I turn my face to his. He dips his head. *Ready?*

I'm not. I'll never be ready. I am too cold, wet and terrified to want to move. But Dad's eyes help me. They are not cross or impatient. They are warm. They are the warmest thing around us. They tell the truth. *We have to go. I'll be with you.*

For a moment, I look out at the sea. I squint my eyes against the stinging rain. The sea's grey turbulent mass is epic, stretching as far as the eye can see, right up to the misty horizon, and it looks angry. Its power, its rage, is enough to fill it all, and it feels like it is directing this power at us. I look back the way we have come. Two coves, we've crossed just two coves. I see the jagged slices of rock separating them, and then I look at how far we still have to go, and I can't look anymore.

I push myself up from the sharp rock. Over the churn of noise, I hear Dad shout, "Good Lad!"

He holds my arm as I slip down to the next ridge, climbing down the rock and edging my way towards Tessa. Dad is close beside me, and he briefly gives her a thumbs up, but she misunderstands. Her trust is so absolute in Dad; her adrenaline is so high that she doesn't think. She takes Dad's brief, *we're okay, we're coming. You're doing great* thumbs up as *GO, GO, GO!* Her face is one of excitement or tension. It's hard to say which, and she nods vigorously, *I got it! I understand!* Without trying to figure out what the tide is doing, she turns and jumps from the rock into the cove.

She hasn't moved back far enough to be clear of the sea's reach. She splashes into the tide and stumbles down, lost beneath the white foam and bubbles.

"NO!" I hear Dad scream.

He tries to step around me to get down to where she jumped off, but he can't. I'm in the way and still too dazed to get out of his way. Instead, he turns and leaps towards where we last saw her. He does his best to jump diagonally up the cove and hits the plume of water as it roars into the cove, disappearing beneath its surging surface.

I flick my head around to clear the hair matted to my face. I can't see them. I can't see either of them. I look out at the wild sea. Has it sucked them out? Has the undertow pulled them low against the sand and swallowed them up? Panic hits in, slicing through the numb cold of my body. I call out, "DAD! TESSA!"

I don't know what to do.

Am I alone?

Will I die here?

Dad bursts out of the water, which is up to his waist. He has Tessa under the arm and half walks, half drags her as he wades to the back of the cove. He falls forward as the water pulls his legs out from under him, but then he's up again. He still has

Tessa, and he makes it to the back of the cove. He sits her on the thinning strip of sand and holds her chin in his hand. He holds her close and then looks at her, talking to her as she wipes her eyes. Dad bows his head in what looks like relief, and then he turns to me. He points that I need to edge along the rock and get right up against the cliff face, so I am over the still untouched stretch of sand.

I sidle along, and he comes to me, arms outstretched, and I lean down into them. I wrap my arms and legs around him.

I thought I had lost him.

I thought I had lost them both.

I thought *I* was lost.

He places on the sand, and we edge along to Tessa, who is now standing, her back pressed against the cliff face, doing all she can to get as far from the sea's grasp as possible. Dad stoops to talk to us both.

"We can climb the next rock, easy, but we have to do it there," he points out to a section that is partially awash with one of the three small waves. "Count the next three big waves. In the three small ones, we can make it out and up. No dawdling. Okay?"

We nod. The first of the three big waves crash in. It sprays and spits at us, but it falls short of being able to reach us. We press our backs against the cliff in fear that the sea might be let off the leash at any moment. If it pulls hard enough, it might just break away from whatever is holding it back. I turn my head away from it. I can't look at it. It might get me if I look at it. I can almost feel the whispering touch of its fine, spraying fingers trying their best to get a firm and solid grip on me. The second wave thunders in. I'm sure it's closer this time, but my eyes are shut tight. I don't want to look. There could be ghosts from the sea swirling around us. Is that what gives the sea its power? Is it host to all the lost souls it has claimed? Is it one huge water army of angry spirits trying to claw at life and suck it within its depths?

The third of the huge waves roar in, and then I hear Dad's voice boom out, "COME ON!"

He has my hand, and we run toward the retreating tide. It throbs and pulses as it recoils. It's as if it has water muscles that ache to be let loose. We run, despite our fear, out into the lull. We splash into the water, up to our knees, and Dad lifts first me and then Tessa up the rock. He climbs, but the first of the next round of big waves is set free. We are clear, but Dad's lower legs are not. The tide hits him hard, and he clings to the sharp handhold he has just managed to grab. I stare at the watery mass that slops around him like a frothing white fist, trying to pull him down like a whirlpool of quicksand.

His face clenches as he draws his legs in, and then he stands on a ridge that is lost somewhere beneath the water. He takes another step up, and he is free. Clear and safe. We brave the wind, climbing up and straddle the top of this slice of rock.

We look out across the coves we still need to cross. They are a series of corridors, each with their own version of the thrashing angry sea monster that lashes and pounds against the rock divisions. I remember Dad showing us what looked like a smooth emerald he found on the beach. It was shaped like a pebble but looked like a jewel. Dad had said that it was once a broken piece of glass, but the sea had worn it down. The sea and worn the jagged bards of glass and reduced it to a smooth oval shape. The sea was so powerful that it could change the very shape of something as harsh and sharp as splintered glass.

I looked at the jagged fangs of the rock we were perched upon. Why hadn't the sea-worn this headland smooth? The sea was powerful. That was why there was a fallen piece of the cliff at the second cove. The tide had pummelled the cliff so hard that a piece had fell off. The sea could erode. I knew that much. These coves were made by the sea thrashing against the rock, day and night. It pushed and shoved its way further into the land. Like licking a lollypop and making it smaller, the sea had licked at the headland. The sea had *real* power and the patience to wear the rocks down over years and years. It was patient, and it was relentless. And it had us trapped. I look at the rock teeth again. Maybe these were the sea's teeth, and the tide was its endless tongue. What it can't bite, it will slurp down and devour with its tongue.

I think of Mum, and the tears come back. What is she doing now? Does she have any idea of what we were going through? She will be warm and dry at home, ironing in front of the tele, watching the Waltons. When will she start to worry? What time is it now? Are we already late? Will she call the police? I want to be home. I want to be warm. I don't know if we will get home.

You know there will always be a happy ending with adventures in the films, right before the credits roll. Will that happen to us? Is this what it is like to be in a film? The characters don't know they will win in the end, do they? They don't know the twists and turns of the script?

I'm shivering. I wrap my arms around myself. The three of us are drenched and peppered with sand. I can feel it rasping against my cold neck. It's under my clothes and in my boots. Everything on me feels like it's a heavy, dead weight. My shoulders and legs tremble independently of me. I can't stop shaking. I look at my knees and *will* them to stop wobbling, but they won't.

Dad is shivering too. He points down into the next cove. This one is set further back again. There is a clean stretch of sand to run across.

"Come on," he shouts over the wind. "We'll get warmer the more we move."

"I want to be at home," Tessa says.

"I know. I'll get you there. Let's get across this next one."

Staying low and feeling the wind whistling over the top of us, we clamber down the other side of the rock wall. Every time I touch the rock, I feel the sharp stab of its teeth. My hands are so cold that it feels like I'm trying to climb down barbed wire. My back shakes. I'm not sure if its due to fear or the cold or both, or if it matters anymore.

Dad eases himself down onto the sand. The sea is a safe distance away. He helps Tessa down and then me, and he holds our hands as we walk quickly across the cove to the next rock. I look at the tide. Our usual path of running around the end of the rock has gone, swallowed by the sea. I can't even make out where it should be.

"Can't we stay here?" Tessa says.

Dad is ready to lift her up but then crouches down on one knee. He groans like a creaking old chair as he does so. He looks at me before he talks to make sure I'm listening.

"This cove seems safe now, but it won't be for long. The tide will fill it very soon, and then we'd be trapped."

"How do you know? How do you know for sure that we won't be okay if we just stay here?" Tessa asks, tears now visible within the rain on her face.

Dad gives us both a smile. He points to the lower half of the rock we are about to climb.

"You see this part of the rock? It's different from the top half. Can you see?"

I look at the rock. I start at the top and shudder at the thought of laying my hands on the spikey ridges that look like rows of shark teeth.

"You see how sharp the rock is up there?"

We both nod. He pats the part of the rock next to us. "You see this part? Does it look the same?"

It doesn't. It looks like a cold elephant or rhinoceros' skin.

"It's smooth at the bottom. That means the sea has been coming in here for years and years. It has worn the jagged parts smooth. The whole rock used to be like it is at the top, but the sea changed it."

He points at the rock and runs his finger along its line. We follow it with our heads and see that the smooth part of the rock runs all the way up the cove to the cliff base. Then he points the way we have just come, back across the cove to the rock we just climbed down. It is the same, smooth all the way into the cliff.

"You see? It will fill this whole area. We need to keep moving. Come on."

He leans on his knee and places all his weight upon it to force himself up. He stands and leans his hand against the elephant skin. He glances over his shoulder at the sea and then looks back at us. He rubs his chin, and I hear the rasp that comes from his greying stubble.

For the first time, I see that Dad is not a young man. I don't know how old he is. I realise that up to now, I've only ever thought that the very young and the very old age. Kids get bigger and old people get smaller, but those in the middle don't seem to change that much. Dad never seems to have changed that much to me. Whereas Tessa and I have gotten taller, her more so than me. Do adults age in the same way kids do?

I take Dad in. He is tall, he always has been, but his face is looking older, or is that just because of today? I see the grey at his temples and on his chin. If he grew a beard, would it be grey and white? Is that what I will look like when I grow up? Will I ever know all the things that he knows? Will I be the same kind of grown-up, the same kind of man he is? How does he see me? Does he see himself in me? Am I the kind of kid he likes?

He looks down at me and smiles, but the smile is half smile half wince. I wonder if he is hurt and hasn't said anything. I want to ask him how he *knows* we will get out of here. Has he seen the script of this adventure? Is that why *he* is so sure?

He gives us an *up* gesture with his hand, and Tessa raises her arms to him. This makes his smile take over his whole face. Has it reminded him of her as a baby asking to be picked up? He lifts her up the rock and looks down at me. I mimic Tessa's arms up baby gesture, and I am relieved to see the same warmth of smile spreads across his face. He loves us both. He just doesn't always show us both in the same way.

At the top of the rock, we look over at the next cove. The cliff face is set further forward here.

"Count the waves!" Dad calls.

The three large waves fill the bay, and I feel my heart sink and my body drop to sub-zero temperatures. We are trapped. The sea beat us. It has claimed this cove permanently and will not retreat to let us pass.

"Dad!" Tessa shouts. Her voice conveys the despair I feel.

"Hang on," he calls back.

He is counting. He watches the waves, his head tilted like a hawk or as if he is working out a complicated sum in his mind. When I look where he is looking, all I can see is the sea. It seems to be one angry mass, frothing and spitting up as it ploughs blindly into the cove, filling it and blocking our route home.

"There!" Dad says, pointing at the tide, "There are the small ones."

I turn to Tessa, who is frowning out at the cove. I look, and he is right. It is slight, but I can see where the sea calms slightly. It looks like it's catching its breath in between outbursts. I recognise the feeling. Just like in sports when I can't run anymore. I have to stop to breathe and then try and run again. Is the sea human after all?

"Let's go," Dad says, and we follow.

We edge up as close to the cliff face as we can. I can't quite remember, but I think this is the highest part of the rock to jump from. We turn and press our backs to the rock and wait. The sea has regained its breath and is back in full force, thrashing around like it is trying its best to tunnel its way further into the headland. And then it slows and draws back. It's worn itself out momentarily. Just for three brief moments, it will sit back and wait to see what we do next.

“JUMP!” Dad shouts.

And we do.

TWENTY-FOUR

Before. A Sunday.

Darkness.

Darkness.

Darkness.

Everywhere is darkness.

Where am I? I'm sure I wasn't here a moment ago. I was somewhere else. Doing something else. Something was happening that was really important. All I can see is black. It's the kind of black that is so dark that it seems to invade you. It wants to take over everything, it wants to get inside you and make you dark. It's not just darkness around you. It is a penetrating darkness.

I think I should be scared, but I don't know why. What am I afraid of, and why am I afraid of it? I recognise this feeling from before. I have felt afraid of the dark some other time. Not when I woke up after having that nightmare from the grown-up film. This is a different time. I was somewhere, and I was surrounded by thick inescapable darkness. But there was something else as well. Something coming, something powerful and unrelenting. Something coming straight for me.

Something...

Something...

Something...

"... Something different!" Tessa calls out.

"Okay, so something new?" Dad asks and leans on the dining room table, looking at the map.

I take a bite of my fried bread; the taste is familiar and satisfying. It will always taste like this. Nothing will change. Sundays will always have their routine, their smell, taste and flavour.

"Let's see," Dad says as he rubs his chin.

He runs his finger along a winding path on the map. It makes me think of running my finger along the swirling patterns in the carpet. The routes I would take if I were to shrink in some experiment by a mad scientist. The path on the map is not as swirling as those on the carpet. It winds but never curves back on itself.

"Yes," Dad says, "This might be good."

He turns in his chair to reach for the cabinet behind him. He tips his chair slightly on the back two legs, the way we are not allowed to because we might fall and hurt ourselves or break the chair. He pulls out another map and opens out all the folded sections, and spreads it over the first map. It is a closer view of a section from the bigger map.

"Hmmm... Yes, I think it goes in a loop. That will be a good run."

"Where?" Tessa asks.

I follow up her question with a silent look.

"Fancy a bike ride?" Dad asks.

The tyres crunch over the fine, dusty gravel, making a sound that reminds me of eating rice crispies. Not cornflakes, they make a bigger sound, but rice crispies have a smaller, narrower crunch to them. Tessa's tyres make an almost indiscernible mark on the path. For a moment, I visualise a black snake, the same width and texture as her bicycle tyres, slithering ahead of me and leading me closer to the grass verge where it has hidden, ready to strike.

I shake the thought away. This is silly. I can see the tyres making the mark on the path with their gentle zigzag pattern. There is no snake, just the three of us out cycling.

Dad is out in front, leading the way as always, setting the pace. I try to move my bike, so my tyres fall into the marks made by Tessa's tyres. That way, anyone tracking us will only think there are two people out cycling instead of three of us.

Dad stops up ahead, and we draw alongside him. There is a thin film of sweat on his forehead. He dabs at it lightly with his jacketed forearm and then looks back down the path, the way we have come. He steps up slightly on his pedals to see a bit further. Maybe he is looking for the person tracking us? I thought I just made that up, but maybe I was right? If so, we should get moving because if they see us, they will know that there are actually three of us instead of just two, and all my skilful cycling in Tessa's wake will be for nothing.

"Everyone okay?" Dad asks, looking at us.

We nod, and he gives our tyres a cursory glance. He points at the path ahead.

"It's not long until the tunnel. Are you ready?"

He gives us both the opportunity to nod, and then he looks down at his own bike, spinning the pedals so that the one on the left is higher than the right, and then he pushes off.

We turn the bend, the trees clear from our view, and we see it. The tunnel. The entrance is like an elongated and surprised mouth. The bricks that follow the shape of the mouth are like deeply embedded teeth. The sandy path, which was once an old train line, flows straight into the tunnel's mouth and its endless darkness. Or is the path the tunnel's tongue? Will it suddenly ripple along to where we stand, throw us from our bikes and then retract, pulling us deep into its tunnel tummy?

I feel a shiver looking at the darkness within. What is in there? Why is there no bright dot at the end? Tunnels always have a bright dot at the end, just like the ones we've gone through when we've been driving.

The grass bank on either side of the path slopes sharply down to the woods but builds back up around the mouth of the tunnel. The trees on either side hug in close, lending the brickwork some of its moss and ivy. I look at the brick teeth, and my eyes follow the arch up to the top where a larger singular brick is placed, like a fanged crown pointing down at its own entrance. The bricks are not flat but bobble out. They seem rough but smoothed out over time and by the weather.

Dad snaps the kickstand with his foot and rests his bike to one side. Tessa does the same, but I don't have a kickstand, so I lay my bike on its side. Dad walks to the mouth of the cave... no, not a cave, a tunnel... and he peers in. I'm half afraid that the fanged rock at the top will snap down upon him, but I join him anyway. We all look into the darkness. The light from behind us makes a dim inverted arch on the path just inside the tunnel. Beyond that, there is solid darkness. It's so dark in there it looks like there could be a black wall inside, sealing the tunnel off from the outside world. I feel a coldness emanating from its depths, and there is a dank smell. It makes me think of digging for worms in the garden. Dad cocks his head to us and points inside.

"Do you hear it?" he asks.

I look at him blankly.

"The water, can you hear it?"

I lean in, not wanting to go too far inside. I hear the distant trickle and splat of water. I snap my head around to Dad.

"Is it flooded?"

He shakes his head.

I listen again. I hear a rhythmic tap, tap tap. I feel the cold coming from the snake-like belly of the tunnel. It reaches out to me, softly breathing its dank breath against my face

"Is it... Is it Captain Saw?" I blurt.

Dad shakes his head and smiles. "No, that's the water from the ground above."

“Eh?” Tessa says.

"The tunnel is covered by the bank above. About halfway along, it cuts into the rock. The ground is full of water, especially after a heavy rainfall like last night. Water finds a way. It's drawn down by gravity. It'll find its way through even the sturdiest things, even tunnels like this which have been around for over a hundred years."

He looks at the tunnel as if immeasurably impressed by something. "Nature always finds a way."

He points at one of the embedded bobbly bricks in the arch. Its grey-brown colour fades into the green on the side nearest us.

“Look at the moss. It grows in the shade wherever it can, just like on the trees,”

We look back at the trees that have grown up around the bank to lean in toward the tunnel. They all have moss on the same side as the brickwork. The trees ivy has spindled across to slither up the tunnel's sides.

Dad stands back to take the tunnel and its surroundings in. He shakes his head in marvel at it.

“One day, this forest may swallow the tunnel up for good.”

I gulp and think that maybe the tunnel will swallow us up first.

Dad comes back to the tunnel's entrance and shouts in. His voice bounces two or three times away down the tunnel. Tessa smiles and leans in, shouting "*HEY!*" and grins when she hears *HEY, HEY, HEY* echo back at us.

I’m about to take my turn when I think of the light that is not at the end of this tunnel.

“Dad, why is there no light at the end of the tunnel?” I ask.

“It’s there. You just can’t see it yet. It’s just around the bend. The tunnel curves in the middle.”

I frown into the darkness. I feel its cold air against my face. I look down, scared to let it touch me. What I see fills me with more dread than a surprise test at school on a Monday. On the path, just in front of the tunnel's mouth, are wisps of fog. Small swirls of mist are slinking out from the tunnel, the light catching it and making it dance around our legs. I move back, trying to step out of it. Is this the breath of the tunnel, like my own breath on a winter's morning?

“Dad! What’s that.” I say.

“Hmmm, spooky isn’t it!” he says.

“Wow! Are they ghosts?” Tessa asks.

“That *would* be spooky. Maybe it's the steam from the ghost of the train that used to run through here."

“Did a train really run through here?” I ask, still mildly panicked by the mist enveloping our legs.

"Of course. This whole pathway was a train line. It's been disused for forty years. There would have been old steam trains running through here." He looks up at the inside of the tunnel's top lip. "Probably a mixture of freight and passenger trains. Can you imagine what it would have been like back then?"

“Dad... Is this stuff really steam from a ghost train?” I say, my voice cracking slightly.

Dad has stepped back to look at the top part of the tunnel's entrance. "Can you feel the cold air coming out? The fog is the cold air from inside, hitting the warmer air out here. It's like something from an old ghost story, isn't it?"

I walk back and stand next to Dad. I watch the mist as it creeps across the path. Bright shafts of light appear across it like slats from a window blind. I think I can hear the distant thrum of something coming our way, but that can't be right. The line hasn't been used for years. Besides, there are no train tracks anymore. The only tracks here are those from our bikes and multiple footprints from walkers of the past.

"There must have been a walkway up there years ago," he says, pointing up past the tunnel's upper lip. "This whole tunnel would have been black with smoke from the steam engines." He shakes his head at a forgotten wonder. "They had such a distinctive smell. You never thought that they would not be around anymore. Everything was coated in thick black soot back then. It was just the way things were. Imagine all the people sitting on the train that came through here. I wonder if they ever thought that this would be a walkway, a landmark for Sunday walkers."

“Are we really going in there?” Tessa asks.

Dad snaps out of his daydream. “Of course. Why not?”

“It looks pretty dark in there.”

“That’s why we have torches!”

Dad takes his bag off and pulls out a torch for each bike. He flicks them on and off again and then attaches them to our handlebars.

“There you go. You’re all set.”

He attaches an additional light to the back of his bike and Tessa’s. He turns them on. These ones are red.

“Right! Tessa, you follow me. Try to go where I go. I’ll avoid any rocks or dips. Make sure you follow the route of my red light. Billy boy, you follow Tessa’s red light. If you get stuck, just shout out.”

We wheel our bikes to the entrance, causing the low-lying fog to swirl, disrupted by our movement.

“Ready?” Dad says, and his voice faintly calls back from the darkness within. He looks surprised by his echo, and this makes me laugh.

I edge further in but remain in the arch of light from the tunnel's mouth and shout "*HELLOOOO!*”

My voice reverberates back out to us. *HELLO, Hello, Hello.* I turn to get on to my bike when I hear Hello, Hello, HELLO! Coming back out of the tunnel. I freeze, my hands on my handlebar grips.

I look at Dad and Tessa, who must have heard this voice as well.

“Was that... my... voice?” I say to them, but before they can answer, the voice comes again, Hello, Hello, HELLO! We all peer into the tunnel.

“I can’t *see* anything," Tessa says.

In the darkness, shapes shift and boil the harder you try to focus on them.

"HELLO!" A voice booms out, making all three of us jump and then a bicycle shoots out as if it has been spat out by the tunnel. The rider is bent low, with no light on the front of his bike. He nimbly weaves between us and calls, "Lovely day for it!" and shoots a motorcycle's speed down the pathway and around the bend.

We look at each other, startled, and then burst into laughter. Tessa clutches at her chest.

“God! That made me jump,” she says.

Dad’s laugh fades away, and he straddles his bike, “Bloomin’ hooray Henry,” he says, “Well, at least we’re sure there is a way out the other side now. Lights on!”

We snap our lights on and begin to cycle into the tunnel's mouth, along its pale, pebble-dashed tongue.

TWENTY-FIVE

Before. A Sunday. The Tunnel.

As we leave the light behind, I focus my eyes on the diming shape of Tessa and her bike, which seems to smear and spread as the darkness takes her in. The cold, damp air embraces me, and I feel a chill sink into my bones. The light fades from the walls on either side, making them look taller and more dramatically arched. A thick black shape looms up as I pass by, making me wobble on my bike. It looks like a shadowed doorway, but as my shaky handlebar light catches it, I realise that this doorway is only shallow. It's bricked up. I turn my head to look at it as I pass. Was there a figure standing inside?

A twig snaps as my front wheel crunches over it, and I almost fall off the bike. I look forward again and focus on pedalling. Was that really someone back there? I only caught a glimpse of a figure or what the shadows made look like a figure. No, it wasn't possible. It wasn't...

I look toward Tessa's red light that bumps and weaves in front of me. Beyond that, I can make out Dad's red light that seems to drift like it's dangling from a rope. If I veer to one side, I could probably see their front lights splashing down on the path, but I don't want to risk riding outside of their route. What if I hit some boulder or a dip that they navigated past? I would fall off and then be left behind here. I didn't want to be left in here on my own. What if there *was* someone in that doorway? They could creep up behind me and snatch me off the -.

Something brushes against my leg, and I yelp.

"You alright back there?" Dad's voice echoes back to me.

Don't be stupid. Don't be STUPID! It was nothing, just a twig from a fallen tree or a vine curled up, its leaf touching you as you went past.

"I'm okay!" I say. My voice comes out louder and more self-assured than I feel. That must be because of the echo.

This tunnel is long, and I still can't see the light at the end. We must not have rounded the bend yet. I stick to the path Tessa's red light burns into my eyes. She cuts to the left and joltingly, I follow.

"Whoa!" she calls out, and her voice ricochets around the domed walls.

Dad's red light stops. "You okay," he calls back.

"Yes!" Tessa says. "I almost fell. Have you stopped?"

I wish I could have been that honest when I almost fell. Why couldn't I have just said I almost fell instead of trying to cover it up.

"Yes. Just stop next to me." Dad says. "Billy, I can see your light. You still on the bike?"

"Yes," I puff out and brake as I come next to them.

I can't see his face, only the misshapen circles of light from our torches. I can see part of Tessa's face as she is closer to me and shorter. Her face has taken on an eerie hooded look as the shadows cast by our lights go up her face instead of down.

"Do you want to see how dark it really is in here?" Dad says with enthusiasm.

"No," Tessa says with blunt assurance.

I turn to look back toward the doorway we passed to see if I can make out any figures lurking there or hulking towards us. What I see strikes me with a different fear. The light of the tunnel's mouth, the one we came through, has gone. I twist my handlebars to face back the way we came. I want to see if there is a looming figure and where the light of the entrance has gone.

I catch a glimpse of the finely pebbled and dusty floor. There are outcrops of weeds and spindly twigs that you don't see on the outside path. There are no holes or hidden pits in the ground. As my light catches the wall, I see another bricked up doorway. I jump and almost drop my bike.

“Billy?”

“Wh- Wh- What's that?” I say.

“What’s what?”

“Why are there all these doorways?”

“Doorways?” Dad asks.

There must have been loads of them on either side of the tunnel. Did this use to be some kind of underground labyrinth junction? Where did they all go? Did smugglers use them? Did Captain Saw roam around down here moving his gold?

“There,” I point my light to the nearest one.

Dad turns his bike so that his light doubles up on mine.

"Ah," he says, "Those weren't doorways. It's a recess. The men who used to work in the tunnels, clearing the lines or making repairs could step back into those if a train came through."

“People worked here when the trains came through?” Tessa asks.

“Yes. The train would sound as it was about to enter the tunnel to warn anyone in here to get off the tracks.”

“That must have been scary!” Tessa says.

“What would they look like?” I asked.

“Who? The men in the tunnels?” Dad says.

“Like HUGE moles!” Tessa says, adopting Dad’s Herman Munster voice.

“Shut up,” I tell her. I want to know what they looked like. Did I really see one?

"Covered in soot probably and wearing old-time clothes. I'd imagine they had workman dungarees on and flat caps. We can look in the history book when we get home."

Flat caps and dungarees. Is that what I saw in the first 'doorway'? Was that really a soot-black figure standing back to let us pass like we were a train? I shiver.

"Where's the light we came from?" I ask, pointing my bike's light back toward Dad.

"It's around the bend. We are at the midpoint of the tunnel. There is a stretch in the middle where you can't see where you came from or where you are going. It's the darkest part." Dad says.

"No man's land," Tessa almost whispers to herself.

"That's right," Dad says.

"And people had to come down here? Here in the dark?" I ask.

"Yes. And they would have only had a gas lamp back in those days, not like our torches today. With a gas lamp, all you could do was light up the area immediately around you. Today we can point our lights at whatever it will reach."

"That must have been so spooky," Tessa says.

"They'd have got used to it. Same as the miners who used to work in a state of darkness all day. They would get so used to the dark that they would find it difficult to be in the daylight."

"I would *not* like to work down here," Tessa says.

"Fancy seeing how dark it *really* is?" Dad says.

"No way!" Tessa says, and I silently echo her thoughts.

"Come on, let's try it."

"Don't try and scare me, OKAY!" I say to Tessa and Dad.

"Promise," Tessa says.

"Promise. No mucking about, anyone." Dad says, looking at us both.

We nod.

“Alright then, come close.”

We edge closer to Dad.

"Tessa, turn your backlight off."

I twist to see over my shoulder. The hot red lights both disappear.

“Okay, find your torch switch,” Dad says.

I lean forward and rest my finger on the plastic button. My eyes fix on the shimmering light that illuminates the wall.

“Okay. On three. One... Two... Three...”

There is a unified click as we all turn our lights off. It's as if the darkness has rushed in to meet us. It hasn't been satisfied by just taking over where our lights were. It has hurried up to our faces, pressing itself against our eyes. I feel like it has somehow gotten in behind my eyes and under my eyelids. I can’t tell whether my eyes are open or closed.

“Dad?” Tessa’s voice rings out.

“Yes,” he says.

“I can’t see *anything*.”

“I know. You never get this kind of darkness, do you! Hold your hand up in front of your face.” he says.

I do. I’ve no idea if Tessa does the same.

“I can’t see it!” I say.

“I know!” Dad says with almost childish excitement. “I have mine right up against my face, and I can’t see anything.”

It slowly dawns on me that if there were a figure that had hidden in the recess, and it had followed us, it could snatch one of us away without the others knowing.

“I don’t think your eyes can ever adjust to this level of darkness,” he says.

"Can we turn our lights back on now?" I ask.

"BOO!!" A voice shouts out, and I let out a high-pitched squeal.

Dad snaps his light on, "Damn it, Tessa!"

My heart is thudding in my throat. *"YOU PROMISED!"* I shout at her. I snap my light on, and it flickers slightly, and then the beam steadies.

"Okay, Billy, it's okay," Dad says to me. And then to Tessa, "Tessa! We promised."

"Sorry, I couldn't resist!" she says.

My fear and tremors of panic are somehow translating into laughter. My legs twitch and shake, but I feel giggles bubbling up from inside of me.

"It... wasn't... Funny!" I say.

Dad lets out a light laugh. "She bloody well scared me," he says.

"Sorry," she says and turns her lights on. "But it *was* funny."

I start to laugh nervously.

"Come on," Dad says and steers his bike towards the way we were going. "Let's go."

We mount our bikes, and as I get on mine, the light flickers again. I'm not sure if I knocked it as I got on. I stare at it for a moment to see if it falters again. It doesn't, but maybe it flickered again when I blinked? I stare at it, trying not to blink. The beam remains constant.

"Ready?" Dad calls from the front.

"Yep," Tessa calls.

I look up from my light. Bright dots bounce across my vision. "Yes," I say and push off, following Tessa's red signal.

This stretch of the tunnel feels bumpier and a lot more jarring. I can see Tessa and Dad's red lights jostling like they are on the end of a fretful fishing line. They look like they are bouncing higher and swinging wildly from left to right. I do my best to focus on them, but the darkness seems to move in around them… Or have they pulled further away? It looks like I am moving towards a black canvas with two diminishing red dots on it.

I am about to shout out when I see a flicker in my torch. Did the light go out for a split second, or did something run in front of me? I stare down at the light and try not to blink. Please don't flicker again, please, please, please! I can see the path flowing underneath me as my light bounces and glides across it. It flickers, just for a moment.

It does it again, and for a split second, maybe even a millisecond, I am plunged into total and absolute darkness. The darkness seems to be waiting just at the periphery of my lights beam, waiting to rush in at the first sign of weakness.

No, no, no! Don’t do this to me. The light flickers again, the ground beneath me disappears into a starless night sky. It comes back on again, and I inwardly plead for it to stay on. What if the light goes off? What if I get stuck here in the dark? What if that figure I thought I saw back there wasn’t just a shadow?

I speed up. If I can go faster, I’ll reach the other end of the tunnel sooner, hopefully before my light completely fails. I look up into the dense dark before me and see nothing. There is nothing but a thick quilt of black. Where have Tessa and Dad gone? Where are their red lights? Have they turned them off to scare me? Or has the shadow got them?

I don't stop. I pedal faster. I must be about to turn the bend in the tunnel. I will see the stretched circle of light that is the mouth of the tunnel any minute… won’t I? The darkness before me seems unending. This thought makes me brake. I hear my tyres skid and scrape on the dusty path. I angle my handlebars around, splashing the light across the path before me and the walls on either side. As I turn the light back towards my left, I freeze. There, cast in its own shadow, is one of the doorways.

What if the figure I saw can move between these doorways?

What if behind the fake bricked up entrance are a series of interconnecting passages. He could have darted from the one at the start of the tunnel and be lying in wait for me here! He may have snatched Dad and Tessa into it already!

Come on! *Come on!* Don't be stupid! This is just my brain making me think of the worst thing possible. Why do I do this too myself? I should call out to Dad, and he will be just around the bend, and he will come speeding on back on his bike to get me.

But if I call out, the shadowy figure, if it *is* there, will know I am close and might jump out and get me. What would MacGyver do? What would Indianan Jones do? Think of it as an adventure. All heroes are in situations that are scary sometimes. This is just like the bullies at school. I need to be brave. I should just call out. Dad will come back.

I could shine my light right at the doorway and see that there is no one there. There is nothing bad here, just my imagination. Come on! Think of it as an adventure! *Think of it as an adventure!*

I take a few straddled steps, pushing my bike beneath me closer to the doorway. Its inner shadow, an exaggerated reflection of its arching shape, grows larger the closer I get to it. I pull alongside and take a deep breath. If there were a figure in there, it would have grabbed me by now, wouldn't it?

I grip my handlebars, the light shaking as my hands tremble, and I turn the light into the doorway.

Bricks. Nothing but bricks. At the bottom, there is a large slab like a doorstep. It does look like a bricked-up doorway. I breathe a sigh of relief and then tense again. I've seen films. I know that it's in the moment of relief when the hero thinks they are finally safe that the horrible things happen. I keep my light on the doorway. Nothing happens. It looks blankly back at me with its crisscross gridded brick face.

Keeping my light trained on the doorway, I shout out.

"DAD!"

Nothing.

"DAD?"

Silence.

"*DAD!!!*" I'm irritated now. Maybe they are hiding in one of the other doorways waiting to scare me. But Dad had promised he wouldn't do that to me. Tessa might, but it would be too dark for her to want to stay there just to scare me.

I turn my handlebars back to the path and spin my pedals to get the left one higher. I am just about to push off when my light flickers again.

"DDDDAAAAAAAAADDDDDDDDDD!!!!!" I shout.

I can hear my own echo. Why can't they hear me? We heard the hooray Henry cyclist when he was deep within the tunnel. Why can't Dad and Tessa hear me now?

The light flickers again, and I plead quietly to myself for it to stay on. Please, please don't go off. Maybe it only goes off when I try to cycle. It's only flickered when I've been cycling. That must be it.

I swing my leg off the bike, stand next to it, and stare at the light's beam. It remains steady. Fine, so if I walk slowly, the light will stay on and eventually, I will make it to the end of the tunnel, or at least be able to *see* the end of the tunnel.

I take a few steps. I hear the crunch of my boots on the path, and then the light goes off.

I stop dead. The darkness huddles into my face. I can't even see my nose. The tunnel feels like it has suddenly dropped in temperature. I look down to where I think my hands are, still gripping the handlebars, and I give them a shake. The light flickers on momentarily and then goes off again. My heart sinks. I feel along the handlebar with one hand until I get to the torch mounted at the centre. I follow the contour of the torch and feel a plastic button. I press it off and on again quickly. Nothing happens. I try again. The darkness remains.

"DDDDDDDAAAAAADDDDDDD!" I scream.

I start to gasp in big, heaving breaths. I turn around, hoping that something will catch my eye, some small impossible shaft of light I may have missed. I hear my bike rattle as it hits the path. I let go of it in my panic. I spin around at the sound of metal on stone.

"DAD! DAD!!! WHERE ARE YOU??!"

I stop. I realise that I can't hear my voice echo down the walls. It's as if the darkness is a thick, soundproof fabric that steals my voice. The silence is oppressive.

"Dad?" I try again, but my voice feels like I am talking into a pillow.

I hold out my hands to feel if there is anything surrounding me. I wave them around, but there is nothing there. Which way was I facing before? Have I turned around? Am I facing the way we've already come? I feel my breathing grow short and shallow. Where am I?

My foot hits something metallic, and I yelp. Surely Dad and Tessa will step out any minute and scare me. Surely this is just some joke. I want to shout out, "Okay, jokes over! Come on out!" but something won't let me. Something has sent a rigid spear of ice down my spine.

There is a noise. It's distant and vaguely recognisable. I turn, and my foot hits the metal thing again. It's my bike. I slowly crouch down, fanning my hands out to catch the frame. My hand hits the chain, and I follow the frame along to the handlebars and lift the bike back up again. I hear the noise again. It's closer now and continuous. It seems to be building.

I fumble for the light and try the button again, but it doesn't work. I want to swear, but I'm not sure I know the right word to say... and... *What* is that noise? I look down the tunnel, and relief flows through me. I must have missed it somehow before when I was panicking. I can see daylight far off in the distance. I must have rounded the bend after all.

I start to wheel my bike towards it and then freeze. There is the sound again, and this time, it's unmistakable. It's a whistle. It's a very loud sounding whistle. I look back down the corridor where it is still dark to see if it has come from that direction, but I already know it hasn't. I turn back towards the light, and it is bigger now. It is getting bigger all the time. I can hear a quiet roar. Is that the sea? It sounds continuous and unrelenting, just like the sea.

The noise gets louder. It's a chuff, chuff, chuff sound.

I drop my bike.

"Oh, Jesus!" I yell to no one. "DAD! DAD!!"

The light is coming closer and fast. It seems to drift all over the place, but it's definitely coming towards me. There is the hard, sharp peel of a whistle and the smell of steam and soot hits me. It's coming towards me, it's a *bloody train,* and it's coming towards me!

I turn and start to run further back into the darkness. The whistle lets out its sharp, piercing call again. How can this be happening? There aren't any tracks on the path!

I run blindly. I can feel the air being pushed through the tunnel and blowing my hair forward as the train bears down on me. As the train's headlight catches me, I see my shadow leap upon the path before me. My shadow gets bigger the closer the train gets to me.

I need to run. I need to run faster. Where are Tessa and Dad? What am I going to do-

The doorways! I need to get into a doorway! I run to the side, but it's all tight bricks. I keep up my run. I can't look behind me to see how close the train is as I might slow down, and it will hit me. The noise is deafening, and if I were to see the light head-on, I know it would be blindingly bright.

My shin hits something, a branch maybe, and I fall forward, feeling the dust and gravel scuff up around me as I slide along the ground. I squeeze my eyes tight, waiting for the impact. The sound of the train roars around the tunnel like an echo chamber, and its whistle lets out a death cry.

I clap my hands over my ears, and I scream out, "DAAAAAAAA-AAAAAAAAAAA-!"

Something snags me under my arms, and I'm dragged sideways through the gravel. I realise I'm moving, so I kick my feet to aid my saviour. I'm pulled to my feet and back into the wall, not against it but inside it. I can see the bricks to my left and right. What looks like an old steam train screams past, the wind pulls at my clothes and hair. I see the huge spinning wheels and the shunting side rod connecting them, driving them forward. The power is immense. The train seems to glow as if covered in luminous blue paint. The engine rips by, and I see the carriages fly past me. I hear the clickety-clack of the wheels on tracks that no longer exist.

There are figures on the train. They are sat in individual carriages and look out at me. Are they looking at me, or are they looking at their gaunt reflections in the windows? They are dressed in olden times clothes. I see kids. Their knees must be on the seats because they are high up against the window, their faces pressed against it. There are groups of men wearing flat caps. One raises his hand as his carriage flashes by. Was he *waving* at me?

I see a woman in what appears to be a lacey dress. Her head turns as she passes. Her hollow eyes are fixed on the part of the wall I am standing inside. I lean out to maintain our eye contact as she whips by, but a broad, flat hand gently presses against my chest, encouraging me to stand back.

I don't feel scared, but I realise now that I am not alone. Someone is standing next to me. It is the person who pulled me from the tracks.

The train lets out one final scream, and the carriages are gone. Silence floods back around me. I am not sure what has just happened or who this figure is next to me.

I am not *inside* the wall as I thought. I am standing in one of the doorways. I can see the slab like a front doorstep beneath my feet. Wait... I can see! I'm not shrouded by complete darkness. There is a soft golden glow falling onto the ground around me.

A reassuring hand rests on my shoulder and eases me back onto the path. I go with its gentle motion and walk to stand in the middle of the track. The tunnel doesn't seem scary now. The golden light that emanates from above me gives everything a warm and safe feeling. I turn to look at the source of the light. It is an old lantern. There is a gentle, flickering orange flame inside. The ring of light it gives off doesn't reach far. An outstretched arm holds the lantern high, away from its body.

The arm that holds the lantern is jet black. It looks like it has been drawn with charcoal, and as it subtly moves, it seems as though it leaves a trace of its shape on the air it had just inhabited. The body of the figure is even darker, and it blends with the impenetrable black of the tunnel.

This figure saved me. It saved me from... what exactly? Was that really a train? It couldn't be. There have been no trains on this track for years. Was it a ghost train? Was any of this really happening?

"Thank you," I say. I don't know what else to say.

The shape seems to nod once, accepting my thanks.

"Who are you?" I ask.

I'm an old man

I strain my eyes to look closer at the figure. Did it talk just then? The words didn't sound like they came from the shape, but I heard them.

The lantern moves and points down the tunnel. I look in the

direction it suggests, and I see something catch the light. It's my bike.

Come on, son.

Without question, I nod and walk just in front of the form, its light spilling out around me, guiding my way. The pool of light reaches my bike. It is unharmed.

"How can that be?" I ask and turn to the figure, "The train should have crushed it?"

The figure lowers its lantern so that I can see the bike properly. I take hold of the handlebars and pull it upright.

You're safe now. You are almost there. Just listen to him. He'll get you home.

"But..." I begin, but the next thing I know, my bike's light comes on. Its white beam rips through the soft light from the figure. I turn back to where it stands, but I am alone. I look down the tunnel, and I see its end. The light is rushing towards me, and with it comes a roaring sound, not of a train but of the sea. I can hear a voice. It's Dad. He is distant but getting closer. He is calling me.

"Billy! Billy! Can you hear me? Bill?"

The light builds, filling the tunnel, but I don't move or try to run. The light is grey, the roar of the sea fills my ears. I feel cold. I feel rain stinging my face. The light is right up against me, and I see Dad's face hanging over me...

TWENTY-SIX

Now. This Sunday.

"Billy! Billy! Can you hear me? Bill?"

I open my eyes. Dad is above me. His face breaks into a smile, and then it dissolves into a relieved concern. He strokes my hair away from my forehead and lets his hand rest against my cheek. He is not usually this tactile with me, but I feel a warmth from this rare show of physical affection.

He leans back. I realise that I am lying down. Dad was crouched over me and now sits near me. I can hear the surge of the tide, and I start to feel the jagged spikes of the rock that are digging into my back. Above me, the sky is grey and swirling. I see two careening seagulls swoop above and below each other as they fight the wind. The rain is falling and stinging my face. I jolt up, remembering where I am, where *we* are.

"It's okay," Dad's voice reassures, "Take it steady."

I sit up slowly, my back aching from lying on the rock.

"What happened?" I ask.

Tessa is crouching on the rock behind me.

"You got caught by the tide. You bumped your head." Dad says.

I look over the way we have come, and we are one cove beyond where I remember.

"We jumped?" I say, pointing back across the bay.

"Yes, but you fell awkwardly," Dad says

"Dad grabbed you and carried you through the tide and up the rock! It was amazing!" Tessa says.

I look at her. I can't remember any of this. I was in a tunnel, wasn't I? This was all a bad dream, wasn't it? How can I still be here, trapped on our coast?

"I thought we were in a tunnel?" I say.

Dad's face almost breaks, and he looks away across the coves we still have to cross.

"How do you feel?" he asks, turning back to me.

"I'm okay, I think."

"Can you stand?"

"Yes."

Dad helps me get up. The wind hits me, and its noise crowds in around me. Dad holds me steady.

"Are you sure you can walk?" he calls over the roar.

"I'm okay!" I shout back.

"Go easy. Stay close to me!"

He helps me across the ridges of this rock, and we start to climb down to the next cove. There is a wider and flatter ridge here above the beach. The roar dulls as we drop down onto it. Dad steady's me and then looks out across the bay.

This cove is set further back, so there is still a stretch of sand we can stand on near the base of the cliff, but the next rock is unclimbable. This is the cove with the V-shaped crack. The gap in the rock is our only way through to the cove beyond, and the big waves are already smashing against it.

Dad points to the stretch of sand. "Come on, let's get down there."

Something dawns on me, and I feel cold panic saturate my body. I feel colder than I did a second ago, if that is even possible.

"Dad!" I say.

He turns and gives me a lopsided smile. "It's okay, Billy, we're just going on to the beach, don't worry."

"No, Dad..."

"Hold on," he says, cutting me off.

He has turned and is lowering Tessa down into the cove. She drops on to the sand and stands to look out at the tide rolling in. She looks strangely calm.

Dad lowers himself onto the beach and then holds his arms up to me. I lean into them, and he gently lets me down onto the sand.

I try to catch his eye, "Dad!"

He glances at me, "How's your head?"

"It's okay, but I need to ask you something."

He looks across at the next rock, at the crack, which is our only way through. He rubs his chin and slowly shakes his head. Tessa has moved off to the side and seems to be trying to find a hand-hold in the rock we have to get around. She's wasting her time. There is no way over this rock. We can only go through it.

Dad is about to call out to her when I tug at his jacket. He turns to look at me. He is about to dismiss me and look away again, but he sees the tears in my eyes.

"Hey," he says, crouching down to look at me on a level, "It's okay, Billy. I'll get you home. We're almost there."

"Dad!" I blurt, "What colour is the timetable?"

"What?" he says and almost smiles at this random question.

I start to sniff, "What colour is the timetable!" I say, desperation cracking my voice.

"Billy," His voice is soft, just like the amber glow of the shadow figures lantern, "Billy, it's okay. We just have a few more coves, and we're home."

I feel my anger at myself surge up. "NO!" I'm crying now; I can feel the tears and snot on my face. "Dad! What colour is the timetable?"

“Hey. It’s okay,” He says in a soothing tone that I usually hear from Mum. “Do you mean the *tide* timetable?”

“Yes!” I cry. I want to stamp my feet.

“It's white. The timetable cover is white.”

I drop my head, and tears spill out of me. It’s my fault. It’s all my fault.

I raise my head and look at him. “I’m sorry, Dad. I’m so sorry!”

“What do you mean, Billy boy, what’s wrong?”

My breathing starts to hitch as I gasp deep breaths around my tears. "It's my fault, Dad. I picked up the blue timetable. I'm sorry, I'm so sorry!"

I push into his chest and hug him. He returns my hug but still seems unsure why I am so upset. He holds me for a few seconds and then pushes me away, holding me by my shoulders.

“Billy, what do you mean? You got the blue timetable instead of the white?”

I sob loudly, “Yes! I got the wrong one. It’s my fault we got caught by the tide!”

Dad seems to step out of himself and looks off across the sea for a moment. I watch him closely. Is he angry or upset? He turns back to me. His face is warm and gentle.

“It’s okay, Billy. It’s not your fault.”

I can feel my anger at myself boil over. It is! It is my fault! He is just saying it’s not my fault to be nice.

“It is! It is my fault!”

Dad stands and looks down at me. He cups my tear-stained cheek in one hand.

"Bill," Dad says. His voice is soft, but it fills my ears and my head. The noise of the storm fades away. I realise he said Bill, not Billy or Billy Boy, but Bill, like I'm a grown-up. I feel warm. I feel calm. Even though he has stood up, he feels close. He pats my cheek.

"Bill."

"Yes, Daddy?"

"Listen to me. It's not your fault. I promise you. I'll get you home."

My eyes fill with warm tears.

"Daddy?"

He has looked off over the tide and turns back to look down at me again. His face is tired but relaxed. He smiles at me.

"I love you," I say.

He holds my cheek in his hand. He says something, but the tide roars to remind us it's there and hungry. His words are lost. I want to ask him what he said, but the sea sounds angry, and we must go. I know we *have to* go.

We stand by the side of the rock and watch the waves as they beat in, the froth and foam drenching the crack we need to get through. Dad rests his hand against the tough grey skin of the rock's side and leans back, looking up at it. He steps away and looks up and down its length. It's like a beached submarine. Its sides are smooth and impossible to scale.

We focus on the sea.

"Right, let's count the waves," Dad says

I try, but they all seem big to me. The tide looks like it's snarling at us.

"There!" Dad says, pointing. "Do you see it?"

The sea still swamps the area around the V shape crack but is not smashing against it.

"We can wade out and climb through. We're going to have to be quick. We are going to have to go one at a time."

I grab his arm.

"It's okay. It's the only way we'll all get across. There is not enough time for us to go together."

"But Dad?" says Tessa.

He turns to her. "It'll be okay. Have you still got the radio?"

She looks dumbly at him for a moment and then reaches into her sodden bag. She pulls out the walkie-talkie. She unwraps the clear plastic bag around it and holds it up. Dad has crouched down and taken his walkie-talkie out. He makes sure both are on and tests them, speaking into his. The radio is crackly, but I can hear his voice coming through.

"Good," he says and puts his back in the plastic bag and then into his jacket pocket, zipping it closed. "Keep yours out. I'm going to go first."

"Please, Dad!" I say.

"We have to try. When I make it through, listen to the radio. I'll count the next waves with you, and then you run like mad to the crack, okay? Billy, you come after me. Tessa, keep the radio. I'll keep talking to you and run when I say. Promise?"

We nod.

He stands and shoulders his bag, looking down at the waves as he does so. From where I stand, I look up at him. I see the underside of his chin. I can see his eyebrows frowning, concentrating on the pattern of the tide.

"Dad!" I call up to him.

He looks down at both of us.

"Please, don't go."

He kneels. "It'll be okay, come here," he holds his arms out, and we sink into him, one of us in each arm. I feel his arm tighten around me, and his mouth press against my head. "Think of it as an adventure," he says quietly to us both.

He stands and looks at the sea.

"Remember," he says, turning back to us, "You will have to run out when the last big wave rolls in. If you miss it, wait for the next round. Keep counting the waves."

He looks out again, and before we can call after him, he sprints out.

It looks like madness. It looks like he is running head on to tackle a ferocious sea beast. The last wave is still high, and he is running straight for it like he's in a crazy game of chicken. But Dad wins. The sea retreats, and his boots splash into the sea. The water is quickly up to his knees, and he is washed by the first of the small waves.

Tessa and I look out at him from the beach. We jump up and down and shout out encouragement.

"Go, Dad! GO, GO, GO!!"

He reaches the break in the rock and climbs up. As the second small wave rolls in, he holds his weight on either side of the crack and pushes his legs through. Suddenly his body jolts down as if something has pulled him from the other side.

"NO!" shouts Tessa. "NO! DAD! GET UP!!"

"WHAT? WHAT'S HAPPENING?" I shout out at her.

"Oh God, I can't watch!" she says, "I think he's slipped!"

I look out at Dad, and he has dropped down in the crack. His rucksack is caught on this side, and his body is on the other side. I can see his head moving as he struggles to regain a foothold and lift himself clear.

The third and last of the small waves churn in.

"OH NO, OH NO! He's stuck!" Tessa shouts.

"DAD! GET UP!!" I call out.

The first of the big waves thrust in as if in victory. It has finally caught one of us in this tidal game of *catch me if you can*. The big waves seem to have grown and become angrier during their short break, and they hit the rock with increased fury. The crack in the rock disappears in the trash of its assault, covering Dad and his snagged rucksack completely.

"NOOOOOOOO!" we shout out, "NO! NO! NO!"

The tide ignores us and draws back for another attack. In the brief moment between waves, we see the crack is now empty.

"WHERE IS HE?" Tessa shouts, "WHERE IS HE?

The second big waves swallow the space again, swirling around like a big mouth rinsing itself out, cleansing its rock teeth of any bits of detritus that may have got stuck in the gaps. The third wave hits the rock, and as it draws back, Tessa points at something in the wash. Dad's rucksack tumbles out with the suck of the tide and disappears.

We are silent. I feel like the sea has quietened in its victory. I try to keep a line of sight on the bag, but it's gone. It must have got dragged deep within the undertow. I feel the backs of my legs start to throb and ache, and then I start to shake.

"Tessa?" I say quietly.

"Tessa?"

"Tessa?"

"Tessa?"

I look up at her. Her face is fixed in shock. I take hold of her arm and shake her.

"Tessa!" I shout. "Tessa!"

She looks down at me and, for a moment, I think she doesn't know me. I half expect her to ask me who I am. When she sees me, her face is blank.

"Tessa, do you think he made it?"

"I... I..." She breaks off and looks back out at the sea. She starts to run out but stops. I go and stand next to her and pull at her arm again.

"Do you think he made it?"

Her eyes are empty but full of tears. She steps backwards out of the water and up the beach.

"I don't know. I..." Then her head jerks around to look down at me. "The radio!"

She turns and runs up the beach to the cliff face. I run after her. She takes her bag off and unwraps the walkie-talkie. She flicks on the button and listens. I crowd into her, trying to push my ear as close as possible to the radio's speaker. There is a rise and fall of static. The tide roars again as if attempting to drown out the radio's sound. Tessa cups her hand around the circle of holes that are the speaker and listens.

"Say something into it!" I say.

She looks at me. Her face registers a reluctance to try. She puts her ear against the speaker, and when she hears nothing but white noise, she presses the orange button.

"Dad. Are you there?"

Crackle.

She looks at me.

"Dad, can you hear me?"

Crackle.

Tears start to slip from her eyes.

"Dad? Please!"

I feel my own tears boil up and over my eyelids. I slump down in the sand next to her. My body heaves as I cry.

Tessa is crying hard now. She holds the radio against her forehead and presses the button weakly.

"Dad... Please. Daddy..."

The radio spits back noise that rises and falls with the swelling tide.

Crackle.

Crackle.

"Daddy… Please…" she says weakly.

"… Tessa! Can you hear me?"

Our heads jerk up and look at the radio. Tessa holds it as if it's made of glass.

"Daddy?"

We look at each other and listen, not quite believing we heard his voice.

"Yes, I'm here. Are you okay?" he says, his voice floating up and down with the wind.

We scream with relief. I hug Tessa so hard that we fall over onto the sand, and she drops the radio.

"Tessa? Can you hear me?"

We fumble for the walkie-talkie. Tessa snatches it up. "Yes! I'm here! Jesus! We thought you were pulled out to sea."

"I'm okay. My bag got caught. Is Billy with you?"

She depresses the button to speak, but I shout over her, "I'm here, Dad!"

"Good. You need to move quickly. The tide is getting further in every minute."

"How did you get out?" Tessa says.

"I got out of my bag. I'll tell you more when you get to the other side. Listen to me," he says, and we press in even further. *"Take your bags off and leave them there. I don't want you getting caught like I did. Did you hear me?"*

"Yes, okay," Tessa says as I dutifully take mine off, stuffing my compass into my pocket.

"Send Billy over first," Dad says. *"Tessa, keep the radio close; I will be right here, okay?"*

She gives a firm nod and then tells the radio, "Yes, okay."

"Remember. You need to run out at the tide when the last big wave comes in. Otherwise, you won't have enough time."

I look from the radio to Tessa and nod. She returns my nod.

"Got it," she says back.

"Good. Let's count the waves."

We draw as near as we dare to the edge of the big waves reach.

"One, two,"

Tessa looks at me, "Ready?"

"THREE!"

A firm push from Tessa sends me off, and I run out at the sea. Its roll is huge, and I think for a moment that we got it wrong, that it is not about to draw back, and it is going swell further in and absorb me into its frothy mass. I shout my defiance against it and the voice within me telling me to turn and run back up the beach. I push forward, and the sea seems to pause and then reluctantly retreats. Was it wondering if it could break the rules and roll in for a fourth time?

It pulls back, and I splash out into the wash, which is up to my waist. I push through as the first of the small waves bumps into me. I'm almost knocked over, but I manage to catch the rock and pull myself up.

The next wave is drawing in its breath to attack. I don't think I will make it. I heave myself up onto the ridge and make for the crack in the rock face. As I draw level with the gap, I realise that a hand and an arm are reaching through.

"DAD!" I yell, and in a split second, I look back up the beach towards Tessa, who is jumping up and down.

"Come on, Billy! The second one has already come in." Dad says.

I slap my hand and forearm into his, and I feel his strength pull me to him. I hold myself up on either side of the crack and push my legs through as the third small wave churns in. I land on the other side of the rock, and Dad snatches my hand, and we leap from the ridge, landing in the shallow of the last small wave as it sucks itself back to the sea, waiting to pounce.

"RUN!" Dad shouts, and we pull our feet against the gravity of the sucking tide. I hear the bellow of the first large wave as it is released and roars after us. I don't look back. I just run. My legs pump, and my heart thumps in my throat. The mist and spray clouds around me, and I am given one hard shunt from Dad's hand, and I fall forward onto the beach. The wave washes over my legs, but it has no firm grip on me and slips back to the sea.

Dad is on the sand next to me on all fours. He's shaking his head as if he can't quite clear his vision. I lunge for him and hug him around his middle. He turns around and hugs me back. I push away and look up at him.

"Dad... I thought... I thought..."

He smiles, his confusion clearing. "I know," he pulls me to him. "For a moment there, I thought so too. Don't worry. I would never leave the two of you." He ruffles my hair, "The adventure is not over yet! Still, one cove to go!"

He pulls the clear bag from his pocket and unwraps the radio, "Tessa! Are you there?"

"I'm here! Is Billy okay?"

"I've got him. Let's get you over here." He pauses to look at the sea as if it is taunting him. He looks up at the rolling clouds that are now plum in colour. He walks down the sea line as if called by it. I get up and stand next to him.

"Dad?"

"The weather is getting worse. The storm is not over yet," he says without looking at me. He jerks the radio to his face, "We've missed the small waves. This is the first of the big ones. Are you ready?"

"YES!" Tessa crackles back.

"Come on then," Dad says out to the tide as the first wave smashes the rock and the beach before us, splattering our feet. I edge back, afraid it might just snag a hold of me, but Dad stays where he is, unflinching.

"Two...", he says into the radio.

The sea rears up for its third and final time this round.

"Three. GO, TESSA!"

He tosses the radio to the sand behind him, and without a backward glance, he launches himself towards the tide. With his head down, he sprints and ploughs through the steaming spray. As the tide draws back, he leaps onto the ridge and pushes his arm through the crack.

I feel the unease and excitement swirl together in my stomach. I feel nausea creep up my gullet. I jump up and down, willing Tessa to appear through the break in the rock.

A small arm jabs through, and Dad seizes hold of it. I look out at the sea. It has sent its second smaller sibling in to splash against the rock. Tessa hoists herself up, and her legs shoot through the gap, and she falls into Dad's arms. Together they jump down as the third small wave draws out.

I start to wave my arms, gesturing for them to run towards me, as if I can pull them with an unseen force, "COME ON! COME ON!"

I can now see what I couldn't when I was running away from the sea with Dad, and it is terrifying. The tide is enormous. It rolls back upon itself like a giant recoiling snake. Then it thrusts forward as if to collapse over them as they run. The frothing white surf is a frenzy of want and anger as it breaks just behind them, sending out its spray to cover them, spitting at them as they run out of its grasp.

Tessa collapses on the floor, her chest heaving as she drags in huge sobbing breaths. Dad stands but bends double, hands on his knees, shaking his head to clear the sea mist.

“Are you okay, Tessa?” he says.

She rolls to her side and nods. Then she gets up and grabs Dad in a hug. He holds her close, his eyes down, looking at the top of her head. I can hear him whisper to her.

“I know, I know... You’re a brave girl. It’s okay. You did well.”

He strokes her hair as she sobs into his chest and his eyes look over her to me. He gives me a nod, and I try to reflect the same nod back to him. He looks out at the sea and frowns.

“We have to go,” he says, loud enough for both of us to hear. “There isn’t much time left.”

He looks down into Tessa's face. "Are you ready?"

I hear her reply, a soft *yes.* He looks at me, and I nod. I’m ready... but I’m not ready all at the same time.

“Let’s go,” he says.

We run across the cove to the next rock. Beyond this is a small narrow cove. It's set forward, so it will be filling up with the sea. After that cove, there is one more rock to climb and then we are in the big bay and safe. We will just have to scrabble up the collapsed cliff and into the cove where the steps are to get home.

Just one more cove.

Dad looks up at the rock, feeling its hard skin as if it were breathing.

"Here," he says, pointing upward. "We climb here."

Tessa goes first, gingerly feeling for solid holds for her hands and then her feet. I follow, hearing the scrape of my rubber boot soles against the hard slate as I climb.

“Watch the wind when you get to the top. Stay low,” Dad calls up.

Tessa finds a place to stop before the crest of the rock and perches beneath it. I join her and sidle to the other side to give Dad room to climb up between us. I want to look over at the cove to see how full it is, but I’m scared to see what is there. What if it's too late. What if the bitter, grey, swirling sea storm has cut us off? We are so close to getting home.

Dad appears between us and, giving us each a glance, looks over the top. The wind hits his face, and then he ducks down again. We look at him, waiting to find out what's next.

"It's pretty full. We will have to get as close as we can to the cliff. I'll go over first. Can you hang on here?"

We nod, the exhaustion holding back our words.

He climbs up and over the rock teeth, and his clothes are slapped and tattered by the wind. His top half remains in view as he gestures for Tessa to climb over. He uses his body to block the wind as best he can to get her over, and then she crouches down out of view. He points to me, and I climb up.

As my head moves above the top of the rock, I am hit with a shotgun blast of wind. It thumps into my mouth and whips away my breath. I am made mute by the wind. I topple backwards, but Dad snatches the front of my jacket. He pulls me back to him, and I feel his arms wrap around me, navigating me over the rock.

We move down one ridge and are splayed flat against the rock by the force of the wind. We try to edge inwards, but the wind beats at us. It whistles between our legs, pulling at us and our clothes like a ripped sail on a weather-torn yacht. I hear a faint noise, and I turn to Dad, who is trying to shout over the wind. He slaps my arm and points downwards. Beneath us is another ridge, but it's close to the frothing tide. He steps down, his boots licked and sprayed by the sea. He gestures toward Tessa, and fearfully, I release one hand and smack her elbow. She does her best to turn as I climb down, and she follows.

The wind dies slightly at this lower level. I look back to Dad, and he waves us on. We edge up as close as we can to the cliff. We each turn and cling to the rock, our hands clenched tight to the cut-glass ridges behind our backs. The sea has taken over the cove, but the small waves are shallow near the base of the cliff.

Dad looks at us, head down against the wind. He shouts out, but his words are whip-cracked away by the storm. He releases one hand and steps around me to be between us. He tries to shout to me again, but I only catch, "Jump together!" I hope I have the gist of it, so I nod. He shouts to Tessa. I feel his cold hand fumble blindly for mine, and I catch hold of it. We look out at the cove and wait.

The third big wave draws back, and I feel Dad's hand tug me forward. He has Tessa in the other hand, and we jump together. I splash into the water, my feet numb in my hollow boots. Water fills them, trying to anchor me down. I still hold Dad's hand, and I feel his strength pulling me forward. The water is up to my waist as I try to pull against the sideways sucking gravity of the sea. With our hands joined above the water, I swing my body side to side to make my way to the next and final rock face. I am bumped by the first small wave, its splash reaching into my mouth, making me gag at the salt taste.

We push through the throng of the second small wave, and we slap against the rock. I am pushed up, and I grip the first row of available rock teeth. My fingers are dead, and my arms are weak as I try to pull myself clear. Tessa is shunted up to my right. Her body is limp and exhausted. She manages to flop herself up above the waterline. Dad hauls himself out of the water, and he catches hold of my back, pushing me up. I get clear of the water, and I hold the rock in a flat hug.

The first of the big waves throws itself in. We did not get high enough. The sea batters against our bodies. The water level is now up to my shoulders. I feel it try to push me. It wants to push me in and up the cove. It wants to beat me against the cliff face.

"JUST HOLD ON!!" Dad's voice defies the sea's roar.

The second wave hits us, ripping my strength from inside. It wants to wear me down, erode my will smooth as it has done to all the rocks it can reach. I want to look at Dad. I want to see if Tessa is still there, still clinging on like I am, but I dare not do anything other than hold on against the endless sea.

"JUST ONE MORE WAVE! HANG ON!" Dad calls.

The third wave thumps in, and like a blind animal, it thrashes from side to side. I am hit repeatedly by violent pulses as the tide throbs and gnashes its foam mouth around me. I feel my boots slip along the uneven ridge under the water, and Dad's arm catches around me, pressing me tight against the slate face.

The tide draws back, and the water level drops to my shins. Dad climbs further up the rock using what must be his last store of strength. He leans back and catches my hand. Our wet hands slip against each other. I feel his slipper grip search to grasp something solid. He settles for my cuff, and I feel him pull me up through my jacket. I am limp within my jacket, and for a moment, I think I might slip out from inside it and fall into the grey tide below. It would have me. It would want me. I feel the armpits of my jacket dig into me and know I won't fall. I push with my empty legs and move higher up the rock.

Dad deposits me like a wet bag of washing at the top of the rock and scrambles down for Tessa. I feel the wind slap and shunt me like a kid with a stick poking at a nearly dead animal. Tessa is lain next to me. She is gasping. She is crying. Dad pats each of us on our thick, wet backs and climbs a step higher and looks into the next and final bay. Just over the crest of this rock is the end. We have made it. I just don't feel it yet.

With a tired and jolting movement, I tilt my head up to look at Dad. My cheek stings as I scrape it across the rock. I'm too exhausted to hold my head up. The wind blows Dad's words, spoken to himself, back to me.

"For God's sake! Give us a break!... Jesus!"

He looks back down at me. I can see his face above the soles of his boots that jut from the ledge above. He looks over at the next cove one more time, and he awkwardly shifts down to us. He turns to face the previous cove, the sea rampaging against the cliffs.

"The tide is up high, beyond where we can drop down from the rock. We will have to drop into the sea and make for the beach," he says.

“No... No, Dad, Please!” Tessa pleads. “I can move anymore.”

He turns away from me to face her. In the gaps between his body and the rock, I see him pat her cheeks and stroke her hair behind her ear. She shakes her head at his words and closes her eyes. I see a pearl-shaped tear run down her cheek, navigating its way across her drenched face, looking for its own route. When she opens her eyes again, she smiles at something he has said, and she even breaks into a grin. A tired and hopeful grin. She gives him a weak nod.

He turns to me, cupping my cheek in his hand.

“How are you feeling, Billy Boy?”

I feel my own tears break over my face.

"I know, I know you're exhausted. But we are so close. One more push, and we're there." He stretches up, looks over the rock, and then hunches back down to me. "I think after this, you'll have a lifetime membership with the A-Team."

I laugh despite feeling hollow.

“What about Indy?” I say.

He moves his face to look me straight in the eyes. “Indy’s got nothing on you anymore.” He pats my face. “Can you come with me?”

I nod. I can.

TWENTY-SEVEN

Now. This Sunday. The last cove.

The wind slaps at us in a flurry of invisible flat palms as we creep over the top of the rock. I feel the collar of my jacket flap violently between my collar bone and my cheek, stinging me with each hit. Dad, between us, guides us along the rock, pointing to footholds, taking our hands and placing them on handholds to grip. Beneath us, the tide swirls and icily boils. It tries to drench us with its spray and slurp its salt tongue around our boots.

The rock we are on runs inward and blends into the cliff face, and beyond that, it is unclimbable. The sea has broken further in and is guarding the cliff face. It smashes against the beach. It has swapped the point where we can safely climb down.

Dad nudges against Tessa, gently shunting her along. He keeps turning to guide me in his wake. My boot slips from the ridge, and my side is snared by the rock teeth. Dad slaps a hand against my outer arm and pushes me up to gain my balance.

I hear Tessa's voice, soft in amongst the sea's roar. She has reached the end of the rock, the edge of the cliff. We can go no further in. Below us, the rolling tide spews with enthusiasm. Dad turns, placing his back against the rock. We do the same, and he shouts over the roar.

"We wait for the small waves. Jump when I jump... and run, scrabble, move like hell up the beach. Don't stop for me or each other. Just move!"

I nod and look down at the watery mass below us. I feel a surge of vertigo, and I look up, hoping it will pass.

"We have to jump as the first of the small waves rolls in, less chance of an undertow. Get it?"

"Got it!" we shout back.

"Good!"

Dad looks down at the tide as it rolls in without a break.

"I can't count the waves!" Tessa calls.

Dad nods but doesn't look at her. His eyes are fixed on the powerful throng below as it seethes and foams. I glance at him, and his face is tight with worry. He looks up at the beach, which doesn't look far away from here, but the tide is violent and unforgiving. A jump at the wrong time will have us snatched and pressed low under the water, weighted down against the slipping shingle, and then it will suck us out to the depths.

He jolts forward as if to give the instruction to jump, but either he has got it wrong, or he has lost his nerve. He bites his lip, and I see him shake off a daze with a slight twitch of his head. I lick my salt cracked lips and wait. The sea seems to have pulsed further up the beach, making our water dash, once we land, a fraction longer.

"Right," he says, nodding to himself. "Be ready to jump."

My legs feel like twitching led.

"Three... That's the break! Jump!"

Dad snatches at our hands, and we half step, half jump, part fall from the ridge. I land in front of Dad, knee-high in water. As the wave draws back, the shingle pours out to sea like sand in an hourglass. I twist towards the beach, but I feel my boots slip on the fluid stones, and I am being pulled out. I turn, but I lose my footing and fall forward. I see my destination. I can see the safety of the sand beyond the shingle, the beach where I can lie down, where I can laugh all this off. But it is being pulled away from me.

My vision is clouded as the froth of the sea boils over me, and I am gone. I slide on the seas shingle tongue as it gulps me down. I open my mouth to scream, but I swallow the sick saltwater. I wretch as it hits my throat, but my gullet is met with more and more bitter seawater.

There is a swirl of colour in the white-grey next to me, and I feel a soft formless hand grope around my middle. It becomes solid. Is it one of the hands of the sea? Is it a pirate ghost looping around me to make sure I join the army of lost souls?

The hand's power pulls against the draw of the sea, and I break the surface. Water spills from my mouth, and I feel the shingle beneath my feet. I stir my legs into action and start to step, soles slipping against wet, shifting stones. I see the beach through stinging red eyes, and I drive my legs harder. I am weak, but I borrow strength from the thing that holds me. Dad, it's Dad! He is feeding me his strength, and he is pushing me on.

My feet spin faster, and I hear the crunch of the shingle. The water draws back, relaxing its grip, just for a moment, and a voice booms.

"RUN!"

A flat solid hand is placed against my back, and I am pushed forward. My feet catch, and I run. With lungs of acid, I am up. I am free. I run up the beach, stones giving way to soft, wet sand. Tessa is slumped in a soaking pile, and I fall next to her.

I am yanked up, and then I am over Dad's knee. He slaps me hard on the back with a flat palm. He slaps again and again. I feel hot, sparking pain through my ice-cold skin with each slap, but a burn comes from inside. I vomit out a stream of saltwater and sand. It bubbles out of me and onto the beach. I cough and spit until I dry heave, and finally, I am placed back on the sand.

My lungs burn, and I clutch at them as if I can stroke them better from the outside. I open my eyes, blinking against the needles of rain. I can see two seagulls pitch and swarm over each other, their fight still ongoing. There is a distant growl of thunder, and the sky splits with a streak of lightning. I thought there was only thunder and lightning at night-time?

I hear the chuff, chuff of a steam engine, or is it the tide? It doesn't sound as terrifying as it did from the other side of the cove. I can hear a tap, tap, tap. Is that a sword against the stone or the dripping cliffs?

My numb fingers plough through the sand next to me, leaving four miniature trenches on either side of me. I turn my head to look at Dad. He is sat up, arms on his knees, looking out at the sea. The wind whispers through his hair. He looks pale against the melting grey. I roll my head to the left and watch Tessa as she gathers herself up. She looks like a pile of soggy mush growing bones again. She flops onto her back and then sits upright, pulling her knees into her.

“Ahhh," she groans like an old lady, "And I thought sports day was tough."

From his partial profile, I see Dad smile.

“I can’t believe we made it!” she says, elation hijacking her exhaustion. “We did it! We beat the tide!”

I grin. “Yeah! A real regular adventure, eh, Dad?”

He looks back at us both, his smile broad. “Yes, a real regular adventure.”

“Oh, man!” Tessa says, “Mum’s going to *kill* us! Look at the state of us.”

“Hmmm,” Dad looks back out to sea. Its roar has hushed to a steady swish. Is the tide really such a poor loser?

“I don’t think she will be,” Dad says. “Not this time.”

I look back out to sea. The whirling dark clouds have smoothed out into a bright grey canvas. The sky has blended with the sea, and a vapour edges toward us. The mist reaches across the lapping water like spider silk, spun by an unseen being.

The sea has lapped into silence. The air and sound are as soft as the plump sand beneath my fingers.

“Dad?” Tessa says, “Look at the fog.”

He stands and looks out at it.

“It’s eerie, isn’t it. But it’s nothing to be afraid of.”

"Should we get over the fallen cliff?" she asks, "The sea won't be in the last cove, will it? Not the one with the stairs?"

Dad dusts the sand from his hands. “No. The tide can’t reach in that far. You only have to get over the fallen cliff, and you’re home.”

“Let’s go,” she says, “This fog is creeping me out.”

We both stand, but Dad makes no move to leave. The grey is bright around us, the mist has reached the shoreline, and I can only just make out the edge of the tide as it ripples against the beach. It is calm now. It is gentle. I look at Dad, and his face is tilted up at the misty sky as if he is engaged in a silent conversation. When he looks back down at us, his eyes start to glisten.

“Do you remember the phone box at the top of the hill?” he says.

“Eh?” Tessa says, and we exchange a look.

“Do you remember how to reverse the charges and make a call?”

“Y... Yes, why?”

“I need you to get up to the phone box and call your Mum. Ask her to get a taxi out here and bring the spare car keys.”

“What?” I say.

“What’s wrong?” Tessa asks, “Are you hurt? Can’t you drive?”

Dad’s face almost breaks. He turns and looks out at the fog behind him. His jaw clenches. When he turns back, there are silver tears in his eyes.

“I can’t go any further than this.” he says, “I have to go back now.”

“*What?*” Tessa says,

Dad takes two, three steps and stands close to us. He cups our faces in each of his hands and looks down at us. I look up at him. His face is in shadow, but I can see his bright eyes in the darkness.

“You are safe,” he says, gripping my chin in his thumb and forefinger. “I love you both, my two little adventurers.”

"Dad..." Tessa says, "What's happening?"

The silence is thick around us. The fog has swept in, obscuring the tide completely. Dad kneels and pulls us both into him, hugging us tightly. His embrace is warm against my cold body. As he holds me, I feel goose pimples roll like a wave to the top of my head. I hug him back. I don’t want to let go. I want to stay in this moment. I want it to last. I want him to be a part of me forever.

His arms loosen and drop. He stands up. He glances back at the grey smear where the sea used to be and nods. He steps towards it and then stops, turning back to us.

“Always think of it as an adventure.”

I’m lost. I don’t know what is happening. The fog surrounding us is eerie, but Dad is right, I’m not afraid of it.

“Tell your mum that I love her... And tell her... I kept my promise. I got you home safe.”

He turns back to the brightening grey and starts to walk out into it. I step forward, my mouth open, about to shout after him but I feel Tessa’s fingers gently close around my arm. I look at her hand and then up at her face. I follow her stare as she watches Dad dissolve into the fog.

I look.

I see.

I watch him as he walks, whisper soft into the mist. As he goes, he leaves no footprints in the sand.

Printed in Great Britain
by Amazon